The Monkey Wrench Kid

COPYRIGHT
Ian C. Watt © 2021

All rights reserved, for all media:
electronic, printed, film and graphic.

email: ianecowatt@gmail.com

The
Monkey Wrench Kid

Ian C. Watt

CHAPTER ONE

DECOCKTION

A cataclysmic thunderstorm is raging directly overhead...

...*KZZ-rak-a-kaa-ZZAK-a-kaa!!...Baffla-daffla-BOOM-doooom-booooom!!*...

My top-floor flat's getting the full force of it. The attic windows are angled up towards the sky, the wind is thrashing rain against them, shaking them in their frames. Almighty great gusts of wind whoosh across the roof, rattling the old slates as they go.

I'm slowly waking up, but not because of the cataclysmic thunder and lightning and rattling and stuff, there's cataclysmic storms all the time these days and I sleep right through them, I'm waking up because I'm being shaken by a huge hairy man.

"Wake up, Daniel!" he's booming at me.

...*KZZ-rak-a-kaa-ZZAK-a-kaa!!...Baffla-daffla-BOOM-doooom-booooom!!*...

I keep on clawing my way slowly up the slippery slopes from deep, deep sleep into confused half-wakefulness, two claws forward, one claw back.

"Wake up, Daniel!" the huge hairy figure booms again. I wonder if I'm still dreaming. I'm pretty sure I'm being shaken though, because I can feel my head thumping up and down on the pillow, with my brain sloshing around inside. Can this really be happening? The strange hairy man seems very agitated, he's breathing hard.

After being shaken a bit more, I feel about as awake as I ever get... yes... dearie, dearie me... this really does seem to be happening... I let out a strangled, very high-pitched, shocked, terror-stricken shriek...

"EEEEEEEEEEEEEEEEEEEEEEEEEEEEK!"

...*KZZ-rak-a-kaa-ZZAK-a-kaa!!...Baffla-daff-*

la-BOOM-doooom-booooom!!.....

Foulburgh's storms have recently gone from normal cataclysmic to some new level altogether... super-cataclysmic? The next series of lightning flashes are so close together they're more like a continuous flickering explosive blaze. I see a bit more detail of the huge hairy man. He has a bush of thick curly black hair around his head, a long, thick black beard with bushy twirled-up moustaches, and an enormous hot air balloon of a chest, also covered in thick black curly hair. The arms and hands shaking me are very large and hairy as well, in fact there's not much to be seen of him except for masses of thick black curly hair. What I can see of his face amongst all the hair is impressive, handsome in an old-fashioned sort of a way, deep purple in colour, and glistens. I notice that a strong, unusual aroma is drifting about him, not exactly pleasant but not exactly unpleasant, sort of spicey, earthy... musky... unusual yet quite familiar...

He has a few white bits, such as the whites of the tiny eyes staring down at me and the rows of huge gleaming white, clenched teeth revealed by his grimace... teeth so white that I'm a bit distracted by them, I'm easily distracted, I start to wonder what sort of dental hygiene routine he has... it's so important to look after your teeth...

"Wake up, Daniel! Focus!"

I expect you've been in a situation like this yourself, so you'll know that you tend not to think logically, your brain just sort of flies apart into bits which whizz about inside your head, bouncing around and bumping into each other in a completely useless panic, like balls in a pinball machine. It's even worse for a perpetually confused person like me, I never have much clue about what's going on around me, I just sort of drift around in a state of continuous confused bafflement, with a very large question mark drifting above my head...

The huge hairy man is still shaking me, he's very agitated, nervous... he booms at me:

"Daniel! Focus! Focus! Listen to me, I'm your penis,

Daniel, I'm your cock! And I'm leaving you!"

This makes no sense to me at all, "What?... Let me go!... Help!.... Who?..."

He tries again:

"I'm your PENIS, Daniel, *your COCK!* And I'm leaving you! I'm your male organ of regeneration, Daniel, and..."

Suddenly, his mood shifts, he's holding back tears...

"... and I'm leaving you, Daniel... I'm so sorry... *sob!*... I just can't... *sniff!*... live with you... *sob!*... any more...."

The huge, hairy man turns and sits on the bed, making me bounce up towards the ceiling, his shoulders are shaking, his head's in his hands.

Can this actually be happening? Of course, girlfriends have left me before, once or twice... well, quite often... but an organ? Then it occurs to me that it might just be one of the guys from work dressed up for a joke... or my old friend Edrigo, heavily disguised, on an escapade... What should I do? Play along I guess... Maybe I'll pretend to comfort the huge man in some way? A hand on his shoulder perhaps? I'm not sure I want to touch anything quite so hairy though. Maybe offer a mug of tea?

"Big Ronny? Gogo? It's you isn't it? ... ha ha..."

"No, Daniel, how many times do I have to tell you? I'm your cock, your penis... and I'm leaving you... If you don't believe me take a look for yourself!"

With this, the shaggy figure stands up and spins around. With one pull he hauls the bedclothes off me, with another pull he hauls down my shorts, then he points to my nether regions. I look down and, in the flashes of lightning and first glimmers of dawn, I get a bit of a terrible shock when I see what he means. I let out another, even higher-pitched shriek... *because my cock has indeed gone!*

...KZZ-rak-a-kaa-ZZAK-a-kaa!!...Baffla-daffla-BOOM-dooooom-booooom-eeeeEEEEKK!!...

Cock, balls, the whole lot gone! The bits of my brain starts to bounce around even faster. Dearie, dearie me! Is this possible? Can your cock actually become a kind of separate person and leave you? I'm familiar with the idea of your various organs having personalities of their own from my treatments with our excellent local complementary therapist, Dr Krakk, (we'll meet him properly just a bit further along in this strange story of ours), but I really haven't ever heard of an organ actually leaving its owner/host before. Just as well it's only something semi-vital and not my lungs, or heart, or brain or something... What on Earth would happen if your brain left you? Actually, come to think of it, you can see what happens when brains leave their owners/hosts all around you here on the streets of Foulburgh...

I pull the bedclothes back up. The figure throws a pile of my stuff off a chair and pulls it up beside the bed. Now he has the tone of an adult talking to a child:

"Danny, Danny, listen to me. I'm sorry... I know it's hard on you, but there's so much going on in my head... I have to sort things out... try to make sense of it all... it's hard for me to explain, but everything is changing! A Tidal Wave of Change is sweeping around the world... the Total Collapse of Everything is upon us! (More cataclysmic thunder and lightning). Humanity must evolve or die, I feel it in my bones... and evolve very quickly if we don't want to take all other life on Earth down with us... Mankind, Man must change... Man's attitude to Women, and Man and Woman's attitude to the Earth..."

This is not the first time I've heard about a tidal wave of change sweeping around the world. Recently, my friend, Edrigo, has been going on about just exactly that, and all the rest of this stuff too, and more, most passionately, going on about how mankind's attitude must change, how the world is changing and we can choose to change our ways now or wait until change is forced upon us... switch from exploitation to regeneration... and stuff to do with male and female attitudes... and attributes...

"Stay awake, Daniel! Focus! Women have just been objects for us to desire, haven't they? Men have lusted after them, seduced them, wanted to possess them, control them... shown them off like just another beautiful thing to own, like a car, or a house, or a watch, just another prize... but we can't go on like that... that attitude must change now... there must be respect!... Stay awake, Daniel! Focus!... Daniel, there must be respect between men and women, and between men and women and the Earth!"

"Well... er... I'm listening... how do you mean?..."

"... that attitude must change! It is changing! It's a poison that's led to so much pain, suffering and unhappiness... to abuse, rape, suppression all around the world... "

Now he sags, crestfallen, gives a deep sigh.

"... and it's you and I, Danny, that are to blame... you must surely feel the terrible weight of all the guilt and the shame?"

"... well... I think so... "

Now he's all passionate resolve.

"Now is the Time for the Rise of the Feminine! For the Rebalancing of the Sexes! Now is the Time for Respect, for Regenerative Relationships! An End to Exploitation!... try to stay awake, please, Daniel, this is important... in Love, in Sexual Relationships, and in all other ways of Life too... Time for the heavy hand of Patriarchy to be lifted up from its Opresive Smothering of so many aspects of our lives, for men as well as for women... "

...KZZ-rak-a-kaa-ZZAK-a-kaa!!...Baffla-daffla-BOOM-doooom-booooom!!...

The huge hairy man sighs again, seems to pull himself together, becomes resolved. I'm beginning to get my head around the idea that maybe he is indeed my cock, however unbelieveable that is, and that, by some sort of bizarre freak lightning or radioactive/chemical leak event of some kind, all too possible here in Foulburgh, he has indeed taken on a whole personage of his own and parted company from the rest of my body.... and become... what?... *Cockman?*

Feeling a bit numb and dazed, I watch as he starts to rummage around my bedroom, looking in my cupboards and drawers, pulling out items of clothing. I watch him try on various things, a long faux fur coat and a pair of urban camouflage trousers, both passed on to me by Edrigo, and a pair of my urban survival wellies. He hauls a purple woolly bobble hat over his head. Everything is far too small for him and there are many bulgings and rippings as he tries to cover his colossal shaggy nakedness. One of his body parts, I can't help noticing, is so huge that it's difficult to cover at all: dangling down between his legs from the thickest bush of curling black hair of all, reaching almost to his knees, there swings the biggest cock I have seen in all my years, even in the world of pornography, very long, and thick with it, and balls like a pair of turnips besides. He rips two pairs of trousers in his attempts to tuck it all away and in the end gives up and just ties my leopard-skin print beach towel about his midriff.

"Well... I'm leaving now Daniel, but before I go I must just say a couple of things to you..." his voice is quivering now and tears are streaming down his face, soaking his beard and moustaches, making them droop, so that tear-drops drip off their ends. I can't help a bit of nervous giggle at this but, not wanting to upset the cockman figure any more than he's already upset, I change it into a gurgling snort, as best I can. The giant hairy man's moods are swinging all over the place, in fact he's a complete emotional wreck... a thought occurs to me...

"I wonder if some counselling might be helpful for you... er... Cockman? A few sessions... you know... you might be able to see things more clearly... I can recommend..."

He flies into a rage at this.

"Counselling?! Counselling?! I'm fine! There's nothing wrong with me!... I just need to sort things out in my head..."

Just as suddenly, he calms down again.

"I'm so sorry, Daniel... it's all so confusing isn't it?... I just know I want more from life than this... I deserve better!... the world deserves better... and yet I don't know what exactly..." now he's muttering, mumbling to himself, "... so much change in the world... have to adapt... so difficult to find my way... to make sense of anything at all..."

Well I have to agree with him on that, confusion is my normal state of mind...

He leaps up and starts pacing to and fro, waving his arms, all passionate resolve, ranting away, but his next words are lost in a fresh burst of thunder...

...KZZ-rak-a-kaa-ZZAK-a-kaa!!...Baffla-daff-la-BOOM-doooom-booooom!!...

The super-cataclysmic storm rages on directly overhead. The first light of dawn is filtering through the filthy Foulburgh air, a dingey, mouldy yellow-grey-green background to the lightning.

The huge hairy cock-man sighs and calms right down again. He sits by the bed, becomes quiet, even gentle.

"So, Daniel, how long is it since you split up with your last girlfriend?" This almost tenderly.

"Well... a while..."

"How long exactly? How many years?"

"... a couple... I think...

"I can tell you, Daniel, it's three and a half years. That's three and half years I've had of your fantasies, unfulfilled lusting, fetishes, chatrooms, pornography, masturbation..."

"Well... er... not continuous... I do go to work sometimes..."

"I want real sex again, Daniel! I want love! I've had enough of being pummelled and thrashed by you, enough of this hideous internet charade!"

He's throbbing and glowing with passion again now.

"...well... it's not that easy to meet someone these days you know..." I chip in, "Edrigo doesn't have parties like he used to... all his models are so busy with Post-Industrial Disruptivism... and gorilla gardening and everything... "

The cock-man figure doesn't hear this at all, now he goes all mystical, seems to be seeing a vision or something...

"Daniel, I have an important part to play in all this...

I don't understand exactly what that part is, but it's a mission of some kind... I dreamed I was riding out on a magnificent wild stallion, through murky woods, by misty lakes, on a quest, a Quest for Lady Destiny herself!... music was thundering in the background, trumpets, horns, trombones, triangles! Mayhap there's a dragon or twain to slay... and Daniel, I will meet her! I will meet her, in human form, very soon, Lady Destiny will appear to me as a magnificent, all-powerful woman... every bone and blood vessel, every joint and tendon, every organ in my body is throbbing, pulsating, telling me so! I will win her hand... and all the rest of her! Ha!... our bodies and hearts and souls will become as one... we will make ecstatic love that will resonate through all Space and Time forever... a spectacular cosmic event, a vital part of the Tidal Wave of Change and the Rebalancing of the Universe!"

His eys are flashing with passion, I can see the blood vessels in his head throbbing and pulsating just like he says, his hair is bobbing about...then suddenly he's holding back the tears again...

"But now I must be on my way... I'm so, so sorry to be leaving you, Daniel, so very, very sorry..."

His lips are quivering, is he going to cry again? No, he sniffs, gets up, grabs another of my towels and blows his nose into it...

"I'm sorry, Daniel... but let's remember all the wonderful, good, fun times we've had together, eh? all the... well... all the, yes, all the good times..." he's sort of stoically cheerful now, "... I'm going now, I cannot be late for my Appointment with Lady Destiny!"

Now he pauses at the bedroom door, and draws himself up into a regal presence.

"And just one last thing, Daniel, from now on I will be known by my full and proper name, not Dick, not Cock, not Cockman, not Willy, not Thingy, not Unit, not Tool... none of those stupid names... but Magnus! King Magnus! *King Magnus the First! King Magnus the Magnificent*! And should we ever by some strange chance meet again, you will call me Your Majesty or Sire! Do I make myself clear? Goodbye!"

"Yes, er... Your Majesty or Sire... I've got that... er... goodbye..."

Then he's gone. I hear the front door open and close, hear his rather squelchy steps going down the many echoing flights of stairs from my flat to ground level. There's a reverberating crash as the main front door slams shut far below, then all is quiet again, save for the storm, the usual traffic noise, road drills, a bird coughing, people cursing and swearing, all the usual drunken singing and fighting down in the street, and the increasing sounds of the super-cataclysmic storm, not just of the thunder and lightning, but now also of the howling wind blowing bits of wood and stone and stuff down the street.

I check down below again, still hoping it's all been some kind of terrible dream or practical joke, but no, no doubt about it, it's all gone... it's taking a while to sink in fully, I'm at about 93.74 % total acceptance, roughly, I would say... cock, balls, definitely gone... a rather strange start to anyone's day, I must say!... I find I can still pee through a small hole, which is a relief.

But what to do now? If there's no waking up from the situation I suppose I'll have to go along with it... should I follow this Cockman/King Magnus/Majesty-Sire entity to see what he gets up to? But then, whether he is or isn't really my cock, part of me is beginning to think that I'm better off without an emotional wreck/Drama Queen/Drama King like that in my life... I reckon I'll follow him... or maybe I won't... I seem to have become even more indecisive than usual all of a sudden... No, I will, some intuition is telling me to... What about work? Well, I don't think they'll miss me too much there for a bit... you'll see why shortly...

I grab some clothes, there's still a few that King Magnus hasn't ripped apart, I stick on some hi-viz work socks and wellies, hi-viz work pants, hi-viz vest, hi-viz work shirt and a couple of hi-viz fleece jackets, my hi-viz fleece hat and my hi-viz storm coat, and head out of the flat, best to be ready for the storm. I go to grab my bike but it's gone! Ha! That mysterious Cockman/King Magnus character must have knicked it to be his mechanical stallion... Well of all the rascally nerve!... I hurry down the twelve flights of stairs to the ground floor... the lifts have never worked since the flats were built... typical Foulburgh...

But by the time I get down the last flight and step through the mesh security gates and other fortifications to the outside world the super-cataclysmic storm has blown over. Now there's not a breath of wind. Even at it's low morning angle, and even though it's having to battle it's way through the chemical grime of the Foulburgh air, the sun is now roasting the city as if it was a giant arthritic old pig on a giant broken down old barbecue... Goodness only knows what the temperature must be, way off any known scale probably. I'm not surprised though, it's just how the weather's been behaving of late, swinging from one extreme to another, then another, Spring in Autumn, Summer in Winter. Of course, I'm hopelessly overdressed, a dazzling beacon of waterproof day-glo protective insulation from head to toe, but I've learned never, ever to cast off a layer these days... another ten minutes and there'll probably be snow, or hail, or I'll be encased in a block of ice...

I look up and down my street, Slaughterhouse Lane, for King Magnus and catch a glimpse of a figure away in the distance, through the shimmering, sun-blasted air, a figure in a faux fur coat and purple wooly bobble hat speeding away on a bike, my bike I see! the regal organic rascal, round the corner into Faraway Close. My eyesight has suddenly become amazingly hawk-like, I can see every detail of his coat-tails getting caught between the chain and the gears, beads of sweat or something flying off him, every strand of wool of the bobble on that purple wooly bobble hat quivering, all with a clarity I've never known before.

I'm just about to head off in that direction when I start to feel a bit odd, well very odd indeed. I don't know whether it was running down all those stairs or being so over-dressed in the sudden intense heat but I suddenly feel as if I'm looking at the world through a huge magnifying glass, or the wrong end of a telescope, or both. My thoughts seem to be happening in a brain that's a long way away, and not quite completely connected up with me, maybe a brain that has just lost some sort of important input or connection from that male regenerative equipment now speeding away on my bike? a brain now flooded with all this newly intense hawklike eyesight detail, and a brain also overwhelmed with newly intense hawklike hearing detail, every snatch of every drunken song, every rasp of every bird wheeze, every hideously out of tune blast of every bagpiping beggar, or is that more road drills? everything's reverberating and crashing around in there in an internal cataclysmic sensory storm... oh dearie, dearie me...

Should I go back and have a little lie down? It's a very appealing idea, but just the thought of clambering up all those stairs makes me feel completely exhausted... what do I do now?

I'm beginning to sag down right there on the street when, with my near-faraway confused but otherwise very detailed vision, I see two figures approaching through the heat haze, two very curious figures, who have a kind of blue-green glow about them, gliding elegantly along, unperturbed by the wreckage of buildings and people they're passing through, smartly dressed in well-fitting suits, one an elegant grey, the other a dashing check, both complete with shirts, ties, shoes, gold cufflinks, waistcoats, gold watch chains, all the trappings of two most dapper gentlemen. But what's especially curious about the two figures is their heads rather than their dress, which are the heads of two scaled-down elephants, and bright pink. On top of these pink heads perch two hats, one a homburg, the other a fedora, both large and rather floppy, which they doff with their trunks as they approach me.

I have the strongest possible feeling that I know the two gentlemen already, have I met them before somewhere? Where on Earth could that have been?

"Aaah, my dear Daniel, just the chap we were hoping

to bump into!" says one. "Allow me to introduce myself, I'm Beebee Heebiegeebie, and this is my friend and colleague, Geegee Heebiegeebie."

The... Heebiegeebies?

"We're just popping round to the Salivation Hotel for a spot of breakfast," says the other, "Would you care to join us? Then we can maybe explain things to you... explain about the... er... departure of your... er... male organ of regeneration... and a couple of other things too..."

Well I never! First my cock leaves me and now it's breakfast with the Heebiegeebies... What a morning... my head's reeling and throbbing, trying to make any sort of sense of it all... and where can I possibly know them from?

"But my dear Daniel, you do look a little poorly..."

"... before breakfast, let us take you round to see the good Dr Krakk..."

"... I think a little treatment from him will be just the thing to help things settle down for you!"

The bits of my brain are whirling around so uselessly and I feel so weak and wobbley that I'd be happily escorted by anyone to more or less anywhere, real or imaginary. Breakfast feels like a very good idea, and so does a visit to Dr Krakk, who has already given me many treatments, but before we go any further with that, or any other part of our extraordinary story, I'd like to tell you a bit more about myself, to sketch in some background as it were, because then things will maybe begin to make a bit more sense to you...

CHAPTER TWO

MY IMPORTANT WORK AT LOZZO INDUSTRIES

My full, proper name is Daniel Thelonius Sprocket, so, at work, as well as "Monkey Wrench Kid" and "Monkey Wrench Kid, son", I'm often called "Dan", or "Danny," as well as "Daniel", "Mr Sprocket", or "Hey you!", or "Hey sonny!", just as you'd expect. Away from work, however, I'm often called "Didi". This more unusual name was given to me by my best friend, Edrigo, when we were kids. He comes from a hot country, where they like to give each other sing-song, rhyming nicknames like that. Edrigo himself is often known as "Gogo".

Anyway, I, Daniel Thelonius Sprocket, work at Lozzo Industries, by far the biggest employer here in Foulburgh, and for a very long way all around, employing people like me either directly, in the reeking sprawl of factories, refineries, workshops, foundries and so on that make up the largest part of the city, with its blocks of flats and shops and what have you scattered here and there amongst the more important industrial stuff, or indirectly, in smaller sprawls of reeking enterprises and homes that supply them, or are supplied by them, in one great big sticky web of interconnected, many-headed, stinking monstrosity.

My exact role at Lozzo's is a bit of a mystery to me. I don't remember ever having been given a job title or a list of duties in any sort of formal way, it could be that such a thing never happened, Lozzo being such a vast, mysterious, rambling labyrinth of industrial goings-on that a little detail like that could easily have been overlooked, particularly as, (there's general agreement on this), the Lozzo management chain is so utterly useless. Or I may well have fallen asleep during some sort of induction process. It doesn't bother me though, I've got used to wandering through my work life, and my notwork life, in a fog of confusion, forever puzzled, never really understanding what's going on around me, just drifting along with the flow as best I can, half-asleep, half-awake at best, with that very large invisible question mark floating over my head. It might seem a bit strange to you, for whom life maybe makes more and more sense as you tootle along through it, but it's just the opposite for me. Things may start out in a fairly normal way, but then, by one tiny step after another, they start to get a bit strange, then a bit stranger still, then, before I know it, they're galloping along very, very strangely until - dearie, dearie me! - I find that things have got very, very, very extra-super-duper, very strange indeed.

I guess I've worked at Lozzo Industries since some time in my teens. I have patchy memories of being taught by, or maybe even apprenticed to, a friendly old master mechanic-craftsman-repair guy kind of character, Shuggy, I think his name was. Shuggy's domain within the infinite Lozzo Industries complex was a rambling collection of workshops and stores, each one leaning onto its neighbour, where he patiently tried to show me how to use the various tools in endless racks on the walls and in box after box on benches, and all the bits of equipment and machinery lying about everywhere. He himself was one of those people who completely understand any bit of equipment or machinery in the world at a glance, a sort of natural understanding I expect he was born with, like a Second Sight for Machinery. Quite possibly he was the Seventh Mechanic Son of a Seventh Mechanic Son.

When our workmates brought round non-functional machines or weird bits of broken down equipment Shuggy always seemed to know exactly what was wrong with them even before they were through the doors. Without any apparent effort, he would wave his hands over some oily entanglement of cylinders and levers in a relaxed blur of activity, the right tool jumping from its resting place into his grip, while cracking one of his two jokes and whistling one of his three tunes, take a couple of old parts off it and fix a couple of new ones on, give it a couple of taps with a hammer, flick a switch or two, stand back, and hey presto! a few sparks, a cloud of black smoke, and that would be the thing working again.

It was fascinating to watch him at work, and I'm sure I could have picked up loads of skills in those days if it weren't for my falling asleep so much. Sadly, people explaining things to me is one of the most irresistible triggers for my narcolepsy. Also, I'm very easily distracted by other things going on in the area at the time, like dust falling, clocks ticking, the bristling of nose hair, ants, the dripping of oil and so on. If you're ever talking to me you may well think that I'm listening to you, but that's very unlikely. Right back when I was at school, I developed a way of escaping the boredom and irrelevance of it all by gazing out of the window up into the clouds, drifting away into their magical shapes, slipping away into sleepy bliss, but at the same time appearing to be fully alert and present by way of a fixed expression of fascination, and the occasional grunt where appropriate, and a kind of daydream-walk became my natural, default, all-day, every day state, a state which stood me in good stead, right through into my working life. So by the time Shuggy retired, or died, I had only picked up a few basic techniques, mostly Taking Things Apart techniques. I had become a bit of an expert with The Sledgehammer however, and had become really good at giving things a couple of good taps with that, though I say it myself. I had also learned the names of quite a few other tools, such as The Spanner, The Screwdriver, The Bolt Cutters, The Hacksaw and, of course, my favourite, *ta da!* The Monkey Wrench, without learning much about how to use any of them. The smattering of Putting It Back Together Again skills I now have were gained largely through guesswork and trial and error on my part.

Anyway, after Shuggy's death or retiral I must have been promoted to the old guy's position by some secret

Lozzo process. It must have been assumed, wrongly, by some incompetent someone, who clearly didn't know me, in some managerial role in some office block somewhere, that I had absorbed Shuggy's knowledge and skills, like a pile of sawdust or a rag, and so could take over his role, whatever that was exactly. A wage goes regularly into my bank account, just enough for me to pay various parts of the Lozzo empire for my basic needs of food, shelter, heat, light, water and now of course air as well, (we're being charged for that too because it is of course so very expensive to clean up the air to any sort of survivable quality these days), in short, all the things a chap needs, in the worry-free dependency of the Lozzo Industrial way of life.

So I just sort of potter along. I suppose I could ask someone for a bit of clarification about my job, but, "if it ain't broke, don't rock the boat", as they say. So many people work here that I expect some file on me has been lost somewhere along the line, and it might actually create a huge amount of work for someone, with better things to do, if I brought the matter to light. By the way, I did once ask one of my workmates just exactly how many people there are working at Lozzo's, "About half of them," he replied...ha ha...

AF TY FIR T

I remember Shuggy going out on what he called "Inspections", dressed from head to toe in h-viz gear, carrying a huge tool of some kind on one shoulder, looking very workman-like and important. I've inherited all his fluorescent yellow work jackets, coats, trousers, hard hats, boots and gloves which must once have had things like, "SAFETY FIRST", "BE SURE, BE SAFE" and "THINK SAFE" written on them. Now, as the "S's" and "E's" don't seem to have been very sticky, they read, "AF TY FIR T", "B UR, B AF" and "THINK AF" etc, which I think adds an intriguing air of mystery to them. Anyhow, I guess Shuggy's remit must have included something to do with Lozzo Safety, or AF TY, Procedures so I feel I might as well keep up this possible tradition. When I feel in an AF TY mood, I dress up in lots of this AF TY gear, put some giant tool or other on my shoulder, grab a clipboard and pen, and head out on an "Inspection" myself.

Generally speaking, no one seems to bother much about AF TY at Lozzo, as long as things seem to be ticking along ok. I suppose if workers at the plant have survived at all they must have some personal idea of AF TY, and be nimble enough to dodge the worst of the flying blades, sheets of flame, showers of acid and so on. It's obviously a really important thing to go through the motions of having AF TY procedures, as long as that doesn't get in the way of efficient production, but there's no expectation for anything beyond that at all.

It's so much fun strolling about the vast complex! It's so huge that you could probably wander about Lozzo Industries all your life without ever visiting the same building twice.

I thought I must be cutting quite a professional, workman-like dash in all my heavily stained but otherwise gleaming clothes, with my enormous monkey wrench over my shoulder and my clipboard in my hand, but I caught site of myself reflected in a window one day. Shuggy, like all the rest of the workers, male and female, etc., in the factories and foundries, except for me, was a great big enormous person, whereas I am on the small side, so his old work gear was hanging about me in fluorescent festoons. With the great big yellow hard hat sitting high on my, not particularly big, head I looked like a kind of day-glow souffleé or something, so I don't bother with the AF TY hat anymore. As you've probably guessed, it's because of carrying the monkey wrench around that I've been given the nickname, "The Monkey Wrench Kid." I don't mind at all, as it's meant in a very friendly way. As I say, I'm not a big guy, and I'm one of those people who, however old they really get, will always just look like they're fresh out of school, particularly when swathed in over-sized day-glo work gear, so it suits me really. With my clumps of blonde hair, huge specs and bemused cherubic grin, I guess

I've become an industrial mascot or something, like a football team would have.

Round the vast compounds and enormous buildings I stroll, marvelling at all the tanks of stuff, pipes, columns and tubes, all bubbling, gurgling and blazing away, through the vast hooting halls full of grinders and welders sparking and flashing, past frantic machinery shrieking and howling, along the endless clattering, rumbling corridors. I scribble down readings on my clipboard from any dials I come across and take notes as I look through inspection windows at stuff seething away, like I imagine a real AF TY expert would do. I'm recognized and waved at from low down in pits and from high up on gantries. Blackened faces on top of huge blackened hulking male and female shapes grin at me from workshops thick with smoke, just eyes and teeth floating and glistening in the billowing gloom. Greetings are shouted at me from all angles:

"Hey it's the Monkey Wrench Kid! Yorayeson?"

"Hey look busy! It's the Monkey Wrench Kid!"

The atmosphere at Lozzo is friendly and welcoming like that, wherever you go. That might surprise an outsider visiting a workplace which at first sight must look utterly grim. In fact it's more than just friendly and welcoming, it's a party-like atmosphere, like some giant family gathering, or some reunion of schoolmates, which, this being the main local employment, it often actually is. Everyone's telling jokes and laughing, except for those eternally miserable people of course, you'll always get some I suppose, however often you tell them your joke. Really, the primary purpose of Lozzo, as far as we workers are concerned, is for everyone to have a laugh and as generally good a time as possible, if any product rolls off the assembly lines that's just a bonus. I haven't ever made this observation to any of the people flitting about in the background everywhere whom I'm told are "managers" - usually in a kind of hissing tone of voice and with a down-turned-mouth expression - who apparently think they have something to do with the running of the place, but I'm sure they would see our work in this way too, if they properly understood it.

MANAGERS - THE MANY KINDS THEREOF

From what I've gathered listening to my workmates over the years, there seem to be various kinds of these "managers". There are middle, branch, regional, department, assistant, shift and front line managers, just for a start, probably also side, back, top, bottom, radial and spiralling arc managers too, and there's also executives, directors, (who have a board... is that like a plank? I wonder, or are they really trying to say that everyone else is "bored" of the directors?), there's supervisors, team leaders... it just goes on and on. If someone counted them all up I bet they'd find there were more managers than workers.

As I say, these people, who tend to be a bit small and weedy in contrast to my enormous hulking co-workers, can often be seen flitting about in the background and trotting along corridors, with the glazed look of calming medication in their eyes, on their way from one "meeting" to another. They wear suits, or white coats, they often carry clipboards like mine, or even briefcases. There's a rumour that some of them have "degrees", whatever that might mean... maybe it just means that they've been de-greased? It's obviously not a passport to common sense, as most of them have none of that, or much of any skill at all. We workers can spot a manager who is particularly useless because they generally get promoted to a higher level. You can spot when that has happened by their clothes, which get just that little bit cleaner and smarter. (By the way, talking of clothes, you can tell the actual bosses at the top of the greasy management pole as their clothes start to get tattered and oily again, just like mine, from climbing up the greasy pole maybe? strange isn't it?)

Managers often have a most unpleasant air of efficiency and officiousness about them, so I avoid them as much as I can. If and when they ever emerge from their "meetings" and make so bold as to approach members of the workforce, they are, of course, completely ignored, if at all possible. Sometimes a manager will instruct a worker to make a completely stupid change of some sort to the way in which they're doing something. The worker, with extreme grumpiness, will sometimes actually adopt the change, just to get a bit of peace, but only until the supervisor or executive is out of sight, of course, then he or she will revert, very sensibly, to their original way of doing whatever it is. Really! the cheek of some of these management people, ever to think that they might know better than people who may have been doing that same job in the same way for maybe fifty, or sixty, or even a hundred years...

I guess if anyone was going to ask me for a report or anything it might be well one of these managers. I'm happy to say that I haven't ever been asked for anything like that, but I do keep a file of scribbled notes with columns of figures I've made up, just in case.

Then right at the very top of the *Lozzo* management pile sits Lord Lozzo himself. I imagine him in his oily, greasy, tattered suit and t-shirt, at his sprawling acres of desk, issuing commands and demanding reports, or peering down through a window at the very top of Lozzo Tower through his telescope, through the filthy air, keeping a beady eye on us all scurrying about down below, the comings and goings, holding all of *Lozzo* Industrial, and Foulburgh too, in the sweaty palm of his control, occasionally being driven out in his colossal black armoured car, through the windows of which you may sometimes catch a glimpse of his shrivelled up, sneering face and ever-snarling mouth.

SECURITY PATROLS

I'd like just to mention another group of people who wander about the Lozzo complex, the gentlemen of the security patrols, because two of them play a brief but important part in our fantastic story later on. These men are a kind of combination of police officer and soldier, always dressed in full armour and swathed with so many weapons that they can barely stand up under the weight. They are, in fact, a division of Lord Lozzo's private army, and can be seen on the residential streets of Foulburgh gunning down miscreants and the like as well as staggering around and about here in the industrial areas. There's absolutely no need for them in the factories because if anyone was foolish enough to break in they would surely be killed almost straight away by the whirling scythes or thundering hammers of some bit of lethal, un-guarded machinery or other. Anyway, they don't come round the factories very much nowadays since some members of the workforce practised with catapults until they were able to ping a nut or bolt off their helmets from a hundred yards away, and since shortly after then when one of these officers of the Lozzo Law was accidentally hoisted up by a crane and dropped, *oops!* into a tank of food waste slurry.

MY LOOSENING-OFF AND DROPPING-IN EVENT

There was a period of time during which, if I was carrying the giant Monkey Wrench around with me, I used to see if there were any nuts on the machines I was passing that needed tightening up or loosening off. I took it in turns to tighten up the first nut I came to, then loosen off the next one. Unfortunately, I once loosened something right off that would probably have been better tightened up even more. A very unhealthy clanking and grinding noise started to come from the machine in question so I thought I'd better have a peek inside it to see what was going on, or not going on. I lifted the cardboard safety shield and looked down into the rolling and churning blades and grinders therein. It appeared to me that a gear? or cog? or ratchet? of some kind had come loose and was sort of bouncing around down there, occasionaly meshing with other gears, cogs or ratchets and having bits torn off it, then bouncing up again. I have to say the noise this was all making was rather unpleasant, a sort of whining, screeching, grinding, clanking, the sort of sound bagpipes would probably make if they were fed through a rock pulveriser, but all the same, looking down into all those whirring, clonking bits and pieces was somehow rather mesmerising and I found myself drifting off into a lovely daydream filled with fluffy mechanical ducks circulating around in great big fluffy clouds filled with such a peaceful, calm, golden light... I think I must have nodded right off because *oops!* the giant Monkey Wrench slipped right out of my hand!

OOPS!

I woke up again to see it floating down into those same gears and cogs and things! As soon as it got enmeshed amongst them the whining, screeching, grinding, clanking, almost bagpipe-like noise went up to a whole new level of unpleasantness which got louder and louder as I backed stealthily away into the shadows. I was rounding the corner into the next department as the grinding and clonking etc. etc. reached a kind of frenzied climax and started to sound like the sound I imagine a machine would make if it was ripping itself apart. Then there was the whizz of metal things whizzing through the air and hitting walls and other machines, then alarm bells and sirens going off, shouts and booted feet running closer. It was actually quite exhilarating, once I got over the initial shock, but I did feel a little concern about how the managers and security gentlemen might react. At least, I thought, I had several more monkey wrenches back in my workshops so I didn't have to worry too much about losing one, even though it was one of the really big ones.

Just as I was thinking that thought, I was picked up off my feet by one of our enormous women co-workers, Big Brenda, or maybe Big Glenda, I think she's called. She bundled me, AF TY gear and all, under her arm and whisked me off down a little-used back staircase. She was grinning from ear to ear and laughing in a very unrestrained way, which made her huge face and body wobble all over, like heavily-muscled jelly, as she carried me swiftly back to my workshops, via more shadows, and popped me safely out of sight in a dark corner.

"Better stay out of the way for a bit, Monkey Wrench Kid, son, till the fuss dies down."

INTRODUCING EDRIGO

Later that day, I told my oldest and best friend, Edrigo, who is an artist, about my Loosening-Off and Dropping-In Event. He laughed too... then, as if he had been struck by lightning, he suddenly froze and stared at me with shock or awe or something, and called me a "genius", which I thought was very nice of him.

"Didi," he said, "You're a natural Post Industrial Genius!"

I wasn't really sure what he meant, but I felt very flattered anyway, since no one has ever called me a genius of any kind before.

"Do you realise you've just invented a whole Art Movement, Didi?"

"Really, Gogo?" I was glowing with pride now.

"You have just invented Kinetic Post Industrial Disruptivism! It's pure genius!"

I got a strange feeling then, one that I quite often get, that everything had changed... but that nothing had changed...

THE HELLO MACHINE

My workshops are equipped with all sorts of metal-working, wood-working and electrical-working tools and machinery. I still have no idea what most of it's for or how to use it, but I do sometimes wander about dusting things down, even giving some of the shiney bits an extra little wash with soapy water, to try and get the last of the oil off them, or I might see if the motors need any more sawdust or sand. There's a storeroom full of what I think must be spare parts for the huge machines out on the factory floors. There's lots of chains, motors and gear wheels, and boxes and boxes of nuts and bolts, all that sort of stuff. I love wandering about amongst the shelves wondering what it's all for. My workshop is tucked away in one of the more remote corners of the Lozzo complex, looking out onto a bit of wasteland where scrubby weeds, stunted bushes and half-dead trees are trying their best to take the area over again, in spite of all the chemicals, metal wreckage and stuff that's been dumped there. Often when I'm "In" and not wandering about "Out" on an Inspection, I'll just gaze out through the huge, cracked, cobweby, grimey or missing windows for a bit, and lose myself in the beautiful, magical, daydream world of the lovely patterns the pale flickers of sunlight make as they struggle through the drifting smoke, the chemical haze, the dead branches and withered leaves and stuff, wondering what that's all for too, until I nod off.

It seems somehow to have been generally decided or accepted on the factory floor, as well as by some inept brood of managers, that I have taken over from Shuggy as some kind of general purpose oddjob/repair man for the complex, as well being some kind of AF TY expert. Colleagues bring in bits and pieces of non-functioning equipment, machinery and so on from time to time. Really they just want to have a bit of a chat, there's no expectation for anything actually to be fixed. Just as well, because apart from my lack of appropriate skills, none of the stuff was ever really designed so it could be easily fixed, as Shuggy was forever saying in an annoyed kind of way. (I made a resolution that if I ever met a designer I'd suggest that he or she starts to think about designing things so they can be easily repaired). Worse still, incredibly, it's even becoming more and more the case that things are being deliberately designed so that they would be very, very difficult to repair! Even, what's more shocking still, designed so that some vital, irreplaceable, irrepairable part of them will break, or stop working, after a certain quite short life, on purpose! So that its manufacturers can make more money by supplying another one! Which is even more un-fixable!

I was deeply shocked when Shuggy explained all that to me, it seems to fly in the face of any kind of manufacturing decency and honesty. It's as if the Industrial World was deliberately sabotaging itself... how completely insane, I thought. I couldn't help having a little nap. I think it's high time designers everywhere were given a good talking-to and were told to pull their socks up. All the same, I often go through the motions of fixing stuff, just for fun, and often manage to take some of the things apart, the sledgehammer is brilliant for that. Sometimes I even manage to put something back together again, but by now it's usually in an even worse state than before and much further away from working again.

So, just for fun, almost by accident, I started putting bits and pieces together from different items into Creations: pretend robots that don't actually do anything, non-perpetual perpetual motion machines, clanking and juddering things and so forth. One day, a huge colleague brought in a bit of equipment that I somehow liked the look of, it had what might have been a motor, or a transformer, or a gearbox, (terms I remember Shuggy using), and an arm, and other bits and pieces. I noticed it had an electrical plug, so I plugged it in to see what would happen. After recovering from the massive electric shock it gave me, I hit it as hard as I could with a sledgehammer here and there, then fixed an old work glove onto the arm and banged a few other bits and pieces onto it where there was room. I set the whole thing up on a bench right under one of the front windows, so now when I - very carefully - switch it on, the arm moves through the air from side to side in an arc. I felt very proud actually to have got something to work again. I called it the Hello Machine, so my visitors would always feel welcome, even if I was "Out", on an inspection, or asleep. When I showed Edrigo a photo of the Hello Machine later he liked my idea very much. He said I was most definitely nothing less than a natural-born, Post Industrial Genius and told me I must keep up my ground-breaking work, which I have done.

I stack up my creations along with all the piles of broken parts and sub-assemblies in a kind of inner storeroom behind the main storeroom - the one with all the spare parts in it - where they go right up to the ceiling. A steady trickle of water is coming down from a hole in the roof right in the middle there and everything is slowly beginning to rust, rot and stick together, it's a fascinating process to watch. I dragged an old abandoned sofa in there from the wasteland, on which I can sit for hours at a time in happy contemplation of the decay, in between naps, and when not reading through the huge piles of comics I found in an old chest of drawers. I liked the look of all the rust and decay so much that I went up onto the roof of the spare part storeroom, took a few slates off, and sledge-hammered a nice big hole in it so that everything in there could start to go that lovely red-brown rusty colour too, and start to stick together in that satisfying way.

THE GOOD MANNERS MACHINE

The grand success of my Hello Machine must have been what brought another of my ideas up into the light of day from where it had been lurking not quite fully-formed deep down in the abyssal lair of my kinetic post-industrial creativity, the idea for my Good Manners Machine.

I'm sure you'll agree that it's terribly sad that people just can't seem to be bothered with good manners these days. Whatever happened to, "Please", "Thank you", and "Sorry"? And another phrase of politeness I would like to hear more often is, "Well done". So, over a period of several months, mostly by accident, I put together a machine, fully motorised and remotely controllable, which can trundle freely about the streets with you, or unaccompanied, shouting out these essential words at random, or on command, to make up for the many times they have not been used when it would have been much better if they had been used. Honestly! trying to encourage some people simply to say "sorry" once in a while... I had no idea just what a hebridean task that would be. I must admit that it's mostly a male failing, but it can most definitely sometimes be a female failing too. It's as if the word "sorry" was some enormous granite gallstone that refused to emerge from some people into the light of day, just lying there obstinately inside them, becoming bigger and bigger, like a bad-mannered festering old troll.

I started tootling round town with the Good Manners Machine on full volume, roaring out, "SORRY! SORRY! SORRY! PLEASE! THANK YOU! WELL DONE! SORRY! SORRY! SORRY!" for hours at a time but, sadly, without ever hearing one single word of good manners in response. In fact, quite the reverse, the machine and me were called all sorts of terribly rude names... why, one ill-mannered nasty malicious cantankerous old bag of an evil horrible smelly old woman even said that the noise was worse than the blank, blank, blank, bagpipes! This awful, awful comment wounded me very deeply, as you can imagine, and I slunk back, quite disheartened, to my workshops and stores, so that the machine and I could brood and sleep on the problem.

What I came up with was partly inspired by a blissful dream and partly by a memory from my early days of kinetic creativity, the memory of that massive electric shock. I added a kind of trailer behind the main section of the Good Manners Machine and piled it up high with the biggest batteries I could lay my hands on, wiring them all up in series, parallel and both, just to be on the safe side, then to the bows of the, now, Articulated Good Manners Juggernaut Machine I attached a kind of bowsprit, cattle-prod, telescopic lance device, the idea being to prod passers-by gently into saying a "please", "thank you", "sorry" or "well done", with a few thousand volts, ohms, amps and watts, etc., when all else had failed.

Sadly, I was never able to try the Articulated Good Manners Juggernaut Machine out on the ill-mannered streets of Foulburgh because there was a supernoval flash of light and thundering explosion when I switched it on for a trial run in the workshop and I was hurled backwards, hitting the wall behind me at great speed, with screams of "SORRY! SORRY! SORRY! THANK YOU! PLEASE! WELL DONE!" pounding through my head. I must have been knocked unconscious as the next thing I remember is being mopped down with oily rags and having vodka poured into me from hip flasks by a group of my, very concerned looking, female enormous co-workers, muttering and cooing over me, like giant pigeons or something, Big Brenda, Big Glenda, also Big Daisy and Big Maisy too, I think, amongst the smouldering wreckage. So the Articulated Good Manners Juggernaut Machine never went into active service.

"Probably just as well," said Edrigo later, "Total genius, all the same, Didi, total genius."

KARMITIS

As it turned out, the Articulated Good Manners Juggernaut Machine was superceded by a natural phenomenon which performed the task I had set out to do, I must admit, much more thoroughly than I could ever have dreamed of, I mean the dreadful disease that slithered up from some hideous pit of pestilential plague at around about that time, the grim affliction which started to afflict the whole world, which came to be known as Karmitis.

No one knew exactly where Karmitis came from, some suspected that it came from the East, others said it must be from the West, others said that the pit of pestilential plague it came from was deep down in the bowels of some secret Lozzo Laboratory, where it was brewed up as a weapon of war, and from where it escaped and mutated in all kinds of ghastly ways, but wherever it came from it was deadly. It was a very selective and unusual disease, in that it only struck down people who had brought it upon themselves and thoroughly deserved it, and its symptoms varied wildly according to the type of person it afflicted. The very first cases appeared amongst people, men and women, who, by some cosmic coincidence with my own experiences, hadn't been able to say the word "sorry". Every time they should really have said the word but hadn't, another thin layer of bitter black basalt had been added around an inner gall stone of remorselessness, building up layer on layer inside them, first in the gall bladder itself, so often painted green in anatomy text books, but more a kind of bloody, mud colour in real life, or for these sorry-less people just plain old black, then spreading from there into the small intestine, duodenum, jejunum, by way of the duodenum/jejunum junction, slowly working its way through all that wiggley stuff, round and round, layer upon layer of stone being laid down as if in some sort of geological process, possibly called stratification or morphicisation or something like that, on and on, round and round, being stonily laid down and down, right round to the often-overlooked but highly important, ileo-cecal valve, and further on even from there, until pretty much all of that wiggley-wobbley stuff had turned to the blackest of black stone and, naturally, stopped working.

Generally, at this point, those afflicted just keeled over, stone dead, with a thud, in the street, or fell out of bed, with a clonk, deader still, to the dismay of all around, and that was that, but in a very few cases it somehow dawned on the sufferers that they just needed to start saying "sorry" for the whole mortal-stoneyfication process to be reversed, so these few people survived through finding a streak of decency inside themselves they never knew they had up till then. However, this first manifestation of Karmitis was just the very beginning of the beginning of its reign of terror, as we shall see later on in our story... no, no, we haven't heard the last of Karmitis at all... but for now we're going to bring our attention back to Lozzo Industries, so I can tell you about some of the stuff we make there.

BOMBS AND BABYFOOD

We do seem to make an absolutely vast range of stuff at Lozzo Industries. There's always trucks and trains coming and going in all directions, piled high with raw materials or finished products. I recognize some of the symbols on their sides: the ones for "Deadly Poison", "Very Deadly Poison", "Extremely Deadly Poison", "Radioactive Waste", "Catastrophically Dangerous Waste More Dangerous Even Than Radioactive Waste", all that sort of thing, which tend to be on the in-coming trucks and trains. The outgoing trucks and trains are usually labelled with a different range of signs: "Super Safe Food Grade Stuff", "Graded Even Safer Than Super Safe Food Grade Stuff", "Safest Possible Happy Kid Breaki Grade", "Even Safer Still Yummytummy Burger Delight Grade", then there's a whole other range of signs and labels: "Super Safe Assault Rifles", "Danger Free Hand-Grenades", "Bouncy-H-Bombs-U-Like", and so on, bombs and baby food apparently being two of our biggest sellers.

Mountains of stuff are tipped into hoppers, go along conveyor belts, are sifted and shaken, mixed and manipulated, battered and baked, before vanishing into dark, locked warehouses. From the other end of the works comes a steady stream of not just once plastic-wrapped, nor just twice plastic-wrapped, but usually thrice plastic-wrapped foodstuff wrapped in even more plastic, to hold any contamination in, or out, or maybe both, in charming bright colours, a bit like the night sky over Foulburgh, shades of volcanic cerise, hyper-fluoro-jaundellow and glowblu-glowblu, so as to appeal to babies and their parents. Of course we make food for grown-ups too out of just the same sorts of sugary sludges, it's cleverly highly-addictive, lowly-nutritive content making it impossible for people to stop shovelling the muck in, their bodies always screaming out for more, never getting enough nutrition, making people constantly needy and dependent on our Lozzo production lines, the sludge conveniently available and all they can afford, making them get fatter and fatter and iller and iller and more and more dependent still, on medication for heart disease, brain disease, gut disease and just general industrial life disease. By the way, these medications are all Lozzo products, so nothing's lost in the end really.

The steady stream of sludge-food is intermingled with a steady stream of shiney new weapons, all gleaming steel barrels with telescopic sights and intricate grips, all shapes and sizes, and multi-coloured hand-grenades as big as your head, all emblazoned with the name or slogan of the buyers' religious or ideological preferences, "Up With ----!", "Down With---!" or, "A Safety First Death To ----!" It's a lovely sight. I'm so happy just strolling about, carrying my enormous Monkey Wrench or something, making my notes, and feeling such an incomprehensibly vital part of this magnificent, fun, and productive industrial Lozzo world.

LOZZO, THE GREAT BENEFACTOR

The Lozzo business has been not just a wonderful provider of jobs and security for the people of Foulburgh but also a wonderful provider of local amenities and services of all sorts for them. Practically on every corner there's something of the kind, the Lozzo Machine Gun Library for example, or the Lozzo Atom Bomb Fogey Farm. The Lozzo Nerve Gas Arts and Crafts Gallery stands proudly right in the centre of the beautiful Lozzo Germ Warfare Plaza, all thanks to the Lozzo Trust Fund set up by the Great Lozzo Benefactor himself with his plutocratic millions, centuries ago, Lord Lozzo the First. Yes, Lord Lozzo the First, that great owner of slaves, feller of forests, builder of mills, miner of mines and general grand exploiter of Earth and human resources - sad, I once thought fleetingly, for the Earth and its people and animals, etc., to be so thoroughly exploited, but then, we are always told to ponder, without that thorough, exhaustive exploitation of natural wealth how could any financial wealth ever have been created? Financial wealth that all of us benefit from, especially the Lozzo Lineage, of course, but financial wealth that trickles right down to benefit even the very lowest levels of the human heap, albeit in ways that many of us down here at the bottom of that heap wouldn't have chosen for ourselves, given the chance, a tiny token drip here and a tiny token drip there.

The current Lord Lozzo continues this tradition of local benevolence through all sorts of projects, big and small, but mostly small. Come to think of it, the only big thing he has donated to the city recently is the wonderful statue of himself, nineteen or twenty foot high, which stands right dead centre in our beautiful Lozzo Germ Warfare Plaza. So high it is that the glorious likeness of His Lordship's, it has to be said, in reality rather shrivelled head can rarely be seen through the ever present Foulburgh fog of chemicals and miscellaneous grime. In fact I do sometimes wonder if the statue is a very good likeness of His Lordship in any way at all, given that in real life he is such a tiny, wrinkled up, ancient sort of a man, clad most often in ill-fitting, tattered, shiny suits on his few appearances in daylight, rather than this god-like figure in its flowing robes, clutching its orb and sceptre. Maybe there's been some kind of mistake? but, no, there on the monumental pedestal it says, "Lord Lozzo of Lozzo XIV", so it must be him.

When the statue of Lord Lozzo of Lozzo XIV was unveiled for the first time, in a magnificent ceremony to which the entire population was enticed with the offer of a free non-alcoholic drink and an artificial nut each, I thought Edrigo was going to die, from an attack he had of some kind, difficult to say what, rapture? or rupture? The people of Foulburgh mostly reacted in a similar sort of way too, and over the following weeks and months, an unofficial competition started up quite spontaneously, citizens seeing how far they could climb up the great work. Then, with a shocking lack of respect for the Great Benefactor, under cover of darkness, they tried to see just how many bizarre and inappropriate items they could decorate it with, items such as soiled underwear, empty cans and bottles, traffic cones, used condoms, bicycle frames, bits of abandoned soft furnishings, tattered lampshades and so on. Condoms, by the way, fit perfectly on the fingers of the hand which holds the orb balanced on its palm. I can't say they add much to the work though, dangling sadly there like deflated soggy balloons after some coital birthday party. Dearie, dearie me... Come to think of it, you might almost think that the sculptor had deliberately made the statute with as many places from which such rude things could be dangled as possible... It's all removed by the Lozzo Police Army the next morning and the great work is scrubbed clean of graffiti and daubings by the community penitential service chain gang... ready for a repeat performance the next night. Dear, dear... such lack of respect for authority and autocracy...

As I say, the Lozzo benevolence still flows freely in small ways too. The Occasional Crust is given out to the Unknown Beggar once a month without fail, and a ceremonial Twig of Divine Right is planted outside the Lozzo Machine Gun Library every year, in the Spring, if there is a Spring...

...but that's enough about my important work at Lozzo Industries for now. We're heading back to where we left me outside my flat, at No. 77 Slaughterhouse Lane, in the blistering heat that followed close behind the super-cataclysmic storm, my head throbbing and reeling with bafflement and confusion, watching my errant male organ of regeneration, aka, cock, or King Magnus, vanishing at the gallop round the corner on my bike, off somewhere to keep his "Appointment with Lady Destiny", then coming face to face with the curious blue-green apparition of the... Heebiegeebies...

CHAPTER THREE

BEINGS OF LIGHT ENTERTAINMENT

So here I am again, back outside my flat at 77 Slaughterhouse Lane with those two curious pink elephant-headed gentlemen, the Heebiegeebies. I'm feeling more than a little poorly, as they put it, my head is throbbing and reeling like crazy, what with the strange event of my male organ of regeneration becoming some sort of separate regal entity, "King Magnus", and leaving me, and the blistering heat following on from the super-cataclysmic storm, all on top of my usual state of bewilderment, so I'm quite happy for them to escort me round to Dr Krakk's clinic as a prelude to breakfast at the Salvation Hotel... especially as I have the strongest feeling that I know them from somewhere... but where?...

DR KRAKK - GENIUS OF ENERGY MEDICINE

As Beebee and Geegee Heebiegeebie escort me away everything goes strangely blurred and sparkles with blue-green light, but before I can wonder too much about what's going on I find myself in the waiting room of our most excellent local complementary therapist, Dr Krakk. I happen to know the good doctor very well as he has treated me many times for Sledgehammerer's Elbow, Monkey Wrencher's Wrist Syndrome and stuff like that, and I must say that he's always had me up sledgehammering and monkeywrenching again in no time at all.

The pink elephant-headed gentlemen take a couple of seats and start to peruse magazines on fishing and restoring vintage cars with intense interest. A door opens and Dr Krakk appears, dazzling us with the reflections from his enormous spectacles. He ushers me through to the familiar peaceful ambience of his treatment room, his little world of muscle and meridian charts, pictures of soothing woodland scenery, crystals and pyramids, walls covered with professional certificates, his writing desk with its piles of notes and jug of water, then he guides me onto his treatment couch.

"How nice to see you again, Daniel, and how are we doing?"

"Well... I'm having rather a strange day... and I feel as if my brains have turned into a steaming, churning mush of some kind..."

Doctor Krakk sits at his desk unperturbed, taking notes, listening with his radar dish-like ears as I sketch in the outline of the day's curious events. He makes empathetic "hmm's" and "sooo's" now and then, giving me gentle, friendly glances through those colossal spectacles.

Doctor Krakk treats his patients on the principle that there's no physical problem that doesn't have some element of an emotional, or energetic, non-physical problem at its heart, and that's where patient and therapist should focus if they really want to make progress, accessing the patient's Inner Wisdom as a guide. In his understanding, life's whole cavalcade of one damn thing after another is just a kind of educational journey of the soul - and the sooner you get your head round whatever the lessons you're supposed to be learning at any particular time might be, the quicker you can sail through the storms of life into calmer waters. I can tell you that it certainly works for Sledgehammerer's Elbow.

"Hmmm... So, this... er... King Magnus, that is... ahem... your penis, has left you, Daniel? Well, well, most curious! Possibly a whole new syndrome... quite possibly the first ever case of Departing Organ Syndrome... still, a wave of change is rippling around the world, we must expect more and more curious things such as this to happen."

Doctor Krakk gives me a physical checkover with many "hmm's" and "sooo's" then sits at the end of the couch and takes a hold of my head. That's another funny thing, wherever your physical problem is, sooner or later he'll start holding your head. He did start to explain why to me once but lost me very quickly... something to do with fluids, or nerves or something. Anyway, on we go...

"So let's see what your Inner Wisdom has to say about all this, Daniel. Breath in slowly... and out... gently... and relaaax....verrry gooood..."

He starts to guide me into my imagination, down inner stairs into my subconscious, as he's done many times before. I generally find I'm pretty good at drifting into my inner imaginary world... so much practice at school and work I guess.

"Now I would like you to keep taking slow deep breaths in... and keep breathing out gently and slowly too... I'd like you to imagine that you're going down a staircase, a long staircase... and that with each slow out breath... and with each slow step down you're relaxing more and more deeply..."

Just listening to his soothing voice is enough to start me off inwards and downwards. I head down into my inner world, down many flights of steps, onto landings leading off in many directions... down more flights of steps. All the time, I'm becoming more and more relaxed, and the imagery is becoming more and more vivid, until I feel I am actually living in the scene itself. You might think that an old narcoleptic like me would fall asleep, but not a bit of it. Though I'm deeply relaxed, I'm becoming much more awake and alert than usual. Dr Krakk's voice is still quite clear and he gently guides me along through doorways and corridors, and down yet more steps.

"Now why don't we look for your Inner Control Room today, Daniel, and see if we can find out anything about today's curious events...."

My subconscious obliges by taking me through a doorway off a landing, heading down more steps, finally leading us to a doorway lettered, "Ye Controlle Roome". It's set in a rather grand stone surround carved with heraldic symbols, mythic creatures and the like. Strange, but this must be it.

I have to say it's a bit of a mess inside the heavy old,

creaking oak door. I push my way through a clutter of boxes and filing cabinets overflowing with papers and folders, parchment manuscripts and carved stone tablets all piled higgledy-piggledy on top of one another. There's cobwebs and dust everywhere, I notice drawers with labels such as: "Memories - Early", "Memories - Youthful", "Memories - Still to Come", there's "Akashic Records - Human", and "Akashic Records - Not Human", all empty. There's a huge empty bookcase carved at the top with the word "school", with empty shelves labelled "French", "Latin", "Greek - Ancient", "Greek - Modern", "Greek - In Between", "Geography", "History", "Statistics", and so on. Hardly anything stored anywhere here at all, and none of it in the right place. The whole area looks as if it has been ransacked by a Mongol Horde.

A hum of equipment and chatter of voices is coming from further in, so I squeeze along through the clutter of the corridor, heading in that direction. I find myself in a large room, a stone vault where operators of some kind sit staring at ancient-looking screens and banks of obsolete-looking switches, levers and dials. I notice that there's a feeling of barely controlled panic in the air. One of the operators, who has an air of authority about him and a hat which says, "Ye Braine Masterre", turns and sees me. I smile to myself on seeing that here, at least, the letters "E" and "S" don't fall off.

"Ye Gods! Mr Daniel, Sire! Please come in! This is a... very pleasant surprise!" He leaps to his feet and bows, the other operatives following his example. "Methinks we're getting ye Great Genital Departure Emergency under control, Sire... doing everything we can of course... but without your normal Testicle-to-Thought connection input, it's touch and go... for, as you well know, those Testicle-Brain units were supplying more than half, well sometimes almost all, of your normal thinking activity... and so consequently your higher brain function layers, such as they are, are desperately thrashing about searching for input, searching for connections, whizzing about, heavily underloaded and overloaded at the same time... they've mostly shut themselves up and down thank goodness, but a Raw Unprocessed Thought Vaccuum Pressure is building up and up!... I'm afraid there is ye significant risk of Ye Mental Meltdownne Implozionne Event... *ad astra non verba!*..."

Well, no wonder I feel a bit odd...

Ye Brain Masterre mutters frantically as he turns back to the screens,"...but methinks we'll avoid Ye Mental Meltdownne if we link up these old reptile brain units we found down in the basement, they're completely obsolete and haven't been used for thousands of years... but they may just give us enough emergency processable input... the lads are bringing the last of them up now... I should stand back for a moment Sire! these old thinking units are very, very unstable..."

Ye Brain Masterre turns away, mumbling to himself, to check on some process or other and I take a look around. My Inner Controlle Roome is a stone-built vault, something between a medieval cathedral, a vampire's lair and a steam railway station, with all sorts of equipment crammed into it, from the sort of stuff medieval alchemists and magicians would have used if they had ever tried to send a man to the Moon, or to create life in the lab from green sludge and bits of dead bodies, all leather, iron nails, wood and glass, to slightly more modern stuff, thermionic valves glowing away, the air shimmering around them, huge cathode ray tubes, there's reel-to-reel tapes creaking away in the background and lots of gently smoking exposed cloth-wrapped wiring, smoke also curls up from transformers the size of cows scattered about. A mummified unicorn floats in a glass tank of fluid, with a bemused grin about its muzzle. Flickering multi-coloured light filters down on the scene through stained-glass windows, and high up in the background a wild-haired figure is hammering out rousing music from the many keyboards, pedals and stops of a cathedral organ.

Well, well... and no wonder I feel a bit confused sometimes...

A crew of dishevelled, unkempt workers of all sorts is scurrying about everywhere. Some wear the white coats of scientists, others the flowing, symbol-embroidered robes of alchemists, others the overalls of mechanics, joiners and carpenters, painters and decorators, all of them are hurrying about with boxes of tools, I think some of them are for measuring, others possibly for welding, and carrying bits of material, wood, sacking, leather and stuff. I notice with great pleasure that there's even a worker wandering about aimlessly with a monkey wrench over his shoulder, tightening up a nut here and loosening another one off there... I wonder for a moment if he has a control room in his little brain where another, very tiny guy is walking around with a monkey wrench over his shoulder and if maybe that very tiny guy has a control room inside his tiny little brain in which another, even tinier still, guy is wandering aimlessly about with a by now very, very tiny monkey wrench over his shoulder... and so on smaller... and smaller... and smaller and so on... until maybe there's little tiny quons and glarks wandering about in there with little sub-atomic adjustable spanners on their shoulders... is there a point at which things just can't get any smaller? Do they instead, at that point, suddenly get bigger again? What on Earth would happen to my poor brain then? This is all too much to ponder over at the moment... so I stop.

A gang of heavily-built, extra-dishevelled and unkempt labourers puff and wheeze as they drag two lumps of dusty, cob-webby extra-ancient looking equipment on creaking cartwheels up a spiral stone staircase into Ye Controlle Roome. The equipment appears through the doorway, two huge wooden crates, reinforced with iron bands, from whose open tops the mouldy sides of glass tanks protrude. I sense that these could be Ye Obsolete Reptilian Thinking Units. There seem to be Things swimming around in the filthy greenish water inside the tanks, every now and then I get a glimpse of slithering scaley coils of something ancient and reptilian... maybe a crocodilisk?... or a basiligator?...

The labourers push the two Obsolete Reptilian Thinking Units right up to the main Controlle Console where half a dozen more are already lined up. Next they take coils and coils of huge cables with clips on their ends down from hooks on the walls - I've seen things like these at work, I think they're called "The Jump Leads" - then with noble disregard for their personal safety, the labourers, wearing stout leather gauntlets, welders masks and chain-mail aprons, reach down into the foul waters with the clips and attach them as best they can to the horrible things sloshing about within. It's a miracle that none of them is injured by the gnashings of teeth and lashings of tails that follow. Worse is to come though when the stout labourers connect the other ends of the cables to Ye Controlle Console and start cranking two giant handles on the fronts of the units. This sets off the most awful noise of obsolete reptilian screeching as the beasts thrash around in the fluid. Bright green sparks and flashes dart all over Ye Controlle Roome, from Ye Obsolete Reptilian Thinking Units and from Ye Controlle Consoles. Cogs and wheels start to grind and mesh in the background, operators stare intently and nervously into their medieval monitors, cables glow, thermionic valves crackle and hum, transformers smoke...

"More power, laddes! Fasterre! Fasterrrre!" shouts Ye Braine Masterre, *"In absentia lucis, absurdum est!"*

With yet more cranking, a spectral dirty grey flickering starts up in one of the dormant monitors, with "Ye Streamme of Consciousnesse" carved into its frame, then moves into another and another, there is a general hubbub of excitement as little by little the banks of screens come to life again, and the atmosphere of panic calms down a notch or two.

"Merciful Heavens!" shouts Ye Masterre, "Sire!... It seems to be working..."

A gong rings out loud and clear through the vault. At the sound of this, a cheer ripples around the crew and there is tremendous general excitement.

"Oh Wondrous Day! Ye Gong of Thought Occurrence rings out anew! Ye Mental Meltdownne be avoided!... *Quad erat desperatum*!... Heavens be praised!..."

And I suddenly feel just a tiny bit better as the throbbing, churning and boiling starts to subside in my brain...

UPGRADE

The gentle voice of Doctor Krakk drifts into this joyous scene.

"We just have ten minutes till the end of our session, Daniel, is there anything we should attend to while we're here? I fear that your brain crew may just have patched things up in there with temporary measures. May I suggest applying some upgrades and modernisation to your control room? I think you'd find that most helpful in the medium and long-term future... how does that feel?"

Krakk's words make me think, yes, perhaps it's time to make a few changes in here... I remember the control room of a starship in some old sci-fi TV series or other...

"Yes... let's upgrade a few things in here!..."

With my subconscious assisted by suggestions from Doctor Krakk, I start bringing Mynne Controlle Roome forwards from Ye Darkke Agees. Out go leather, oaken cupboards, iron filing cabinets, tablets of stone and cauldrons of goo, in come hi-tech materials from the future, super-efficient, high-speed storage, and solid-state pondering units.

With Doctor Krakk's helpful advice, I install a Logic and Metaphysics Quantum Pondering Suite and something he describes as a Five-Fold High Frequency Intuition Resonator, for Co-Immersion with Global Consciousness or something, also a Sheep Uncounting Accessory Unit, to help me to stay awake through Tiresome Times, as well as a Shuggy Machine Instant Comprehension Repair Re-purpose and Design Channel, which speaks for itself, and some other state-of-the-art brain stuff which can't actually be described in any Earth language.

I make all these changes and also set up a brain staff retraining and grooming rota for good measure. By the time Doctor Krakk starts to guide me back to the surface again the upgrade is well under way. I come around slowly, feeling a bit better, sort of slightly un-deranged and re-connected or something, and strangely awake, and Dr Krakk ushers me back to the waiting room.

"Ah there you are", says Beebee Heebiegeebie, "Helpful treatment I trust, young Daniel? Now, breakfast!"

The three of us now take a leisurely stroll back through the dishevelled streets of Foulburgh, streets that are no longer being thrashed by a super-cataclysmic thunderstorm, nor being roasted by a super-heated heat wave, no no, not at all, streets that are now frozen solid. Honestly, the seasons are switching about so quickly and randomly these days that there's hardly time to register whether it's Spring, Autumn, or whatever... better just to think of it being a kind of continuous Highly Variable Clag Season. At the moment, there seems to be an inch or two of ice on everything and the going is very slippy indeed. Citizens of Foulburgh are falling flat on their faces and arses all around us, though they're still managing to fight, curse, do drug deals, beg and play the bagpipes.

Fortunately, my Lozzo Industrial work wellies are fitted with excellent studs, giving me a fine grip of the icey pavements, and the Heebiegeebies glide along quite serenely, apparently not really needing any foot-ground traction for their progress, chatting away as we go. Sadly, I don't hear a word of this as my brain is busy adjusting to Dr Krakk's treatment, and I'm taking in the wonders of Foulburgh almost as if I've never seen them before. It's a funny thing, but I suddenly seem to notice everything around me in ever sharper and sharper detail... are my senses getting stronger and stronger? or is all the dereliction and decay suddenly getting much much worse?

ABANDONED SOFAS

Foulburgh has been falling down for years, but the rate at which it's been falling down seems to have gone falling right up recently. Wherever you go round town, you see paint peeling and flaking, signs with missing letters, buildings subsiding and cracking, metalwork rusting completely away, broken down sofas and prams abandoned on the pavements, straggly bushes and weeds growing in the once delightfully neat car parks, dead and dying trees. Talking of trees, the one place where they do seem to be flourishing is up amongst the roofs and chimney pots. They seem to love it up there, but it's the beginning of the end for a building when tree roots grow down into its chimney stacks, on through the roof, get their woody fingers into the walls and slowly start to tear it all apart.

Things are never repaired properly in Foulburgh, new paint in random colours, mostly in shades of grey or brown, brown mainly, because that's usually the colour you get when you mix all your left over paint together, random brown that's slapped straight on top of those old rotten, peeling boards. Broken windows are patched up with any old scrap of salvaged wood or plastic packaging. Sagging walls and roofs are propped up with tree trunks and piles of old broken blocks of concrete. Damp seeps through everything in every direction, up, down, sideways, leaving patches of mould, mildew and fungus growing everywhere.

Long ago, there were shops everywhere selling all kinds of stuff, but they're all gone now. Trade has mostly moved out to giant fortified mega-stores away from the centre, or onto the flickering screens of the internet, leaving a sad abandoned, gutted shell. The boards of the dead shops' windows have been ripped off and carried away to fix up a broken window or something somewhere else leaving a sad mess visible inside. Anything at all useable having been looted, all that's left is piles of un-opened mail, dead electrical fittings, smashed crockery, broken furniture and so on.

The saddest shells, however, are the old dead bars, once rollicking drinking dens alive and kicking from dawn to dusk with intellectual discussion and general merriment, even... actual musicians playing actual music!... not any more...

Now, this morning, I feel bombarded even more intensely than usual by all these inputs, the sights, sounds, and smells of decay. But the strongest impression I get is from the light, the still faint yellow morning light glinting through the frozen grime on the trees, squeezing its way through the swirling purpley-green clouds of chemicals billowing from the Lozzo factories, battling with the flickering orange streetlights and neon signs, it's a light that gives everything the sort of look that I imagine Venus must have on a particularly acidic Monday morning.

The wind suddenly picks up again, in a storm that must be getting to the very top of the super-cataclysmic range now, bits of building are getting blown past, whizzing along on the ice, and the ground itself seems to be shaking. Fortunately, my hi-viz Lozzo afty work coat is one of my longest and toughest. Work gear has to be extra-extra tough at Lozzo Industries, naturally, to cope with all the awful chemical and other hazards flying about. I gather the day-glo yellow chemical and storm resistant material around me and pull the hood up over my head. It's one of the many coats and jackets I inherited from Shuggy, who was a huge tall hulk of a guy, so it comes down right to my ankles. The hailstones, fresh streaks of lightning and bits of building all just bounce off me. None of this seems to bother the Heebiegeebies in the slightest, they just seem to swoosh gracefully along in their blue-green glow, their smart appearance quite unruffled. We're at the Salivation Hotel in no time at all.

AT THE SALIVATION HOTEL

The Eat All You Like All Day Every Day Full And I Mean Full Traditional Breakfast Buffet at the Salivation is a magnificent event. It was first put on several hundred years ago when the hotel opened and has been going non-stop all day and all night ever since, with a couple of changes of staff of course. Serving tables, hot plates, hot cabinets and gas burners are arranged all along one wall of the vast dining hall. Diners by the hundred are shuffling along the steaming display piling up their plates with every possible breakfast item: nine different types of bacon, cooked to various levels of carbonisation, eggs, (poached, fried, scrambled, coddled, boiled, in omellettes), sausages, of various content and shape, black pudding, white pudding, grey pudding, haggis, beans, more beans, tomatoes, mushrooms, chips, waffles, pancakes, bread pan-fried in bacon fat rather than that abomination of being dipped in the deep-fat fryer, toast, (brown, white, wholemeal, gluten free), croissants, morning rolls, marmalade, jams, various, butter, non-dairy spread, coffee, tea, dairy and non-dairy milk and cream, sugar, brown and white - all the main staples as you'd expect. A team of huge, tattooed chefs, waiters and waitresses, all in their stained and tattered breakfast costumes, rush about serving, bringing out fresh trays and tureens of food and flagons of fruit juices, various, through the kitchen doors, passing it through hatchways, taking it from lifts and ferrying it around on trolleys. For the more adventurous there's devilled kidneys, kippers, haddock, salmon, mackerel, trout, kedgeree... right at the very end there's even a healthy option or two, a yoghurt, a wheatgrass stem, part of an apple, a pineapple chunk, and so on, all looking rather jaded having sat there unwanted for at least a century. There's not many takers for any of that kind of stuff of course, this being Foulburgh, world capital of unhealthy eating. We pile up our plates and a waiter shows us to a table. The noise in the hall is deafening, rattling plates and cutlery, the sloshing of hot drinks and the roar of conversation. This doesn't stop me chatting with my new, familiar-seeming, elephant-headed friends though, as I now find that as well as having sharpened senses, I can communicate telepathically with them... well, I think, that's strange... but handy too, as you can chat and eat without any pause at all, except to catch a breath now and then.

THE HEEBIEGEEBIES, BEINGS OF LIGHT

- Quite an interesting day already, eh, Daniel? Let me tell you a little about myself and Geegee...

Beebee and Geegee go on to explain that they are beings of pure energy rather than physical matter, originally from a remote cluster of stars and planets, who normally zoom about the Universe in blissful beams of pure love and light but who have brought the frequencies of their life force vibrations way, way, waaaay down from their own level so that they can appear as fleshy versions of themselves in our Earth plane, where they have come to study such subjects as Life and Stupidity, as in their own world they are what we would describe as students. They tell me they can't put this all to me in much detail because our primitive Earth languages don't have the words for it, and my primitive Earthling brain would simply explode if they transferred their full understanding of it all to me telepathically, even with all my recent upgrades from Dr Krakk's treatment session. It turns out, by the way, that Dr Krakk is a friend of theirs from long, long ago, another being of pure energy rather than physical matter, from a different cluster of stars and planets to the Heebiegeebies' cluster, tucked away in the back of the cosmic beyond, who also normally zooms about the Universe in a blissful beam of pure love and light. Well, well... I had wondered more than once before if he was from another planet or something...

Anyway, the Heebiegeebies do transfer a few of their basic concepts to me: Space and Time are so completely enfolded that Scale and Location are meaningless, big things are really wrapped up inside small things as well as vice versa, further dimensions are folded up around us and down within us, and Space and Time are multi-phasic, multiple strands of reality travelling in enfolded waves... and there is no beginning or end to the Universe or Time or anything, how could there be? What would come before or after it? Everything is just sort of bouncing and flickering between being and not-being all the time... or something like that anyway.

Normally, stuff like that would have put me to sleep in seconds but their telepathy just sort of pops into my head without my having to concentrate at all, and I do feel a bit... more awake, even receptive, now, after my treatment session and brain upgrades...

- So, if you don't mind me asking, if you Heebiegeebies have evolved over trillions and trillions of Earth years into beings who mostly just tootle around the Universe in blissful beams of pure love and light, why would you want to visit a ghastly place like Foulburgh? Couldn't you study something nice? in more pleasant surroundings?

- Well you see, Daniel, taking on physical bodies for a while allows us to appreciate and understand things at a core, primal level, to experience a much wider range of emotions, and so much more fully... not just pure bliss, but all the other stuff you human beings feel every day, anger, fear, joy, humour, sadness, contentment, the pleasure of eating an excellent all-day-breakfast... Think back to the last time you felt anger, for example, it wasn't just in your mind was it? Your whole body became angry, didn't it? heart pounding, jaw clenching, blood boiling, hair standing on end and waving about... making the experience so much more intense.

Yes, I know just what he means...

- Heebiegeebies have been visiting Earth for billions of years, but in this present age, Earth life has reached the most extraordinary point. You human beings, in your insane, short-sighted, fossil-fuelled, industrial exploitation of your planet, have brought it to a point from which there may very well be no going back, a point leading in an ever more destructive downwards spiral to mass extinction, to the inevitable loss of almost all life here, to a point where Life on Earth is teetering on the edge of the Total Collapse of Everything...

This is just the sort of thing Edrigo has been saying recently...

-... yes, your friend Edrigo sees this all very clearly... leading to such degradation of your environment that it will reach a state in which it can support barely a ghost of the wonderful diversity it has seen in the recent past, and never develop that same wonderful diversity ever again before it is swallowed up by the Sun...

-...you have beings all over the Universe watching, gripped in horror and fascination, on the edge of our seats and perches. We can't believe your stupidity. This dire spectacle on Earth has drawn many other student Heebiegeebies here, and other entities too, by the way... like the dreadful K'oll-eE-Wobbuls... (they both wince and hiss telepathically at the thought of these beings)... we'll tell you more about those dastardly mischief makers later...

-... the suspense is so intense! Will you Earthlings destroy almost all life as you know it on your planet or come to your senses in the nick of time? and there is indeed a tidal wave of change rippling around the planet! Perhaps it's not too late... Though the general thinking in the sentient cosmos is that there will be a widespread and very upsetting total and general collapse of all the human and environmental systems of your industrial way of life before anything like enough of you, politicians and everyday people alike, make anything other than the most pathetic token gestures towards sustainable living.

- You and Edrigo were assigned to Beebee and me, Daniel, not long after you were born, as two of our own personal study cases, and we really must thank you for all the excellent entertainment and enlightening insight into human being behaviour you have given us.

It takes a moment for this to register with me...

- You mean... you've been studying me all my life?

This is a bit of a shocker for me... it could explain why they seem so familiar though...

- Well... yes...

- Everything I've been doing?... at school... at work and... eating and sleeping and... everything else?... like going to the toilet and... having sex... and everything?...

- Yes, Daniel! and the "Earthenders" series of programmes we've been making about you and Edrigo and the Collapse of Life on Earth have made you into two of the biggest entertainment, and educational, stars in the whole Universe! Isn't that wonderful!

- What!?... (I'm feeling several different emotions with my whole body now)... you mean you've been making programmes about us and all the... intimate detail of our lives... and broadcasting them... throughout the whole Universe?...

THE HEEBIEGEEBIES
BEINGS OF LIGHT ENTERTAINMENT

It takes me a lot of sausages and bacon to get my head around this idea at all. It seems that what the Heebiegeebies started as a kind of series of Natural History broadcasts for bored Light Beings, basically a bit of student fun, turned out to be tremendously popular, as well as educational, and evolved into a kind of regular student tragi-comic video programme, "Earthenders". It developed a life of its own. It began with a few mad escapades from my life and Edrigo's, so many to choose from in the days of our crazy collapsing industrial world, and slowly but surely took off until now every episode is watched by squadrillions of beings from every corner of every galaxy, both near and far, far away, a kind of multi-galactic tragi-comic soap opera, or something, constantly discussed and speculated about between episodes by hordes of universal university professors, therapists, entertainment pundits and all the rest of the great cosmic audience.

- You mean that squadrillions of beings have watched me having sex... for entertainment? I'm a kind of... cosmic porn star?...

- Well, no, really Edrigo is a little bit more of a star in that department, you have more of a name for comedy, Daniel, falling asleep at inappropriate moments, creating industrial mayhem, that sort of thing, oh! the pleasure you have given to so many entities!... well... yes, for entertainment... er... but in the name of Science ultimately, to help us to understand Behavioural Patterns and so on... all the episodes are repeated over and over again, there's always something new to be seen in them! classic entertainment... and so educational...

- Well, I don't remember giving anyone permission to watch me all the time.

- But, Daniel, when your own Natural Scientists here on Earth are studying insects and animals do they ask them for their permission? No! And, by the way, what's the first aspect of life they focus on? Why, you're hardly five of your Earth minutes into the programme before the subjects are engaging in full-on carnal knowledge of one another. They're not aware that they're being watched at all are they? And neither have you been... up till now... and I think we'll be more than making up with you for any intrusion, Daniel, we'll tell you all about that later...

The idea of being some kind of insect or animal for Extra-Terrestrials to study and make tragi-comic soap operas about is really making my brains bubble and slosh about in a whole new different way now, this is all just getting stranger and stranger... I move on to something else...

- Changing the subject a bit - I think back to them - it's a strange thing but no one here seems to be have spotted your elephant-shaped heads, if you don't mind me saying.

- Very observant of you, Daniel, yes, well, people just don't seem to notice an elephant in a room do they? That's exactly why we use this disguise on Earth, so that we can mingle amongst you and watch you without being seen ourselves.

- But I can see you...

- That's because you're waking up, Daniel. Haven't you noticed that everything seems a bit more in focus, more detailed today? After your... er... Decocktion Process, and Brain Upgrades you'll probably keep on finding your senses get sharper and sharper, and all sorts of other possibilities and abilities will open up for you too.

- Now that you mention it, yes, I suppose things do seem a bit clearer today...

- Look round the room, Daniel, I wonder if you can spot anymore Heebiegeebies having breakfast at the moment?

I look carefully around the crowded hall and see a tell-tale faint blue-green haze here and there. There's quite a scattering of pink-headed, big-eared gentlemen, and some pink-headed, big-eared ladies too, floppy hats are raised, and pink hands and trunks are waved in greeting from all around the room when they're spotted.

- Most of our production crew come here for breakfast when we're putting the latest show together, it's very grounding. That's our editors over there, the sisters Chopchop and Stikistiki Heebiegeebie, they do a vital task most ably, well done and thank you ladies! Keep those scissors snipping!

The two smartly suited ladies go even pinker and grin from floppy ear to floppy ear.

- And that's our ancient commentator over there, Sir Boatey McBoatface Beebeecee Heebiegeebie... aaah! how soothing are the friendly, cultured tones of that familiar voice, as he describes yet another scene of carnal knowledge... it's an honour to work with you, Sir Boatey!

Sir Boatey doffs his floppy hat and smiles his lop-sided venerable smile at us.

- And over there, Daniel, look who we have composing the music for this whole current series, it's the immortal Zizi Heebiegeebies! One, Two and Three...

Geegee points out three particularly impressive looking elephant-headed gentlemen, very sharply dressed even by Heebiegeebie standards, with embroidered jackets and gold jewellery galore, two of them with long, luxuriant beards, all three of them with dark glasses. The Zizi Heebigeebies nod the heads under their magnificently embroidered hats and raise their gold encrusted pink fingers in effortlessly cool acknowledgement. No surpise that their fame should have spread throughout the Universe, you only get that good when you've been making music together for a long, long time.

MORE COFFEE, SIR?

Throughout our telepathic conversation, the Heebie-geebies and I have been tucking into a little breakfast top-up with gusto. For beings with the elephant-shaped heads you might have associated with vegetarianism, they can certainly put away the bacon and sausages. The great thing about telepathy is that you can eat and talk at the same time, as fast as you like, without bits of food coming flying out of your mouth and spattering your companions, and without egg yolk and stuff dribbling down your chin.

In the Salivation's very civilised manner, waiters and waitresses have been flitting attentively from table to table with steaming trays and trolleys, keeping our plates and mugs topped up. More coffee, sir? More bacon? More toast, sir? Brown or white? Gluten free? Gluten encrusted? Crusts on? Crusts off, sir? Two extra-heavily built waiters are doing the rounds with a giant cauldron of beans suspended from a pole which they carry on their shoulders, ladling the stuff out to any takers as they go. Another two come along with a similar arrangement for those whole tomatoes in sauce that are a vital part of any truly "full" breakfast spread.

Being the world's oldest hotel, the Salivation is crumbling apart even faster and more thoroughly than most of the rest of Foulburgh. Part of a wall falls onto the serving tables just now as the waiters, waitresses and chefs work away, but they carry nobly on, calmly straightening their huge hats and uniforms, propping the wall back up with old chairs and wardrobes. Nobody is hurt and they deftly scoop bits of plaster and lathe out of the chips and eggs. The sound of kitchen equipment exploding and smoke, screeches and curses billow out from the kitchen doors whenever they open, we catch glimpses of cleavers and crates of sausages flying through the air within. No one seems in the least bit surprised or concerned. The Heebiegeebies and I carry on chomping.

Even when part of the ceiling collapses on top of a neighbouring table bringing down with it part of the bedroom above, complete with a bed occupied by a couple having boisterous carnal knowledge of each other, we diners munch on as if nothing had happened, save for one woman at a neighbouring table:

"Wilbur!" she shrieks, "You... you... Depraved Naughty Monster!"

She picks up the nearest heavy object, a length of lead piping from some bit of broken plumbing or other, and chases the naked couple around and out of the dining room. They leave a trail of torn and soggy bedlinen, and more curses and screams behind them.

"You....you.... LITTLE RASCAAAAAL!" ...and worse...

Across the hall, part of the floor caves in, rotten I suppose, swallowing up a table and its four diners whole. They manage to cling to the edges of the carpet and scramble back out. In a flash, the floor is fixed with a couple of palettes, and some twigs and paper, a fresh table is laid for them, fresh breakfasts are conjured up and all is well again.

EARTH - WHICH WAY WILL IT GO?

- Yes, Daniel, you Earthlings have beings all over the Universe watching "Earthenders" on the edge of our seats, gripping our perches with whitened talons, eyes out on stalks, literally, in many cases. The last episode was simply appalling, no sentient life form anywhere can believe your hideous, cruelty towards each other...

- ...the senseless brutality of your wars, the destruction, the appalling everyday mindless violence...

- ...such unbelievable stupidity, short-sighted ignorance, vanity... and that's in your leadership...

- ...your self-seeking, unthinking incompetence and barbarity...

- ...can a species really be quite so stupid? To be comprenhensively destroying the very biosphere that keeps it alive, in spite of years and years of scientific reports and forecasts detailing the devastation of your land and ocean, the trends becoming more and more obvious... now you see the super-cataclysmic floods, storms and fires with your own eyes, and yet you still choose to ignore it all, call it a hoax, make empty proclamations of emergency and pathetic gestures towards change but still carry mindlessly on with your stupid, wanton, industrial, exploitative way of life... it's a hideous, ghastly spectacle...

- I'm getting the idea, I interrupt, but if it's so appalling why do you watch us?

- Well, Daniel, thinks Beebee, chomping on a sausage while holding his mug of coffee with his trunk, the thing is, it's appalling yet fascinating at the same time. I mean what sort of entertainment do you have here yourselves? It's all murders and wars and blood isn't it? How many of your films, soap operas, plays or books start happily, carry on happily and end happily? You watch, read and listen out of a sort of horror-struck fascination don't you? It's appalling but you're hooked aren't you? And there are such wonderful, funny, touching, heart warming moments too in your tragi-comic soap-opera lives... in spite of all your cruelty and stupidity, en masse, when we get to know individual human beings better we find that you can actually be quite pleasant, co-operative and capable of such a wonderful generosity of spirit... we do believe that you're mostly all decent beings deep down inside, albeit very, very, abysmally deep in some cases, and we can't help but become a bit fond of some of you... contradictions at every turn with you Earthlings! All the light entertainment critics are absolutely gibbering about "Earthenders", by the way...

- ...and things may yet turn out well for the human race, and all life on your planet, a wave of change is rippling around your world... Mother Nature is reasserting and re-balancing herself in all sorts of small and large events... your decocktion is just one of many of these,

Daniel, a long overdue re-balancing of the attributes and influences of gender in your daily lives, the beginning of the end of the ghastly, baleful, stranglehold of patriarchy...

- ...even at this eleventh hour you may escape from the jaws of the total collapse of everything.

- There's other worlds out there where things, you may find this hard to believe, have been in an even worse state than here on Earth! And yet Nature has managed to restore herself.

- Now... the thing is, Daniel, there's a huge audience of Earthenders fanatics who are desperate for the show to keep on running, and would just hate it if you did kill yourselves off, and Beebee and I have a feeling that we might be able to nudge things in the right direction...

- ...though we couldn't actually interfere in Earth events at all... as that would tamper with the Flow of Reality... and who knows where that would lead...

- ...but we might just pop a few ideas into your heads, teach you a few techniques, that sort of thing, all stuff that you're on the verge of understanding anyway, gently shove your evolution along a bit in the general direction of the flow of the succession of Life and Consciousness, which is continually in process here already anyway... even if it's got a bit stuck at the moment... or actually seems to be going backwards at times...

- ...your treatment with our friend from afar, the good Doctor Klakk, was just the start of all that. There's a couple of techniques we'd like to show you next... but not until we've quite finished breakfast, of course! Anyone else for more toast? Oh, and before we start your training let us just tell you about the dreadful K'oll-eE-Wobbuls...

THE DREADFUL K'OLL-EE-WOBBULS

Beebee and Geegee Heebiegeebie go on to tell me a little bit about the dreadful, dastardly K'oll-eE-Wobbuls. They're another race of beings of pure energy rather than physical matter, but it's mostly not very pleasant energy at all. They're often to be found zooming about the Universe in beams of hate and darkness. They are the sort of beings who take pleasure in seeing trouble and strife, a thoroughly nasty lot of mischief-makers, forever stirring up turmoil here on Earth and elsewhere, even when you might have thought that things couldn't get much worse. The Heebiegeebies think that the K'oll-eE-Wobbuls may be trying to stir up even more trouble by giving away some of the secrets of their advanced technology to some Earthling, or Earthlings, in exchange for... well, they can't imagine what...

- We're hoping hard that our Heebiegeebie Techniques will help you all to thwart the K'oll-eE-Wobbul's and their terrible ways...

- Now, how about a last little top-up smidgin of breakfast all round before we get started?

THE BEAM OF PEACE

We get to the point where we can't fit in one more egg or bean, then the whole scene at the Salivation, our three bodies and everything around us, starts to dissolve into tiny sparkling blobs. For a moment we seem to float in a shimmering space of multi-coloured light before we take on physical forms again. All three of us are now dressed in dramatic, flowing, hooded, symbol-embroidered robes - I must say the Heebiegeebies have an eye for style if nothing else. A different scene altogether shimmers into being around us, I recognise it as another street in Foulburgh, one of the network of alleys by the main blast furnace complex, it's the mankier end of Concreted-Over-Gardens Street. There's no storm here, just a fitful greasy wind drifting through the abandoned furniture and supermarket trolleys, a wind which can hardly be bothered to stir up the litter and filth, or ruffle the dead vegetation, and a chilly drizzle - about as good as it gets in our foul city.

- That was the Shimmer Technique, Daniel, which we mostly use for travel in the physical manifestation of the Universe. We'll show you that later, as it's a bit advanced. To start your Energy Training, we're going to show you something simpler, the Beam of Peace Technique, a couple of your Earth years should do the trick...

- A couple of years!

- ...though, of course, you'll be practising and refining these techniques forever! But don't be concerned about the passing years, we've shimmered into a different, backwater phase-strand of time... when we drop you back into your usual phase-strand it will seem as if no time has passed there at all.

Human wreckage is also drifting about Concreted-Over-Gardens Street. One of the tottering hulks, a zombolzoid, notices us and staggers in our direction. On his head there's a threadbare orange cap bearing the slogan, "Proud to be Stupid". He's carrying a hand gun of some kind, not a Lozzo model, I note with surprise. For no obvious reason, the zombolzoid seems to have taken an intense dislike to Beebee. He raises the gun and points it at him, I can see his finger moving onto the trigger. At the same time, the usual green-blue glow around Beebee becomes more intense, and extends out to the gun and forms all around it too. The zombolzoid pulls the trigger but nothing happens, he tries again and again, shakes the gun, bangs it with his fist, but still nothing happens. In zombalzoidal frustration, he raises the gun behind his head to throw it at Beebee... now the greenish-blue glow intensifies further and envelopes him completely. Suddenly he drops the gun and his sneering, menacing attitude melts away.

"Oh... I'm so sorry," the attacker says, "Please forgive me..." His body softens, and sags. Then he seems to gather himself together, he straightens up, there's even the faintest glimmer of the beginnings of some kind of basic intelligence in his eyes. "Thank you, master! Thank you for this precious lesson!"

He starts to shimmer into sparkling light, we hear his last words, "I love you!", fading away into some etheric distance as he dematerialises... and he's gone.

Well, and isn't that just the sort of thing I was trying

to achieve with my Articulated Good Manners Juggernaut Machine!

-Yes, you had something in the vein of the basic concept there, Daniel, it just required a little refinement...

The Heebiegeebies call this technique the Beam of Peace and explain that, as well as neutralising the mental threat of aggression, it can be used to switch off or override the control or operating system of any weapon with any kind of mechanism, be it a bomb, a gun, a missile, a hand-grenade, a land-mine... I'm staggered... this goes way beyond good manners...

- Any weapon at all?

- Yes.

- Any weapon at all can just be... switched off?... with your projected mental energy control?... so that it's completely useless?

- Yes, basically, that's it, yes.

The implications of this start to whizz around in my mind... *wheeee!*... my jaw drops open with a thud... *thhuddd!*... so what on Earth will my enormous co-workers at Lozzo Industries make instead of all those guns and bombs?...

- Focus Daniel! Now we'll show you some more Peace Beaming, we're going to go and play with some tanks!

- It's so much fun! You'll see...

We shimmer to a different scene altogether, a vast wasteland somewhere with a varied, undulating terrain of hills, craters and bogs. Dotted amongst it stand the smoking ruins of buildings. It's a bit like Foulburgh but without all the zombaloids and lunkanumpties staggering about.

We're standing on the highest of the hills watching a seething mass of tanks lumbering about at speed down below us and all around, firing off shells at one another. Shells explode all over the place, making more craters in the bogs or hitting another tank now and again, leaving varying degrees of damage. Beebee and Geegee stand still and focus their attention, sending out the most slender of intense greenish-blue beams towards each of the huge machines. The tanks all stop dead in their tracks for a moment, then rumble into the largest open space and group themselves into a circular formation. Lovely classical waltz music starts to blare out from their loud hailing systems, and they start to perform a kind of weaving-in-and-out dance routine, then reform into various square and triangular patterns, finally coming to rest in a single giant heart shape... shells come flying out of their barrels but turn into bunches of flowers and flocks of birds. The crews emerge, all hug one another and saunter off into the distance arms in arms, while the tanks all quickly rust and rot away back into the Earth before our very eyes.

The Heebiegeebies tell me that it's possible to defend against any weapon with a mechanism using the Beam of Peace technique, some you can only switch off but others can even be taken over and played with, like these tanks. The secret is to focus into their energy fields, and to look for their weakest links. There's always something: a circuit, something that generates a spark or a signal, an aiming device or a detonator, something that can be switched off or interrupted, whether it's a bomb, or a gun, or a missile. The more complicated the weapon, the easier it is to interrupt. Tanks and warplanes are most easily disrupted, as, for all their size, they often have some very sensitive energy fields, whereas the fields of guns, hand grenades and other similar devices are much cruder and harder to work with. In the case of a weapon with no mechanism, such as a cudgel, a knife or a shillelagh, the non-aggressor has to shine his or her Beam of Peace directly onto the attacker, to neutralise their urge to fight.

The implications of all this are still dawning on me and becoming more and more amazing - all weapons can be neutralised?... that means no more fighting?... no more wars?... will my enormous co-workers be out of their jobs? Just how much baby-food can we shovel down baby throats? Perhaps we can sell more grown up food? It's all just the same few kind of sludge after all... maybe if we add loads more sugar it will become even more addictive and even less nutritive, and so people will need more and more of it?...

- Don't worry, Daniel, things will become clearer and clearer to you as we proceed with your training.

HEEBIEGEEBIE TRAINING

My training with the Heebiegeebies went on for what would have been many, many Earth years, had we not been in a backwater phase-strand of time. I studied with them in many different settings, in the courtyard of an ancient stone-built monastery high up in the boulders and pine trees of a mountainside, amongst the cacti, ravines and mesas of a vast desert, in a beautiful garden by a lakeside, and many others. They devised practical situations with various shimmered-up attackers so that I could practise my Arts of Peace.

I trained with assailants armed with everything from assegais to yatagans, and devices from land mines to atom bombs, improving little by little. It's one thing to find and work from deep inner calm into the fields of a distant nuclear weapon, but quite another to find that same calm while being attacked by a screaming warrior, charging at you with a knobkerry.

- You are such an excellent pupil, Daniel, it's a wonderful opportunity to work with someone whose mind is quite so empty of any kind of previous learning or training. Usually, when we're training someone, we have to spend years and years helping them to un-learn stuff they've had rammed into them at schools, colleges and universities, most of it completely useless and inappropriate for these times of radical change...

- ...but you're a kind of mental blank canvas...

- ...or, you could say, an empty mental bucket...

I glowed with pride on hearing this.

FOCUS!

I hear this word again and again. One of the basic keys to the Heebiegeebie's training is learning to focus the attention: internally, becoming aware of all the fields, and fields within fields, which make up the energy body and working with the flow of life force energy through them - they call it cheese, I think - noticing whether it's a negative or positive flow, a drawing in or a sending out, and working towards finding a balanced, neutral state of stillness, then externally, looking for the fields of a separate object or being, and connecting with them. The Beam of Peace isn't in fact about taking control of anyone or anything else, it's more about connecting with their true inner nature, which in Heebiegeebie thinking must always be essentially peaceful, and encouraging them towards that.

- After all - says Beebee - if you think about it, the Universe must essentially be Life-friendly, musn't it?... or we wouldn't be here, would we?

But just where exactly are we I wonder?...

PRACTISE, PRACTISE, PRACTISE...

Practise! This was another word I heard all through my years of training. Learning the Heebiegeebies' arts of peace was mostly a case of practising them over and over again. I spent weeks and weeks in the various training locations looking for the deepest, stillest "neutral" possible. Finally, sitting with them on a mountain-top one morning, gazing at the view of distant snowy peaks emerging from clouds in the light of the rising sun, I felt a new very, very still kind of inner stillness - and completely without falling asleep. I saw and felt for the first time how the energy fields of all things were not just connected, but all part of one greater, all-inclusive field.

- Very good, Daniel - said Geegee - Verrrry goood...

THE SHIMMER TECHNIQUE

As for the Shimmer Technique, I found this much harder, but after many, many more years of backwater-time practice, I found I could focus into my own energy fields, and for a brief moment channel all my being into them. Then after yet more and more years of practice, I was able to focus at the same time into the energies of the enfolded space around me and merge with them. One day I finally managed to dematerialise from my physical body and rematerialise in a different place. Maybe only a few yards away, but it was a definite shimmer.

- Verry goood, thought Beebee, the greatest journey starts with a single shimmer...

- ...it's just a question of practice for you now, thought Geegee, we are very proud of you indeed, Daniel. Beebee and I would like to congratulate you on attaining Basic Heebiegeebie Training Level Novice Grade Z No-Belt.

- And now we must focus our own attentions! ...on putting together the finishing touches of the latest episode of Earthenders...

- ...so we're going to drop you off back home in Foulburgh. Good luck in the adventures that lie ahead of you! Things may get very strange and chaotic for you now as the Total Collapse of Everything picks up speed, but just stay calm inside and practise our peaceful techniques. You'll find that your brain upgrades will start to help you more and more, and other help will come your way, often when you least expect it. We'll see you again one day very soon, well done, Daniel! Goodbye for now!

- Focus! I hear through the air as it starts to shimmer, and, then fading slowly away, I hear:

- Practise! Practise! Pra.......ct....isssseeee.......

EX ECK'S

Just as they promised, no time at all seems to have passed when I rematerialise from the Heebiegeebies' shimmering back in Foulburgh, right outside 77 Slaughterhouse Lane. My brain is whizzing and bouncing about processing all the events, upgrades and training of the day, or years, so far and I feel the need to sit down quietly for a moment or two with a large cup of coffee.

There's a lull in the super-cataclysmic storm and in the dramatic swings of temperature, in fact there now seems to be no weather at all, just an oppressive, thick, leaden feeling in the air. You have to push your way through it, swimming with your arms, just as if you were up to your neck in mud. I'm sure it would prove to be a kind of record-breaking humidity never before experienced on Earth, if it could be measured at all. A couple of birds are clinging, wheezing, to the dead trees, having given up all attempts at flight. Alcolunks and giant numptettes are sprawled here and there, even more exhausted than usual, as if glued to the various bits of abandoned furniture, the last bits of life having been sucked out of the sagging frames and split-open cushions of everything and everyone. The acidity of the yellow-grey-orange-black-blue-purple-green light has gone way, waayyy up and there's an ominous low hum or vibration of some kind coming and going from deep down, dowwnnn in the ground. Home again...

I trudge with leaden booted feet round to Eck's Place, my local coffee house, just a couple of blocks away in Low Street, but when I get there I can't believe my eyes... Eck's has gone! There's just a smoking crater where it used to be, emergency vehicles of all sorts are parked up in the street, strangely dazed looking people are staggering about in tattered and stained rags amongst the shattered furniture, piles of masonry and pools of... liquid... of some sort... I pass the steaming remains of what looks distinctly like my leopard-skin print beach towel!... but I'm not drawn to inspect it too closely. And, if I'm not very much mistaken, that's my bike lying abandoned off to one side, with bits of shredded faux-fur stuck in its chain...

What dire event have I just missed here? ...and I wonder if there's the remotest possibility that that peculiar King Magnus character might have had something to do with it?

It's an Ex Eck's, I suppose you could say. One table has survived intact though, and there, sitting amongst the rubble and drifting smoke, sits none other than my old friend Edrigo, a pleasant surprise, but I can see at a glance that all is not well with him. He looks just as bewildered and confused as I feel. His clothes, what's left of them, normally a bit paint stained, are now spattered all over in multi-coloured splodges, the tatters gently smoking and steaming. His scarlet hair, usually wild, but in an artistic sort of way, now sits in a knotted heap on top of his head, with bits of patterned stuff... curtain material? carpet?... and what looks like pizza, maybe, and a couple of chips stuck in it. He sits quite oblivious to the record-breaking humidity and destruction around him, his eyes are focused far away into some internal distance...

"Gogo!"

It takes him a minute even to hear me.

"Gogo! Are you alright?"

After a while he seems to re-enter his body. He slowly starts to focus his eyes back onto our immediate surroundings, and recognizes me.

"Didi... it's very good to see you... oh deeerie, deeerie mee... what a morneeng...."

"Ha! Same here!"

Little by little, we start to share our mornings' experiences. Around us, Eck's noble and versatile staff are re-assembling and adjusting what's left of their clothing as best they can and starting to put the place back together. Before long, they have hammered and wrenched some brewing equipment back into operation and we have some coffee in front of us. Gathering his wits again, Edrigo starts to tell the tale of his morning...

...but before we hear any of that exciting stuff, and find out what's happened to Eck's Place, and whether King Magnus had anything to do with it, let's pause things a bit, go back in our strange tale, and find out some more about my old friend Edrigo's exotic and colourful background, before coming right back up to this present moment again later on...

CHAPTER FOUR
EDRIGO

Soooo... yes, it's high time I told you a bit more about my oldest and best friend, the artist, Edrigo. He's appeared here and there in our story already, if you remember, he was very amused by my Loosening-Off and Dropping-In Event when I told him about it, and very complimentary about my Hello Machine. He called me a natural "Post Industrial Genius" and even said that I had invented a whole new art movement, Kinetic Post Industrial Disruptivism! I was very pleased indeed, as no one had ever admired my efforts with machinery before, nor had anyone ever called me a genius of any kind, and I don't think I've invented any other art movements.

I've known Edrigo since we were kids, back when his family moved to Foulburgh, we'd have both been about five or six. They came from a hot country somewhere, a country where people speak in a kind of sing-song way, they pronounce "chips" as "cheeps" and "pips" as "peeps", for example, which was funny and sort of exotic too. He had, and still has, a magnificent mop of dazzlingly bright red hair - hair couldn't get much more dazzling without being on fire, or redder without being dipped in paint - which suits the wildly passionate and energetic nature he's always had.

Edrigo and I pretty much grew up together. We might be in the same class for something at school together, or we'd often be at the same party, or seeing the same band and we just sort of drifted naturally into one of those very close friendships that can really only start when you're young - even if it's just young at heart - that are completely natural and happen quite by chance.

Even though we have always had quite different levels and types of skills and abilities, and while I went on to work at Lozzo Industrial and Edrigo went on to do all sorts of artistic things, painting, sculpture and so on, we've always remained the very best of friends. His artistic career really took off and he became the only artist I've ever known who ever sold any of his stuff, and he sold lots of it, enabling him to buy a vast abandoned warehouse, the old lard and treacle store at 88 Trickle-up Drive, not far from my flat on Slaughterhouse Lane. He filled up the entire top floor with studio equipment and artwork except for an area he partitioned off to make a flat for himself, living quarters with a generously proportioned kitchen, general lounging about room, bathroom etc. and a bedroom of a grandeur befitting an artistic genius. Any light that had managed to squeeze its way through the filthy Foulburgh air shone down through huge windows set in the roof, which was otherwise flat, its flatness turning out to be a very useful feature, as you'll hear later on.

THE POWERHOUSE IS BORN

Edrigo's warehouse attracted a steady stream of other creative types, artists and also musicians, poets, thinkers, authors, actors and cartoon script-writers, etc. etc., also their friends, models and lovers, much of this talent being of an underground, misfit and drop-out nature, drop-in-drop-outs artists you might call them, who were soon filling up the other floors until the place was bulging. By the way, Edrigo pointed out that there's two types of drop-out, one type being the drop-out who drops out because he feels a complete stranger in the modern, industrial world, which type he welcomed with open arms as a fellow chip from the same block - "After all," said Edrigo, "Who would want to feel they fitted in with this crazee world?" - the other type is the drop-out who has been dropped out rather than dropped out himself of his own inclination, often through being a complete pain in the arse generally, for which type Edrigo had no patience at all, quickly showing him or her the door. So, soon, the old warehouse was stuffed full with marvellous misfits, and rocking and heaving to its foundations, and even lower down, in the subterranean caverns below, with wonderful, crazy, creative goings-on. There might be ten different kinds of music being made and twenty artists splashing paint about in an absolute riot of sound and colour, all in amongst a continuous combination of party and orgy. Edrigo bounced about on the top floor, soaking up all the sounds of twanging and sloshing, reaching ever more extreme levels of passion and energy, creating art by the acre. Someone called the warehouse a "powerhouse" of creativity, well, that's just exactly what it had become, and that's what it came to be called. A couple of floors below Edrigo's floor in the Powerhouse lay the lair of the poets and thinkers, a layer of calm sandwiched in a storm of exploding misfitting craziness. Here, Y.Y. Miltoff-Chalky and the other poets gazed out of the windows, occasionally writing down a line or two, reading them over and over again, making many corrections and additions, then scratching the whole lot out and going back to their gazing. The thinkers seemed to find that deep thinking was something best done lying down, under the influence of some sort of herbal mixture, or mushroom derivative, in a state which looked awfully like sleep to me... but they would sometimes surprise you by sitting up with a start, eyes flashing and staring, mouths seeming almost to be about to form a word... before, usually, collapsing flat out on the bed or floor again...

...While deep, deep down in the deepest underground Powerhouse pit the cartoon script writer Infernal Vern, "A Vern for the Worse", scribbled away at his diabolical, underground frames, creating content so wickedly super-subversive that even the other subversive writers raised their eyebrows, whistled, drew in gasps of breath and asked each other if such wicked stuff should ever see the light of day...

Infernal Vern had a "Do Not Disturb" sign hanging on his writing-chamber door but we wondered what the point of it was, because he was pretty disturbed already... ha, ha, we laughed.

The Powerhouse became a kind of crazy galleon of art, crashing through mountainous windswept seas of conformity, acres of square rigged creative canvas bulging and straining in the storm of fresh ideas and paint, flags fluttering, her crew laughing and shrieking as they tended to the ropes and rigging, and there at the helm, Edrigo! blazing hair flying, cackling with glee... well something like that...

LUST AND GRAVITY

As I was saying, Edrigo has always done everything he did with full-on, over-proof, passion and energy. His art was bursting with it. Earlier on in his career, he was always experimenting, flinging weird clashing colours and shapes onto huge canvasses in every possible way, inspired by the natural and man-made forms around us, trees, bits of broken machinery, mountains, blocks of concrete, abandoned furniture, and, above all, by male and female nudity. I don't think Edrigo will mind me saying that he has always been obsessed with sex, in fact, I know he'll be very pleased. Are they all like that in hot countries? or did he fall into a vat of testosterone when he was a baby? Who knows, but he grew up into the most rampantly lustful teenager you could hope to meet, then just got ever more rampantly lustful as the years went by. Fortunately for Edrigo he was naturally so extraordinarily attractive that he drew lovers and partners to him, male, female and everything in between and beyond, by the hundred with whom to share his dynamic sexuality. Was it just the lure of that painfully red hair that drew them to him? Of course, any redhead will tell you just how powerful an attractant even a few wayward tufts of the stuff can be, and Edrigo had forests of it, but he seemed to have some other irresistible appeal too, as if he were another force of Nature, like Gravity or Magnetism, or Beetroot. And he was lustful in such an open, cheerful, friendly, passionate, energetic, polite, considerate and natural way that after being with him for a day or two, people used to wonder if Edrigo's multi-voracious path wasn't a more natural way for everyone, and most of us were just poor repressed pedestrians beside this jet propelled love-lust-god. Also, his behaviour was always passionate in a gentlemanly, chivalrous way, I'm happy to say, and he could take no for an answer, unlike some people you meet. Why did his lovers never get jealous of one another? Well, I don't know. Maybe they just realised that trying to tame a passion like Edrigo's would have been as hopeless as trying to teach a volcano to play the harpsichord, or only to erupt on Thursdays.

The other thing that people noticed straightaway about Edrigo, other than that painfully bright red hair was the intensity of his gaze. His eyes always seemed to be that bit more open than anyone else's, they seemed to be soaking up every detail of everything around and seemed to follow you about like a pair of blazing bloodhounds.

"People don't really look at theengs, Didi," I remember him saying, "They just glance at theengs, just enough to register that the theeng is there, then they continue with their preconceptions about it, what they've been told to theenk. Try it yourself! Really look at something, or someone, I bet you'll see they're nothing like you thought they were..."

I did try this myself, several times, but I'm afraid I just nodded off. I think I know what he meant though...

Nudity and the male and female organs of regeneration featured predominantly in Edrigo's paintings early on in his career, things that he'd obviously been looking at very closely indeed. I was mystified as to how he actually made any money as he never seemed to sell any of these giant works. After all, it's not just everyone that wants a ten foot orange and aquamarine vagina on their living-room wall. I have a couple of giant raspberry vaginas and a cock and balls in cobalt and midnight cerise up in my flat, gifts from the man, and I have to say they get a mixed reaction from visitors, especially girlfriends' mothers.

Edrigo's models and lovers couldn't have been more varied in their blends of the masculine and the feminine, if there was a border, they pushed it, or jumped over or round it.

"Didi, our souls are neither male nor female are they? So why should we restrict the gender of our partners in our sex lives? And, I don't believe there can only be two sexes in the universe! There must be more! Maybe one day there will be a third sex, and a fourth sex here on Earth... and a whole new kind of love!..." I remember him saying, with a wistful look in his eye, reaching for a large brush.

"I thought 'decadent' was a kind of toothpaste till I met you, Gogo," one of the models said.

"Oh thank you sooo muuch," replied Edrigo.

So the Powerhouse throbbed and groaned on all levels, with Life and the making of art, music and love. There were no rules as such, except for one. The continuous orgy flowed from one room to another, including the many kitchens, and it was found that whereas a single couple can mingle food preparation and eating with having carnal knowledge of one another in lots of imaginative and fun ways this doesn't work so well for multiple couplings. Blazin Pianna Pete had a close shave with a chopper and Glenda the Gender Bender with the blender. They said it was all putting her/him/etc. off her/his/etc.'s porridge. So Edrigo made the one and only Powerhouse Rule then and there, that there was to be "No Sex in the Kitchens Please".

NEW OLD MASTERS

Generally he loved to show people his work, but he was secretive about a small room, an inner studio, off to one side of his main studio, which he kept locked up and screened off, I think I was one of only a very few people who were ever shown inside. Here were different works, some of them seemed somehow familiar, they were on a smaller scale, more delicate and precise. They were a bit like photographs but even more real, these paintings featured fruit, dead birds, glasses, carved urns and distant gardens, barely a genital in sight, all painted with the most wonderful delicacy.

"They're my fakes, Didi!" he said, in a mischievous whisper.

Edrigo had found some time ago that he had a talent for imitating the work of a certain school of artists, from a few hundred years earlier. Not in the league of the famous household names that we've all heard of, Patisse, Wali and Da Winkie, and so on, more of a kind of second layer of artists, but ones whose works still fetched good cash when "lost" or "previously unknown" examples turned up at auction. Though Edrigo's own-label work never sold particularly well, there was most definitely a market for his fakes, and that's where the secret of his success lay, in the timeless masterpieces he cooked up in his inner studio, with such finely executed brushwork, so different to the orgasmic explosions of colour of his main work.

"The secret is that they're not really fakes, or copies, because these wonderful old masters live again through me! I become Jan van Shpronkenclompen! I become Pieter Weenerpoop! Willem Wittlwattl, the Elder, lives again in me and through my brush!"

Edrigo could only produce a few of these new old masterpieces. It took him a long time to paint them and almost as long again to prepare the old or aged frames and canvases, the pigments for the old colours, and to fake the old receipts, letters and anything else he could think of to help to back up their authenticity. The commercial art world was only too eager to gobble up the paintings if they were at all plausibly presented, the dealers, auction houses and collectors lapped them up like slavering dogs. Edrigo was a little cynical about the art world I have to say, especially about the collectors:

"They don't care about Art, Didi, they only care about money, and what other people will theenk of them and their contrived, so-called taste. Or they buy Art as an investment!" He shuddered. "They bury these beautiful things, which they don't even like or appreciate in any way other than by way of their monetary value, they bury them away in vaults and bunkers, never to see the light of day again. It's seeeckening, it's deeesgusting. They are monsters! Monsters of Greed and Vanity. They deserve to be streeppcd of their millions. One day the world will see my own works as the divine masterpieces they truly are. Until then my little new old masterpieces can keep us all in bread and vodka."

Edrigo spent the money he made through his fakery wheeze freely and generously on general high living, on good food and drink, and on beautiful clothes, for himself, his assorted friends, models and lovers, and for all the other marvellously misfitting, drop-out inhabitants of the Powerhouse. It was sometimes difficult to tell whether the scene in Edrigo's top floor studio at the warehouse was in party mode or work mode as in both cases his friends, models and lovers spent a lot of their time lying about scantily clad, if clad at all, either posing for paintings or getting stoned, or reeling about in time to the music throbbing away on the floors below, or they might rouse themselves to join in the continuous orgy flowing about everywhere, except for the forbidden kitchen, or to grab a bite to eat. Call me a romantic fool, but I miss those days... There were always lovely, available women to meet - even Edrigo couldn't possibly have sex with all of them all of the time - and I was very popular with them. I don't know exactly what instinct I woke inside them, I would have said a mothering instinct, I'm quite sure that mothers shouldn't behave like they behaved with me with their children. Perhaps I was a kind of slightly chubby little mascot, like I am at Lozzo Industries, with my clumps of blond hair, great big round spectacles, cherubic smirk and generally forever young appearance, the Powerhouse Studios' Good Luck Charm.

POST SHPRONKENCLOMPEN

After a while, Edrigo moved on from School of Shpronkenclompen forgeries to channel another movement altogether, keeping all of us friends, lovers, artists and other misfits in even more mountains of bread, rivers of vodka, and acres of faux fur. This was Minimalism. In fact, he invented a whole new sub-movement, Super Minimalism, then developed that even further, into Super-Duper Minimalism. Edrigo said that it was actually one of the art dealers that gave him the idea, the little rascal. On receving Edrigo's latest New Old Master, an exquisite lost Jeemi Klanknsplankn, this rascally dealer-gentleman made a very broad hint that there was a style of work which he could turn out much quicker, it basically being just one or two simple shapes of colour, generally in shades of black. Edrigo got the idea immediately and before long no major collector or museum was without a colossal square of deep black darkness, or deeper still black brooding gloom. Then, being a creative type, Edrigo couldn't help but develop the idea even further still, supplying the rascally dealer with huge canvasses daubed with perhaps just a single blob of ultimate black, or maybe with just the slightest suggestion of where a very dark black black smear might have been smeared if the artist had felt able to smear it there, but then hadn't, so saving paint as well as time. These, too, were soon hanging all over the world. In a stroke of typical genius, Edrigo developed this further into Super-Super-Duper-Duper Minimalism, discarding not just any kind of paint or frame, but even canvas. However, although these fantastic works could be very quickly produced, the rascally dealers found that they couldn't be quite so easily sold. Some collectors and galleries even wondered if the works were actually there at all...

Normally, ever adaptable, Edrigo would simply have moved into a different movement but at that point his art, and life, went careering off, with his usual passion and energy, in a different direction altogether, when he was struck by some sort of internal lightning...

EDRIGO THE ENVIRONMENTAL ACTIVIST

One evening, I had popped round to Edrigo's after work and found quite an unusual scene. There was not a model or lover in sight, either clothed or unclothed, nor was there a poet, musician, sculptor, writer or thinker, male or female, etc., anywhere to be seen anywhere in the whole building, it was as if the Powerhouse had been switched off... There was the usual party and orgy wreckage strewn about Edrigo's studio, but mixed in with it were newspapers and magazines with headlines like:

!! ICE CAPS - GOING FAST !!
!! COP-OUT 99 - TOTAL WASTE OF TIME !!
!! RAINFOREST - WHAT RAINFOREST ?? !!
!! SUPER-HISTORIC DROUGHT !!
!! MORE PLASTIC THAN WATER IN OCEANS !!
!! FIRE !! FIRE !! FIRE !!
!! SUPER-DUPER CATASTROPHIC FLOODS !!
!! METHANE - THE SLUMBERING GIANT OF DEATH AND DISASTER AWAKENS !!
!! REALITY STAR TRIPS ON BANANA SKIN !!
!! PLAGUES DEFROSTING FROM GLACIERS !!
!! ANTHRAX AND YOU !!
!! BILLIONS OF REFUGEES !!
!! OCEANS, LAND, AIR, INSECTS, PLANTS, ANIMALS - ALL DYING !!
!! TRILLIONS WITHOUT WATER !!
!! SUPER-DUPER CATACLYSMIC WEATHER NOW NORMAL !!

...and so on and on. Edrigo himself was sitting absolutely motionless, brooding in front of a TV screen, something he never usually did, there was no programme on, it was just flickering and hissing.

"Gogo... are you alright?"

He stirred himself, "Didi... so good to see you..." he

was muttering to himself, "...what have we done?... what have we done?..." He settled back into his brooding silence for a while, I could tell something was brewing up inside him, some Idea or Realisation...

Then we hardly saw him for days, he shut himself up in his bedroom... alone!... We friends, models, lovers and various artistic misfits started to drop by and hang about outside his door, tip-toeing nervously and concernedly about, or just sitting or lying down, like faithful dogs waiting for their master to re-appear, wondering what on Earth was going on... the place was like a ghost warehouse without Edrigo's energy and passion... we were waiting... waiting for... waiting for... for what? ...an extra-extra big painting or sex episode? ... an explosion of colour or emotion... or both?

From time to time he would emerge from his room to answer the call of nature. He would shuffle to the window, look out at the filthy sky, let out a long, long sigh, then shuffle back to his room. We looked at one another, mystified...

By the way, it actually takes quite some time for even, say, twelve people to look at each other, even if it's just for a passing glance, let alone deep scrutinisation, so although we weren't really doing anything we were actually quite busy...

GLANCING WITH GONGS

If you think about it, you'll see that if every member of a group of, for example, twelve people is going to look at every other member they must each make eleven separate glances, and we should really consider the glancee being glanced at as a separate event to the glancer glancing, because that's what it is. So at a rough guess we may have a possible twelve times eleven, one hundred and twenty-three, divided by two, i.e. sixty-seven glances, to fit in, I make it, and then we should probably double that to take into account the separate glances of the glancees, taking us back up to one hundred and thirty-four. But surely if the glancee is looking at the glancer when he's being glanced and notices or even acknowledges the glance in some way that's quite a different kind of event to the possible event where the glancee is not looking at the glancer and so couldn't possibly notice or acknowledge this glancing event? How many possibilities does that bring us up to now? Can we say two hundred and seventy-eight? I haven't a clue. Maybe we should round that up to three hundred. And what about the degree of intensity of scrutiny with which each glancer is glancing his glance? Should we take that into account? I think so, but that would surely make the event infinitely long? And what if someone blinks? Or if someone's mind has wandered off somewhere? Would that make it longer than infinity? Should you start again? Really, if twelve people were going to look at one another at all thoroughly the event would have to be choregraphed, and maybe synchronised with a metronome, or a gong, the long lasting notes of which would give each glance plenty of time to play out. Maybe each member of the glancing group should have a gong? Or two gongs? One for glancing and the other for being glanced upon. Come to think of it, this might make a wonderful work of art, a musical performance really, let's call it, "Glancing with Gongs", an infinitely long musical-theatrical piece for twelve players and twenty-four gongs... the gongs would have to be on stands so that the glancers and glancees could strike them with gong-beaters, or small sledgehammers... and in any case, I'm not exactly sure how many of us were gathered outside Edrigo's room, sometimes I counted seventeen, then I counted thirty-one, then...

Sadly, the world was never treated, at least up until then, to a complete first performance of "Glancing with Gongs" - that comes much later on in our extraordinary tale - because after a couple of days of our filling in the Edrigo-less vacuum in our lives with looking at each other, sadly without any gongs, just with a general emptiness, Edrigo interrupted us by hurtling out of his room like a startled moose, vermillion hair flying and blazing, and eyes staring and flashing.

"Wake up! Everyone! WAKE UP!"

His hands were bundled into fists, every muscle in his body was drawn up tight, he was shouting, quivering with passion and rage. Some sort of internal lightning had struck, or some sort of bubble had burst.

"It's time to do something! Time to ACT!"

He went to one of the huge windows and flung it open, then screeched down to the street far below...

"Wake up! Wake up! WAKE UP!!"

Down below nothing much changed, a zombonumptik stopped in his tracks for a moment, looked around to see where the noise was coming from, then fell over. A naked couple being chased down the street by a woman brandishing a length of lead piping also paused for a moment, looked up, saw the mad-looking, red-haired figure looking down at them waving its arms about, shrugged then carried on running.

Edrigo calmed down, just a notch, and turned back to us.

"I have a Veesion! a Veesion of the Future!... a Veesion of the Now! It's time to wake up!...

THE VEESION

"The time for conferences and writing articles is over!.. a wave of change is sweeping around the world, Mother Nature is rising up, Man thought he could control Her... ha!... you, me, all of us, must help Her in any way we can... Man and Woman, and everyone in between, and around the edges, we must be ready for change! ...be ready to change our way of life completely... we must evolve! We must evolve consciously!"

He was jumping up and down on the spot. Tears were running down into his beard, making it all soggy, while that bright red hair was waving about with electrostatic passion. Words spewed out of him...

"Friends! Models! Lovers! My Fellow Artists and Misfits! It's Humankind's last chance to avoid Mass Extinction *now*... There's no part of the Earth that we haven't ravaged with our industrial way of life... from the depths of the oceans to the peaks of the mountains... we can't exploit, drain our dear Mother Earth a day longer... we must flick the switch from Exploitation to Regeneration! We must live much, much simpler lives, live on what we can produce locally, naturally... If we don't make radical change, Mother Nature will make it for us, She'll swallow us up whole and spit us out into tiny little pieces..."

He'd often talked about trees and oceans and stuff in the past, and about how we should be getting ready for the Total Collapse of Everything and the inevitable Post-Industrial World, but there was a throbbing field of urgency about him now.

"But Gogo..." said Priapic Youth in Cobalt with Chrome Vegetables, one of the friends, models and lovers, "Didn't the Government declare a Climate Emergency just a little while ago? Aren't they going to sort everything out?"

I had never actually seen smoke come out of someone's ears before... but instead of a fresh, even bigger, explosion Edrigo sank into a state of deep, deep gloom and sadness, a state I'd never seen him in before...

"And what exactly has changed since then, Priapic Youth in Cobalt with Chrome Vegetables?" said Edrigo, sad but calm now, "A few less plastic bags in the shops? A few more recycled beer cans? There's a bit of tinkering about and a lot of talk but the Industrial Machine of Exploitation and Consumption is still thundering along... and we're all still a part of it... carbon's building up and building up in the atmosphere... we're still burning coal! The cars and trucks are still running mostly on oil, although there's sentient agreement that the remaining oil should stay in the ground... not only that, we're even subsidising fossil fuels! It wouldn't make economic sense to extract it without those subsidies!... We're just making pathetic token gestures... not even scratching the surface of the surface of the real problem...

"There's only so long you can exploit a system without allowing and helping it to restore itself before it starts to collapse... it's as true of a slave as it is of a forest... isn't that blazingly obvious?... can't we see that collapse beginning to happen all around us?... everything creaking at the seams... not just in the environment, in peoples' lives too... peoples' health getting worse and worse, mentally and phsically... so many people struggling harder and harder to get by... the quality of their lives going down and down... bombarded with adverts of some fantasy sunny world filled with shiny cars, beautiful homes and happy people consuming more and more and more, a fantasy world so few people will ever attain... the dissaffection, the bitterness, hopelessness... a world looming of blackouts, shortages, empty supermarket shelves..."

He went over to the window and pointed down to the street.

"Humankind is in a death walk, just like those zombolloids down there, a death walk over a cliff... there's barely any general understanding or awareness of the issues, of the scale of change required, and no one has any intention of making anything but the most trivial changes in their own lives... except for us! ...We, we my dear artist-friends, misfits, musicians and lovers, we are going to ACT!"

"But what can we do, Gogo? What difference can a few people make?" said Phosphorescent Green Woman with Bits of Guitar.

"Phosphorescent Green Woman with Bits of Guitar! It's only individuals, and groups of a few people like us that can make a difference! There's really no 'us' and 'them', there's just 'us'! You and I, we can act of our own free will, and what are governments, and industries but collections of individuals? You and I, all of us, we are going to explore and show what a truly sustainable, earth-friendly way of life is like, a simpler way, based on what we can produce locally ourselves... with simple hand tools... in natural processes... regenerating local diversity and abundance... starting by growing some food!..."

"What? Growing food right here in hideously polluted

Foulburgh?" asked Blazing Pianna Pete.

"Yes, Blazing Pianna Pete! Mother Nature will clean up our disgusting mess with us, given half a chance, we will make forest gardens for food, materials and all our other basic needs, so as and when the General Collapse of Everything happens, and it can't be far away, we will be as ready as we can be... and we are in fact going to hasten that collapse, the quicker it comes the less Mother Earth will suffer..."

He paused for a moment and started to grin.

"...and, we are going to have a lot of fun with it! The time has come... enough is enough! Didi's vision of Post Industrial Disruptivism has been sent to show us Our Way! We have been given a mission by Mother Nature... to hasten the Collapse of the Industrial World... with Art! ...with Kinetic Post Industrial Disruptivart!"

KINETIC POST INDUSTRIAL DISRUPTIVART

There was tremendous excitement. It was impossible not to be drawn in by Edrigo's passion and energy. All of us friends, models, lovers, artists, musicians and other misfits and drop-outs were charged up by his colossal batteries with our own passion and energy. Tremendous artistic creativity and all sorts of skills and craftsmanship were shown, we all started to come up with ideas and hatch plots, putting the best of them into action over the next few weeks and months.

We printed fake money, but soon found that money was already fake, so that didn't have much impact, we printed licences and identity cards and made fake uniforms, with which to infiltrate officialdom, undermine the status quo, and initiate sporadic chaos, and by night we painted the town green, until we ran out of paint. The models, stoners and deep thinkers whose special skill was keeping so still you wondered if they were still alive, were painted with Urban Camouflage designs so that they could hide in control rooms and communications hubs during the day. Then, after dark, they would pop out from hiding and disconnect things that should have really been kept connected and connect them up again with things they shouldn't have been connected to, also switching things off that would have been better left on, and switching on things that would have been better left off, all with exciting results. A thinker by the name of Stinker, Stinker the Thinker, awoke with a start one afternoon with probably her best idea ever, nothing less than the infiltration of the Lozzo Industrial Management School. We were all thrilled with the audacity of her brain wave...

"What will bring about the death of the Industrial Way of Life quicker than anything?" asked Stinker the Thinker, "Why, simple, more and even worse management!"

"Is that actually possible?" we asked.

"Why, incredibly, yes it is..."

Stinker outlined her brilliant plan, she and some of the other most deeply creative thinkers would infiltrate the exam board of the Lozzo Industrial Management School and alter the marks given to its students so that those with highest marks would fail and those with the lowest would pass with flying colours and go straight into the jobs with the most responsibility, creating disaster and dischord wherever they went, much as things are at the moment, most obvious in the field of politics and country-scale management, though present at all levels, but getting even worse. One of the actors, T.R. Ed the Boards, was keen to try some teaching there too, to see if he could make up lessons even more redundant and laughable than the stuff being taught at present. We all wished him luck.

We printed fake news pamphlets and broadcasted ridiculous completely false news items from our fake radio station, Radio Gogo, which people fell for hook link and sinker, if it was something they wanted to believe. This work evolved into one of our most extraordinary escapades, the creation of Po Tay Toe...

PO... TAY... TOE!

When Edrigo saw to just what an amazing degree people would believe any daft thing we printed or broadcast if it was convenient for them to believe it, or if they felt it would protect them from something they had been made to be afraid of, or lull them into the feeling that there was no need to make any kind of change in their way of life, he thought it would be good disruptive fun to take the whole thing a step further, and create such an obviously moronic political figure that people surely couldn't possibly take the whole bonkers political-industrial cavalcade seriously any longer and would at last see the hand of the Industrial War Machine behind it all, pulling the population's puppet strings. So we created the miniature political leader-character Po Tay Toe out of a very, very large vegetable of the same name, giving him arms and legs with which he could gesticulate and do weird sort of movement things, a sort of un-coordinated stumble-dance, augmenting his eyes so that they could squint, roll, wink, leer and open up extra-wide, and sculpting a mouth for him, much like an arsehole, which could open and close, pucker up, grin with fake intelligence and sneer fiendishly. Then they made a whole wardrobe for this and his other personae including totally bizarre wigs, ranging from a glued-on, glued-up, jet-black sticky thing, to an orange-grey-blonde wrap-over, strangely dishevelled floppy mullet, to a silver-gold-platinum electric corona, to his thinning putrid emperor look, and also including a variety of miniature well-starched suits of various costly material in shades of black, grey, purple and orange, and made a little miniature cardboard studio for him, with a lovely onion-based interviewer to ask him questions, such as "What do you think about the current state of the economy, Mr Po Tay Toe, Sir?" or, "Do you think the armed forces and police war squads should be doubled in size or quadrupled, Mr Po Tay Toe, Your Imperial Excellency?" The rest of the script was easy, because all Po Tay Toe ever said was, "Po Taaay Tooooeee!"

Edrigo hadn't reckoned with the stupidity of his audience though, nor with just how much the brain of his typical viewer had been reduced to catatonic mush by medication and hypnotic dumbed-down TV and internet bombardment, they believed Po Tay Toe was real! even believed he was some kind of saviour who would magically restore a mythic good old day paradise for them. Po Tay Toe was a star!...

The people couldn't get enough of him, they sent in questions for him, repeated his every utterance as a kind of prayer,

"Po Tay Toe! Po Tay Toe! Poo Taaay Tooooe!"

"I know he just says his name over and over again, but it's the way that he says it! Po Tay Toe! He means, Trust in Him and Everything will be Alright Again!" they said. "We won't have to think for ourselves at all, ever again! Shine the light of your glorious golden shower of wisdom on us, Po Tay Tooooe!"

Before long they were demanding that he be made king, then God...

"That's it," said Edrigo, "A joke is a joke but this has gone way too far. It's time to kill him off."

But though we tried everything, boiling, chipping, mashing, dauphinoising him, even roasting him live on social media, he just wouldn't die, the people said that it was all just faked. There were marches and riots.

"I don't know what else we can do, Didi... he just refuses to be cooked and killed off in any way at all..."

Fortunately for all concerned, one of the models, the inspiration for "Variously Gendered Boulders and Bicycles 57", had a brilliant idea:

"Vodka!"

VODKA!

"It's a bit early for me, Variously Gendered Boulders and Bicycles 57, but help yourself, there's stacks in the kitchen."

"No! We turn him into vodka!"

"We distil him? Why would that work when all else has failed?"

"No we don't distil him, we issue a statement saying that he has decided that the best thing he can do for his followers is to become Po Tay Toe the Spirit, that he is going to lay down his life for them and convert himself into vodka, so that people everywhere can for ever more be one with him again, simply by having a couple of shots of vodka!"

"That is just Pure Unadulterated Over-Proof Strength Post-Industrial Genius!"

They set everything up, the statement went out, there was general dismay and mourning, but also much rejoicing and chanting in the streets, as everyone swigged back vodka with a fervour bordering on the religiously fanatical.

"Great is the Po Tay Toe Shhpirit!"

"Eternal Po Tay Toe, guide ush forever with your - hic! - Word and your Shhpirit of Truth!"

Edrigo had rather sneakily added a subliminal message to Po Tay Toe's last statement to the effect that his followers could also honour his name by growing a few potatoes and other vegetables for themselves. So it was without really understanding why they were doing it that people started to dig up bits of car park and concrete wasteland and start little gardens, in between terrible hangovers.

"The Po Tay Toe Spirit works in mysterious ways, Didi..."

SURVIVAL OF THE ARTIEST

Of course, it wasn't long before the Lozzo Industrial Local Government started to take an interest in Edrigo and us misfits, and in our Kinetic Post Industrial Disruptivart. Squads of policestormtroopers were dispatched to hunt us down before we could rock the status quo any further. We were one jump ahead though, we had disguised the Powerhouse as a germ warfare research institute, complete with mock dead festering bodies in bins at the back, and leaks of bright green, stinking, fizzing slime trickling down the walls outside from boarded-up windows. We took it in turns to wander about outside in green and purple make-up, with fake boils, coughing and moaning. The squads of policestormtroopers would come, take a quick look round, then flee, summoning another squad to take their place.

GORILLA GARDENING

And, as if all that weren't enough to keep us misfits busy, Edrigo had us flitting about town at night doing what he called, "Gorilla Gardening".

"One day people will wake up and there won't be anything on the supermarket shelves," he said, "who knows which bit of the collapse will come first, will it be the collapse of the supply chain, of the transport system? Will it be the collapse of the internet or the financial system? Will some terrible disease wipe out a swathe of the population? Or will it be a colossal natural disaster, storm, flood, fire on a scale beyond anything we've seen yet? Will an inter-galactic mega-electrical storm surge wipe out all the satellites? Maybe one will trigger off another and we'll have the whole lot at once, but we can prepare ourselves as best we can for any and all of that by exploring the same natural, Earth-friendly way of life, by growing food and as many of the other things we need to meet our basic needs as we can, in simple, local systems that mimic Nature and look after themselves, as much as possible. Think about gorillas, my friends, misfits and lovers, think about how they wander through the forest, through acres and acres of everything they need for their simple lives. They're gardening as they go, interacting with their world with every footstep they take and every mouthful they chomp, making pathways for other creatures, spreading seeds, encouraging new growth. Yes, they're consuming but they're a positive part of their landscape, helping the process of diverse regeneration around them all day long. There's our Gorilla Gardening model, my friends!"

MORE KARMITIS

Of course, when Edrigo mentions disease, you will remember how that dreadful natural phenomenon, the terrible affliction of Karmitis, has already slithered up from its pit of pestilence, back in Chapter Two, and was very unusually selective for a disease, in that it only struck down people who had brought it upon themselves and thoroughly deserved it, its symptoms varying wildly according to the type of person it infected, but starting, as we heard, with those ill-mannered, rude people who couldn't say sorry. Now Karmitis strengthened its clutch on the peoples' innards. It now started to have a very powerful effect on that kind of pompous, know-all, control-freak kind of personality all too familiar to many of us, often found in teachers, both professional and amateur, often with great big barrel chests for storing up wind with which to blast out their pronouncements, coupled with a big red sneering face with which to direct scorn and sarcasm at their poor pupils - I bet there was someone like that at your school - poor pupils who don't pick up much of what this wobbling windbag is trying to teach them because he or she is so un-inspiring and boring, yet so vain and self-centred that they couldn't possibly have a higher opinion of himself or herself if they were some kind of god of education. Karmitis now started to attack this kind of personality by closing down its windpipe. No more proclamations could issue from these ghastly gasbags, they all just started to store up inside them. They started to inflate! My goodness me! They went on swelling up and up and up until they started to float away into the darkening skies, their voluminous robes rent asunder by the pressure of all that bloating, until *schhhkkwwppppplllloppppp!* They burst! and went whizzing around the clouds on a hideously smelly fart-gale, bursting into flames should they pass too close to a jet engine or the flight of a burning arrow, tatters of smelly, greasy clothing falling back down to the ground. If they could find some humility and remorse inside themselves this dreadful process might be turned around, but very few of them recovered.

Karmitis spread on through the population, striking down rapists, those people who can't take no for an answer, in a similar way and was particularly hard on those who take advantage of positions of power and trust and their apparent personal sanctity to abuse children and the vulnerable, and particularly hard on those who were, at the same time, presenting themselves as any kind of authority on what people should and should not do, on how they should behave and even on what they should believe and think. Awful things happened to them, their genitals migrated to their forheads, turned a throbbing green and then rotted away, *sssschwws-sssschwsssssshhh!* while the rest of them rotted slowly from the feet up. There was some hope for them if they, like the terrible teachers, could find remorse and humility inside themselves, and devote the rest of their lives to doing everything they could to make amends up for their miserable former ways, but again, not many of them recovered and there were yet more piles of smelly, greasy robes to be burned...

... but back to Edrigo and his Gorilla Gardening for now...

So we went out into the acres and acres of wasteland, into the concrete canyons of the urban jungle, sowing seeds amongst the derelict warehouses and factories, abandoned sofas and piles of shattered building blocks, planting plants, tending them until they could spread themselves about. We made compost and stored water. Down in the dank dark Powerhouse basements we set up beds for growing mushrooms, and up on those conveniently flat bits of the slightly less dank and dark roof tops of Edrigo's building, and on the flat bits of my own roof at 77 Slaughterhouse Lane, we made more gardens, planted hedges, nut trees, fruit trees and bushes, and all sorts of other herbs and other foodstuffs, which can all grow in a surprisingly shallow layer of soil, by the way, brought up from ground level by teams of us misfits and drop-outs or made from our own compost on the spot.

"What else are we going to need?" asked Edrigo.

"Vodka?" said Infernal Vern, that most subversive of underground cartoon script-writers.

"Yes, Infernal Vern! For drinking but also as a fuel, because there won't be any petrol in the petrol stations, so we are going to need a kitchen and brewing and distilling equipment, and it will have to be fuelled by charcoal, as there won't be much in the way of electricity. And storage! we are going to need lots and lots of storage equipment, and we are going to have to learn how to preserve food for when there's nothing in our gardens to harvest..."

"Guns?" asked the poet, Y.Y. Miltoff-Chalky, "What do we do when the zomboids and alkolunks come to steal our food and stuff?"

"I can't tell you exactly how, Y.Y. Miltoff-Chalky," said Edrigo, "but we will evolve so that weapons will be obsolete. I saw it in my Veesion. If there are still human beings on Earth in a hundred years from now, they will have evolved into more peaceful, co-operative people. In my Veesion, we won't try to solve problems with violence, which has just got be the most stupid thing in the world anyway, when you think about it, we will have developed a global intelligence, and solve problems by pondering them out globally... and this will work at a local level too.

"Which, my fellow creative drop-outs and misfits, brings me to my next topic, Leadership. Up to now I have been in charge here at the Powerhouse myself, but I also saw in my Veesion that one single person should never be in charge of a project, especially not someone who wants to be in charge of it, why would anyone want the responsibility? there's a danger they're on some sort of megalomaniac power trip. One single person should never be able to make all of a project's plans and decisions, all of its members should have an equal say in designing and developing it, whether it's a small local project like our own, or a whole country. So, my dear friends, I am handing over the running of the Powerhouse to all of us."

You can imagine the gasps of shock and surprise that ran around the room. Edrigo's idea was that everyone should take a turn at running things, a chairperson being nominated from a randomly chosen rota. Quite how this would work in practice when the chosen chairperson was almost always asleep was not immediately clear, but after chatting about Edrigo's proposal for a while we could see how chairpersons who were often awake would keep bringing fresh ideas into the project, and anyway, don't creativity and art thrive on a bit of random input, so wouldn't the exploration and development of sustainable living thrive in that way too?

But we're going to leave Edrigo and the rest of us misfits busily at our increasingly random merry mischief for now, and turn our attention to a different neck of the woods, where an extraordinary event is about to happen, another manifestation of the Tidal Wave of Change sweeping around the World, of the Rebalancing of the Universe, of the Rebirth of The Feminine and of Mother Nature Herself, yes, another such manifestation is stirring deep underground not very far from Foulburgh, in a misty, mystical remnant of ancient forest...

CHAPTER FIVE

THE REBIRTH OF REJENIFFUR

Yes... meanwhile, deep underground beneath a clearing in the woods not far from Foulburgh's crumbling walls, another dormant being is waking up, responding to the Wave of Change sweeping all around and within the Earth. One event is setting off another, just as when one building collapses any others built leaning on to it fall down too.

Daniel Thelonius Sprocket's errant male organ of regeneration is not the only regenerative being stirring awake today. Just at the very same moment as that event is happening down in the foul city, here in the ancient forest of Mystical Keenool another entity is stirring, deep underground, an entity older than Time and Space themselves, nothing less than the ultimate, essential living spirit of regeneration, the life force that powers and shapes the growth of all living things, the Queen of the Underground, the Earth Goddess, Regina Rejeniffur awakens.

Deep in the woodland layers of Mystical Keenool there lies a remnant of the old forest that once used to cover the whole country. No human hand or foot has left its print in this ancient grove, it lies unspoiled, as Mother Nature intended. Within the most secret, tangliest part of the grove there stands a circle of stones, not a man-made circle, but an Earth-made one. The space enclosed by the stones is clear of trees and undergrowth, an open mound covered in velvet moss. All around in the space outside of the circle, dogs have been gathering for days, restless, sensing that their mistress of old is about to return.

The ground inside the circle has slowly started to throb, and a humming sound has started to well up from within the Earth far below. A sound containing all frequencies, from off the scale, very low, to off the scale, very high, way beyond the range of human hearing, and everything in between. The sound slowly gets louder and louder, the throbbing gets stronger and stronger, and the dogs start to howl... all in all it's a pretty effective kind of wake up call of a sound...

Then the mossy circle of ground starts to vibrate and seems to turn liquid, a light starts to glow within the ground, green, yellow, gold, getting brighter and brighter. Now ripples appear in the liquid mossy surface as a shape rises up through it, the dogs are beside themselves with joyful anticipation, running about, barking and howling... and the shape of a head rises up through the rippling ground.

It's a beautiful head, shaped in perfect proportions from living wood and molten stone. The apparition continues to rise up, a slurry of mud, rootlets, mycellial threads and other undergound stuff flows down off its most definitely female form, neck, breasts, torso and limbs, as she slowly appears, her skin steaming in the low dawn light, skin that's something between green fur and speckled birch bark, glistening and glowing. She stretches and shakes her powerful limbs then raises her magnificent head, shakes out her flowing green-gold hair, looks around with her flashing eyes and lets out a cry, somewhere between a shriek and a shout, with a bit of roar in it.

Behold Rejeniffur! The Queen of the Underground! The Earth Goddess, Regina Rejeniffur, reborn into the surface of the Earth in all her wondrous, naked, startling beauty and power. She raises her hand, and looks around at the dogs, now running around yelping in frantic excitement, with her glittering eyes. Her body has come from the Earth but the light in her eyes shines from the stars.

She utters a single word in her beautiful, piercing voice,

"SSIII-TTTT!!"

The dogs immediately settle down, panting, and gaze

with adoration at their mistress.

"Hello again, dear forest friends, Rescue Dogs and Wild Ones, Waifs and Strays. We have much work to do together, but you must wait for me a little longer, stay here and watch over Mystical Keenool till I call you and give each of you your task.

"I have an appointment to keep, an Appointment with Destiny."

With this Rejeniffur strides from the circle and heads out through the forest, down towards Foulburgh...

AN APPOINTMENT WITH DESTINY

So, let's catch up with me again. If you remember, I had trudged round, through the record-breaking humidity, to Eck's Place, my local coffee shop and meeting place, after I was dropped off by the Heebiegees outside my flat, being somewhat thirsty and need of a little pause to re-gather my wits, such as they are, only to find the place completely gone!... it was a wrecked Ex Eck's you might have said...

People were staggering about in tattered and stained rags amongst the emergency vehicles, shattered furniture, piles of masonry, timber and other wreckage, and pools of... mysterious liquids... I didn't look too closely... I saw the steaming remains of what looked distinctly like my leopard-skin print beach towel and my very own bike with bits of faux fur stuck in its chain... which signs could only mean one thing... that the entity, my errant male organ of regeneration, cock, if you like, now to be known as King Magnus must have had something to do with all the devastation... but what?

And, then, who did I find but my old friend Edrigo sitting motionless at the one intact table, crumpled and dishevelled, gazing into deep inner space, his usually artistically rumpled scarlet hair now in a wild entanglement with odd bits of food? material? stuck in it... what on Earth's been going on?

Well, to rewind Time a bit, it's to Eck's Place that King

Magnus gallops off on my bike after leaving me, drawn by chivalry, lust, coffee and romantic intuition, like an iron filing moth to the flaming insect-attracting magnet, to keep his mysterious appointment with "Lady Destiny".

King Magnus is just settling into the Eck's Place relaxed bustle and hubbub, casting an appraising eye over the women gathered there, admiring a lovely pair of ladies and considering sidling up to them with a twirl of his luxurious moustaches and a "Do you mind if I join you, wenches?" when the door slams open, is thrown off its hinges in fact, by a female figure who strides inside, ducking to avoid hitting her golden-green, jungle-haired head on the lintel.

Behold Rejeniffur! Again! The Earth Goddess, fresh from her rebirth deep within Mystical Keenool, in all her ripplingly muscular, magnificently naked feminine furry glory, naked, save for some twigs, bits of lichen, mycelial threads, moss, various liverworts, mud and other underground and foresty stuff. She looks around the room, her piercing starlight gaze falls on magnificently masculine King Magnus and fixes on him with a royal grade of stellar fixation. King Magnus is himself immediately transfixed by this six foot six personification of throbbing womanhood. His jaw drops with a *thhhuddd!* to his chest, her eyes flash glittering galactic beams at his heart, he growls, she makes a gurgley snarl, they approach, slowly, drawn irresistibly together by interplanetary-scale gravity, Destiny and good old lust.

"Coffee!" Rejeniffur sends Eck's crew scurrying to her bidding, "Coffee, big black! Strong!... Two.... No eight!..."

Rejeniffur and Magnus, magnificent regal entities that they are, continue to approach each other with guttural rumblings, much curling of lips and standing-on-end of fur and neck hair. He starts to swell up and glow bright purple, making a lovely contrast to her golden-green. Not exactly short before, he swells up now until he must be six foot nine, or even seven foot, tall, what an impressive couple they make!

With a thump of inevitability they embrace, she tears

off his purple bobble hat, faux fur coat and leopard-skin print beach towel with a shriek, revealing a tree-trunk-stiff male member the size of another arm or leg, he clutches her buttocks, breasts, hair, legs, all in one go somehow... big hands, I guess... they pause only for a couple of swigs of coffee before at last that same colossal member sinks with a *ssshhplurrrp!* into Rejeniffer's receptive cleft as if it had a life of its own. He enters her, she swallows him up whole and they start to go at it like a pair of steam engines, standing up, sitting down, on the tables, on the bar stools, on the floor, pressed against the walls and windows, there's lots of possibilities at Eck's...

Eck's clientele react in many different ways, there's shock, fascinated horror, delight, awed arousal, you name it. Mothers-in-law shriek with disapproval and head for the door, trying not to slip and fall over in the puddles of fluids of one sort and another forming around the place. Men and women in all possible combinations, the customers, the staff, those who haven't fled, passers-by, all cheer and join in themselves, there must be something in the air, or in the coffee. Someone summons the emergency services - but which one do they need? Fire? Police? Ambulance? They go for all three. When the firemen, firewomen, policemen, policewomen, ambulancemen and ambulancewomen arrive they all join in too, in a mayhem of feverish cavorting. King Magnus and Rejeniffur pause in having their carnal knowledge of each other just long enough now and then for a couple more swigs of their coffees and a few deep breaths before going at it again like two giant marine gas turbines or something.

Things are building up though, there's a crescendo in the racket of their rumping and pumping, and a steady increase in the rate of their thrashing and thrusting. The whole room starts to resonate in sympathy, walls, floor and ceiling throbbing and bobbing up and down. All those mobile phones, recently so busy with social messaging, now start to resonate together in sympathy with full blast music, all completely out of time and tune with each other, and without any common melody or rhythm, like a streetful of terrible buskers, but without the bagpipes thank god, then they start to blend together into a super-racket, a pounding soundtrack of abandonment, getting faster and faster and faster... The royal couple and all those other assorted couples, trios, quartets and other groups, are cavorting together in magnificent accelerating unison, it's an awesome sight, and an awesome sound too... what a growling and howling, what a shrieking and creaking, what a moaning and groaning there is! Soon everyone is moving so fast that they have become just a single blurred blob of frenzied flesh, then a bright white light starts to shine from the lustful pair at the centre of the whole cavortion, growing stronger and stronger until it's too bright to look at. The light gets even stronger and stronger still, a new sound is building up too, a rumbling jet engine whine, louder and louder until it becomes a deafening howling roar, surely it can't get any louder? well, no, it can't, there's an absolutely colossal explosion...

...*kkkkRRRRRAAAKKKKAAAdaaaBBBOOOOOMMMMMM!!*...

...the room fills up to the ceiling with light, sound and the splashings of yet more fluid. Then begins a slow ebbing, a sighing out of breath, a gurgle of more coffee going down throats, a relaxation of tension.

As the light returns to normal levels it reveals a scene of utter devastation. Collapsed, entangled groups of two, three, four or more people lie about in exhaustion amongst the broken furniture, and torn and discarded clothing, there's a strong smell of carnal abandonment lingering in the air, but of King Magnus and Rejeniffur there's neither sight, nor sound....

ENTER EDRIGO

It's at this point that we see Edrigo drop by, looking dazed and walking rather stiffly for some reason, no doubt hoping for a quiet moment's reflection with a restorative cuppa. So dazed is he, that he doesn't seem to notice that Eck's is now just a crater of devastation. He takes a seat at the one intact table standing amongst the wreckage, and gazes off into an inner nothingness, while all around dazed looking people start to disentangle themselves and drift about, reassembling what they can of their clothing.

ENTER ME

It's at another point, not very long after that point, that I myself drop by, also hoping for a quiet moment's reflection on all the transformative experiences of my morning so far, and coffee, and am shocked to round the corner into Low Street and find this wrecked Ex Eck's where Eck's once used to be...

It's a pleasant surprise, though, for me to see my old friend Edrigo sitting there amongst the ruins, but it's obvious that all is not well with him. Smoke and steam drift up from his ripped and spattered clothing, and strange bits and pieces of... well what? wallpaper? rug? waffle? pizza? are sticking out of the usually stylishly wild but now tangled mess of his long scarlet hair.

"Gogo!... Gogo! Are you alright?"

It's a minute or two before he turns, bringing his focus back from that inner infinity to our immediate surroundings, and recognizes me.

"Didi... it's very good to see you... oh deeerie, deeerie me... what a morning...."

"Ha! Same here!"

Ex-Eck's versatile staff stagger deftly about, restoring the place to Normal Eck's, the walls and ceiling are soon back up, the windows are re-glazed, and a coffee machine is wrenched and hammered back into service. More tables are repaired with hammers and nails, and spanners and bolts. Customers drift back to their seats, take up their conversations where they left off, and all is soon as normal as it ever was before.

"Can I get you gentlemen anything?" asks a waitress, her cheeks rather flushed.

"Two coffees, extra large, black, please... by the way, was there an explosion of some kind here... or something...?"

The waitress begins to speak but seems a bit flustered and confused, and wanders off, mumbling and adjusting her overalls. Over our coffee, Edrigo and I start to to tell each other about our mornings' experiences. It turns out that Edrigo has had a rather trying time...

SAMMY THE SEXBOT

"Well, Didi, as you know, I've been keeping all my friends, models, lovers and misfits so busy with our Kinetic Post Industrial Disruptivism projects, Gorilla Gardening and so on, that they don't have nearly enough time for sex with me now... so I thought it might be a good moment to try out a robot built for that purpose. Naturally, I've been curious about what making love with a machine might be like ever since I heard of their existence.

"So, I ordered one up on Amabonk and just a few days ago there came a knock at the door. It was Sammy delivering herself. I have to say that she looked utterly ravishing... as it turns out ravishing is a very good word for her... and I escorted her straight through to the bedroom to get acquainted with her controls. It was a bit strange at first I have to say, I think they need to work on that rubbery smell, but once I got used to the clanking and whirring it actually became most exciteeeng."

Edrigo takes a large swig of coffee at this point, tries to smooth out his hair, removing a couple of bits of charred material of some kind, possibly upholstery cloth, and what I think is a couple of chips.

"Someone very clever has put a lot of work into developing this new generation of sexbots. It takes a while to get the hang of the control panel, it's so complicated! but you can make their hair go long or short, or anything in between, and any colour you like, from the natural shades of blonde, brunette, red and black as well as green, blue, through to checks and stripes, silky straight or wavey, and you can even make their skin go any shade you like too, natural or unnatural, black, white, gold, silver... anything you fancy... With a couple of flicks of a switch I could pump her breasts up and down from VVV Petites to Super Grandes XXXL and back again. I'd chosen the TechnoFace ™ optional extra, another feature with which you can get their facial muscles to mould themselves into different personalities, the likeness of say, a film star, or a pop singer you have the hots for - so much to explore and play with, Didi!

"And as if that were not enough, the Sammy Range has a huge variety of voice and personality modes, you can choose from Coyly Encouraging Submissive - "Oooh, Big Boy, beeep beep beeep, your'e so naughty aren't you?" - through to Deranged Fantasising Nymphomaniac and Wickedly Stern Domineering Mistress... I'll leave the sort of things those two say to your imagination...

"Well, Didi, I had several days of the most intense erotic pleasure with Sammy and was even beginning to get quite fond of her. It might seem strange that you could feel affection for a machine, but then think how people grow fond of their cars, how they talk to them as if they were people too, get upset when they come to the end of their repairable lives, or shed a tear when they trade them in for a superior or younger model, it's just the same but stronger with sexbots.

"So it was all going very well indeed... until this morning..." Edrigo pauses to take a very large swig of coffee. "I don't know if you remember how the thunder and lightning reached a new level of super-cataclysmic ferocity this morning, Didi?"

"Yes I do, Gogo... I'm not likely to forget it... "

"Well, I think it must have caused some sort of power surge or capacitance overload event in Sammy's brain. We were going at it hammer and tongs on the kitchen table when an extra large flash of lightning seemed to trip some kind of switch or circuit inside her... Her eyes suddenly started to flash with a bright yellow light, the air around her started to glow and ionize or something, then...." Edrigo goes quiet for a moment and bites his lip...

"What Gogo?... what happened then?"

"Well, Didi, she threw me off onto the floor, planted a shapely robotic thigh-high black patent leather booted foot on my chest... and I could only watch in disbelief as she... *transformed!*"

"My god! Into a truck? Into a plane?"

"No! I watched helpless as her sex organs transformed... her lovely vagina and lips remained much the same, but what had been her clitoris swelled up... then swelled up some more, protruded, kept on protruding... formed into a shaft... a long, thick curving shaft... it was a cock! Didi, she had grown a truly enormous cock! My god, I had no idea she had that capability... to become a man at the same time as a woman... of course I've fantasised about and painted such things, but to see a woman-cock quivering, throbbing and glistening in real life right there in front of you... prepared for action... well, it was a bit of a shock... remind me to read product descriptions better in future, Didi..."

"Dearie, dearie me, Gogo... what depraved, fiendish imagination can have dreamed up such a thing?... so what happened next?"

"Well, 'Right then, Big Boy, beep beep beep', she, (now also he), said, in a somewhat deeper and definitely dominating robotic lilt, 'My turn now, baby!... clank! whirr!... Spread 'em tiger! beep beep beep...' And with that she/he lifted me up off the floor, she/he is very strong, I don't think I mentioned that, plonked me face down on the table, whacked some butter up my arse and proceeded to have her/his wicked way with me... with all the frantic tireless machine energy she/he could muster..."

"My god, Gogo, how awful..."

"Well, I have to admit I did get a certain thrill of excitement and even pleasure from the new experience for a moment... of course, as you know, I've had lots of male as well as female lovers, but not rolled into one machine before, and she/he simply wouldn't stop, or even slow down! before long I was begging her/him for mercy... but it was no use! My cries fell on unreceptive audible spectrum receptor units! 'Ooooh yes, yes, yes! baby! baby! beep beep beep, how's that for size, eh, Big Boy? etc etc'. was all she/he said. Didi, I've often wondered, is it better to give than to receive? well in the case of robotic anal sex I don't think there can be any doubt about it... goodness only knows where it would all have ended, but fortunately there was another extra-cataclysmic flash of lightning, which shorted out, or connected up something else inside her/him. With grinding gears, and much flashing and beeping she threw me aside and turned her attentions to the freedge-freezer! Before long the poor thing was nothing but bits and pieces of smoking machinery spattered with defrosting food."

"I was wondering how you got pizza, chips and waffles in your hair, Gogo."

"The freedge-freezer clearly didn't even come close to satisfying her/his lusts and she/he went on to rampage her/his way through the washing machine, the tumble dryer, the dishwasher, a standard lamp, my clock-radio, the cooker, the toaster, the TV, the computer... any and every piece of electrical equipment in my flat... it's all just a pile of smoking, sparking, mangled wreckage now... "

"It sounds a bit like my workshop..."

"My poor flat ruined... I have to say that Sammy her/himself was looking a bit the worse for wear too. One arm was hanging rather low from her/his shoulder, her/his eyes were rotating in opposite directions and smoke and steam were issuing from her/his nether regions. By the way, I think it's good advice for people and robots everywhere to avoid having sex with toasters, or if there's no stopping you, at least unplug the damn theeng... There was a smell of burning oil, scorched silicone and overloaded electrical circuits in the air. Sammy was staggering about bumping into things, accidentally destroying all the furniture, carpets, curtains and bed linen too. 'Must go... beep, beep, beep... to sexbot repair shop... beep, beep, beep... ciao, Big Boy...'

"And with that she/he stumbled, clanking and whirring out of my flat and off down town, making her way to that sexbot repairguy on Grot Street, I imagine."

Neither of us says anything for a while, we just sit and mull these events over internally. Finally, Edrigo says,

"And how has you're morning been, Didi?"

PECKISH

So I tell Edrigo all about King Magnus leaving me, about my treatment from Dr Krakk and my brain upgrades, and about my years of training in a different, backwater strand of our Time Phase with the Heebiegeebies over another couple of coffees, much to Edrigo's astonished entertainment. We both find that all the talking and listening is making us feel a bit peckish, so chomp up some elevenses in the form of carrot cake, florentines, various pastries, black forest gateau, croissants, madeleines and chocolate brownies, all of which only makes us realise just how really extra-hungry our exploits have made us, so we decide to head round to the supermarket equidistant between our flats, the Festerco's Extreme on Downunder Street, pick up some food and drink there, then head round to my flat for a bite of lunch, what with Edrigo's flat being a bit out of order...

CHAPTER SIX

FESTERCO'S EXTREME

Edrigo and I make our way round to the Festerco's Extreme on Downunder Street, weaving our way through the medicated mongolloids and living-dead zombalunks staggering around, always particularly thick on the ground around here, ground that has started to throb with a very low frequency hum and to shake a bit, weaving our way through falling stonework, cracking pavements and through the bits of plastic, scrap metal and decaying furniture being blown about by the super-cataclysmic storm, now on the rise again after that leaden lull of hyper-humidity, bringing it with it snow, fog, hail, mist, sleet, haar, rain, clag and drizzle, along with flooding, a drought and blazing, scalp-frying heat.

The Festerco's on Downunder Street has recently been de-modernised in a ground-breaking Lozzo Industrial Political Democratic Dictatorship Public Interaction Department Diet and Health Awareness project. The Lozzo Industrial Political Democratic Dictatorship Public Interaction Department has been becoming increasingly concerned about the truly abysmal general level of health of the average Foulburgher, not of course because they care about people at all but because they worry that before long there might be no one fit enough to toil for them or tend the massive machinery in the fields and factories, or strong enough to be worth enslaving, or healthy enough to have medication and food additives tested on them and shovelled down them, or alive enough to be sold stuff to, or just generally existing to be made completely dependent on that same Lozzo Industrial Political Democratic Dictatorship Public Interaction Department, thus justifying its own existence. After all, if people could take care of all their needs themselves would there actually be any requirement for the Lozzo Industrial Political Democratic Dictatorship, or any of its millions of departments?

So, yes, in the hope that the project will address these concerns, a whole new experimental shopping experience has been devised for the people of Foulburgh. Though still in its early days, it's showing signs of being a typical triumph of thoughtful planning and efficient use of resources, and even making a token but nevertheless almost significant gesture towards doing something about the Impending Mass Extinction Climate Emergency Thing in the process by preventing a food mile or two, or even using a square inch of shrink-wrap less, as a kind of fringe benefit, now that everyone is aware of the importance of these issues... yes! yes! and here it is!... the Festerco's Lozzo Industrial Political Urban In-Store Hunting and Gathering Re-enactment and Rewilding Unit!

THE
LOZZO INDUSTRIAL GOVERNMENT RECOMMENDED WAY OF THE MODERN HUNTER-GATHERER

In this wonderful project, our local store on Downunder Street has been planted up with mini-environments, re-creating the huge range of different habitats from which our food comes, such as jungle, estuary, coastal salt marsh, woodland glade, the river bank, heathland, mountain-top and bog, and has been stocked up with lots of wild animals, both prey animals for us to hunt: gazelles, rabbits, deer and the like, and hunter animals to hunt us: wolves, lions, jaguars and so on, also taking the opportunity to bring back a few animals from extinction or near-extinction such as the sabre-toothed tiger, the bison and the auroch, to keep these magnificent beasts alive, the basic idea being to keep us on our toes and make us fitter, and to help us to return to a more sustainable way of life, the way of the hunter-gatherer, but all of this being done in a planned, sensible way in line with the modern wisdom of the Lozzo Industrial Government so that Profit, Growth, Control and Dependency will be maintained. Already, average levels of

Foulburgher fitness and health, by all government measurements, have indeed rocketed up and the numbers of the unfit and unhealthy are rocketing down. Why, only yesterday, three diabetics and a manic depressive were carried off by lionesses, to be fed to their young. I have to say I think it's all been a wonderful success and it certainly makes shopping so much more fun.

Along with the planting of trees, bushes, shrubs etc. from the different habitats, fruit and veg has also been placed, directly into the soil or tied onto the branches of trees, not really ripe but capable of being ripened at home and eaten a few days or weeks later, to mimic nature, all properly labelled, thoroughly washed, debacterialised, irradiated, disinfected and safely wrapped in many, many layers of plastic, so that shoppers will not be too shocked by having to search for things that they won't recognise or be subjected to Germs etc. through the lack of packaging. So there's also plenty of in-store opportunities for gathering and foraging, as well as hunting and being hunted, all in complete safety and government-industry-approved Harmony with Nature.

I pick up a spear, a machete and a wicker basket at the entrance and head on into the leafy aisles. To be frank, Edrigo looks a bit shagged out and in need of a little rest, so I leave him sprawled over the misinformation and manipulation stand by the door, to stand guard and protect our escape route. I've heard that the feral McCludgie Family, who have taken up residence between aisles seven and eight, (climax forest, household cleaning products, tinned fish, and, alpine ridge, hair-care, confectionery, respectively), have been giving a bit of bother recently, since they turned cannibal, by picking off and eating some of the less nimble shoppers, so I tread softly as I head on into the gloomy branches, vines and creepers.

There's often a prey animal drinking at the water hole at the end of aisle five, (emergent layer, tea, coffee, condiments), so I set off cautiously that way, keeping an eye open for the glint of a big cat's fang or a McCludgie's cudgel. It gets darker and more humid the further I go, plant tendrils brush against me making my neck hair stand on end. Here and there I have to hack my way through thorny overgrowing undergrowth, as quietly as I can. It's amazing how quickly Mother Nature will reclaim an area given half a chance! The McCludgies have built themselves an encampment, occupying the central territory of the store, complete with yurts, composting toilets and sharpened palings to fend off marauding bears and elephants, all made from zebra hides, reclaimed packaging, buffalo bones and the like, which I have to hack my way round with the utmost stealth, lest I end up in their cauldron.

Peeking round a corner I see that Edrigo and I have picked a good time for our shopping trip as the McCludgies are taking their mid-day break, gathered round the steaming cauldron, bubbling away on its fire, with various human remains, arms and legs etc. poking out of the deep fat, clearly still a little underdone, chomping on various other cuts and joints also of obvious human origin. The mother of the clan, Beryl "the Feral" McCludgie, gnaws on the remains of a deep-fried human thigh, getting every last scrap of marrow and gristle from it with hideous scrunching and slurping sounds. It's hard to believe that this matriarch of mank was once a respected teacher, or possibly lawyer, or accountant or something, but it's true. No doubt it was the stress of her work, or possibly the dawning on her one dark day that she had missed her true calling, that set her off on a downward spiral of drink, drugs, foul language and complete disregard for personal hygiene. I guess it was a small step for her to go from screeching abuse at passers-by, while demanding money, from her plot outside the post office, to moving her operation across the road and indoors, with her family, to take up residence at our Downunder Street Festerco's Lozzo Urban In-Store Hunting and Gathering Re-enactment and Rewilding Unit.

Though I have to admire the family's handiwork, their yurts and other constructions have been put together with a definite touch of rustic craftsmanship and an eye for style, (it takes someone like me, a post-industrial artistic genius, to appreciate this), their encampment isn't an inspiring sight in any other way. If there's a time of day when the McCludgies are at their most manky and revolting it's mealtime. It's difficult to say which one is the most filthy. The Sul'phrous Maw herself, Beryl the Feral, ranks high, way, way off the Mankfort Scale at a disgusting Force 14, but then so does her partner, the Sul'phrous Paw, Dudgie the Sludgie McCludgie, coming in at an easy Force 13, with the ghastly, continuously bickering boys, Reckie, Feckie and Smeckie not far behind with a strong Force 12, and their revolting sisters, held together with lipstick, gaffa tape, bile and more foul language, fouler even than their Maw's, Pudji, Spludji and Grudji McCludgie, bringing up the rear at a still extremely foul smelling Force 11, so the entire clan is very close knit, in respect of filthiness. Mealtimes add a whole dimension of ghastliness to the McCludgies with all the fighting over eyeballs and other treats, the slavering and cursing, the flinging of human bones over shoulders, the ripping and scrunching of deep-fried human muscle and fat etc etc., all the more hideous for me than usual now that I have my freshly sharpened senses and Dr Krakk brain augmentation.

As I say, finding the McCludgies at mealtime gives me my best chance of slipping past them unnoticed whilst they are busy at their refreshments and grabbing an antelope or something down at the waterhole. I crawl on hands and knees past their stockade, blotting out their noise and smell as best I can with inner chanting, and mindful deep breathing exercises, which the Heebiegeebies also taught me but which I forgot to mention.

There is indeed a deer at the waterhole. Moving ever so carefully, I get as close as I can then fling my spear towards its heart, which is a bit behind its front legs in case you ever need to know. But just as I'm throwing, the creature senses my presence and is off like a flash into the undergrowth. My spear bounces of a tree trunk, flies up into the air then comes whooshing down again to skewer Reckie, Feckie or Smeckie straight through the brain, not doing much actual harm to this vestigial organ but making him howl and stirring up all the rest of the McCludgies like a nest of banshees. There's a frightful clan screeching, even worse than buskers' bagpiping, when I'm spotted and they come lurching towards me from their encampment.

I realise I don't have much time and will have to make a run for it if I don't want to end up in their pot or grisly larder. Though stuffed full of human flesh and blood, they're picking up speed as they head down the central thoroughfare towards me... Dudgie the Sludgie McCludgie is off to a good start and well in the lead, keeping tight in to the inner edge of the track where the going is reasonably firm... Beryl the Feral is pretty much out of the running as she has stuck to something very manky indeed on her log chair and it's slowing her down... Reckie, Feckie and Smeckie are neck and neck right in the centre of the field... with their youthful vigour and reasonable traction they're drawing up closer to their dear papa... it's going to be a tight race, the lads have had a generally good season, they've been finding that extra turn of speed when they've really needed it... but out on the far edge of the track, what a sensation! the horrid sisters have dug deep and found some hidden reserve of acceleration, with their flanks steaming and nostrils flaring Pudji, Spludji and Grudji draw up and even overtake their poor old tiring pa! my god what an extraordinary performance from these horrible young women... and as we come into the vitally important first turn it's Spludji McLudgie ahead by a whisker from Pudji then it's Grudji then Reckie, Feckie and Smeckie neck and neck leading Dudgie the Sludgie McCludgie frankly tiring now and bringing up the rear still stuck by hideously revolting mank to her log chair it's Beryl the Feral, all lather and curses...

The screams, roars and the thunder of feral feet are getting nearer and nearer, the McCludgies are so close now that I can feel the wind from their brandished knives and homemade cudgels, see the reds of their eyes, their wild matted hair and beards flowing, their snot and drool flying, as we round that first bend and head off down the back straight, it's all a bit blood-curdling. I realise there's no time even for a very short nap to recharge my batteries for extra shopping speed so, remembering my Heebiegeebie training, I send out the biggest Beam of Peace I can muster under the daunting circumstances. It slows the grim pack down a little and at least gives me enough time to gather a few essential supplies.

As quickly as I can, I fill my wicker basket with mangoes, raspberries, breadfruit, an oven-ready swan, bananas, pomegranates, hazelnuts, pineapples, brazil nuts and dragon fruit, fillet steak, bread, diced chicken breasts, lard, also some strawberries, pre-peeled potatoes, pre-chewed beef jerky, passionfruit... it all takes a little time as they will keep moving stuff around these stores! you can never find the things you really need... and also cashews, apples, hazelnuts and walnuts, not forgetting bottles of gin, vodka, whisky, rum, schnapps, agua dente, wine, beer, absinthe and cider, my path fortunately taking me along aisle two, (alpine pasture, alcohol and paper products), with a feeling of relief I head for the door... but what am I thinking! no snacks! no crisps, waffles or chocolate biscuits! I'm going to have to make another circuit...

Oh dear! the McCludgies are rousing themselves from their Beam of Peace induced torpor and picking up speed again, steadily gaining solid aisle two ground, and they're even more venomously angry and horrifically bloodthirsty than before... my goodness me!... now there's a surprise burst of speed from Beryl the Feral, she has extricated herself with a *sshsshsshkkkww-wpppllllloooooop!* from whatever ghastly thing it was, better not to know, sticking her to her log chair, howling with rage and terrible oaths she hurls herself at a frenzied ultra-gallop past the rest of the clan....... and...... pause for breath here........ and as I head down the grassy furlongs of aisle thirteen I'm ahead by a couple of lengths from Beryl the Feral with Reckie Feckie and Smeckie hard on her heels the lads have got a second wind from somewhere and it's Pudji Spludji and Grudji drawing up again to the front of the pack with thundering feet all of them clawing the air hissing and screeching as I hastily gather up plain salt'n'vinegar bacon tomato ketchup and giraffe flavour multipacks of crisps and multipacks also of tea cakes chocolate digestives bourbons ginger snaps custard creams hobkits and katnobs but I'm a little bit overloaded now and tottering under the weight and as I turn the last corner there's just the waterhole jump between me and the door and with a fiendishly cunning upgraded brain wave I scatter some banana skins and pour some extra virgin olive oil around the take-off side of the jump ha! ha! as I clear it myself with a massive leap born of terror only dropping a few less vital multipacks like the rich teas and digestives which I'm not really all that fond of anyway and though I land badly and fall in a heap snacks and drink spilling out everywhere the McCludgies are soon slipping and sliding all over the place crashing into each other wounding each other with their knives and fangs as they come to the waterhole before wading through it roaring and cursing heading towards me now with super-enraged fury so as we come into the last furlong with the misinformation and manipulation stand and Edrigo clearly in sight by the door it's me ahead by a couple of lengths from Beryl the Feral and the horrid sisters then it's Reckie Feckie and Smeckie neck and neck bickering away fit to bust and Dudgie the Sludgie at the rear of the pack obviously tiring now snorting and wheezing still a hideously bloodthirsty sight all of them steadily gaining on me that's a me that's tottering and staggering under the weight of food and drink the McCludgies are closing on me their legs and feet are just a blur... they're reaching out for me with their talons and fangs... I can't send out another Beam of Peace holding on to all this shopping... oh dearie, dearie me... the door's so near... but so far... they've caught up!... it's the cauldron for me!...

... but oh no it's not! now several things all happen more or less at once, a panther and a jaguar, the cat not the car, pounce on Dudgie the Sludgie McCludgie at the rear of the pack, which distracts the McCludgies for a vital moment, and tins of special bargain beans and mango pulp start to roll past on the floor and fly through the air at them, followed by spears, flying machetes and more rolling and flying tins, also holding them up, Edrigo, bless him! has roused himself from his post-robotic-coital fatigue and is flinging everything he can lay his hands on from the open doorway, and furthermore, out on the street behind Edrigo stand four enormous stone-faced storm-trooper-traffic-warden-police-soldiers of the Lozzo Industrial Private Army, in their usual full riot-warfare gear, bristling with stubble and weapons. The eight long hairy arms of those four storm-officers of the law are holding a variety of automatic Lozzo weapons, flamethrowers and bazookas pointed at the McCludgies... and so by the skin of our teeth, we escape to the street, leaving the McCludgies screaming the foulest of foul abuse, "I'll put a hexagenarian on you, you jolly bad person," etc. etc. and making the most hideous gestures at us through the closing doors as they slowly start to slink, panting and sweating, back into the leafy Festerco's gloom.

"Mr Daniel Thelonius Sprocket, Sir?" asks one of the storm-police-troopers.

"... er... well, why... yes..."

"Would you please come with us at once, Sir!"

CHAPTER SEVEN
INTERMISSION

After all that frantic excitement, by way of a little intermission, here's a charming work by the poet, Y.Y. Miltoff-Chalky, which describes the first appearance of the monkey wrench in the human realm, and should be quite soothing.

So read on if you like, or you could maybe pop out to the foyer for a hot dog, or just wander around a bit to stretch your legs...

THE SONG OF CEDRIC

explaining how the Magnificent Gift of the Monkey Wrench was given to Mankind, Womankind and Genderfluidkind, from On High

PROLOGUE

Stout Cedric rose up from his bed one night to have a pee

But just when he was going back again, a Voice came: "List to me!

Stout-hearted Cedric, list thee to me!"

Quoth Cedric, "What thon fucke wast that? Good gracious me

Mayhap a weird thingge of the nichtte or a banshee?"

He betook himme to the windy and keekit oot

But couldnee see any such nastty thingge aboot.

His herrt was pundin and in a spinn, when that same Thereal Voice came on the air aginn,

Full cleerre it spake to himme in tones most deare and dread,

And now I will wricht doon exactly what it said:

I

"Stout Cedric! My Sonne of Iron, my Workshoppe Denizon,

You moun go uppe into the hilles and mounts, my dearre old sonne

For something bides up therre magnificent I sweerre, for good of all,

So upp thou goest to grabbit from on high, yay upp ye go my sonne and then

You moun bringge it back richht doun aggen, is that quite cleerre?

For 'tis a thing will proove to be a Boone to all Mankind

And Womankind besides, especiallee women who feel inclined to fix up old carres

And bikes and stuffe like that, with nuttes and bolttes bothe loose and ticchhte

For why should Menne have all the funne dain thinggs like thotts? Nay, nay, indeed

Menfolk should take their turn at hanging oot ye washingge and thinningge ye carrottes,

Onnyway, enuffe o that fer noo, it's time fer yu to goo,

Pit on yer bittes and muffler lad and have nae fearre

For I'll be ever heerre to guide those bittes of thine so tacketee

On thonder path and that's a facketee"

II

Stout Cedric he was somewhat stunned by all this it must be said, what the

Fucke was that unearthlee voice that spoke to mee, thochte hee? Butte he knew

Better than to disobey any strrange unearrthlee voice afterr listening to so many tales

Of supernaturral thingges as a wee small boyy, in which thingges go Very Badly Wronggge for

Characters who do not do what unearrthlee voices say, coming to a Stickee Endd one way

Or another, so back into ye bedroome he popped and said cheereeo to his wifeey dearrey

Lying therre snorring like a drain, alone, her golden hair in luscious billows lay

Across thon pillows, a sweeter sicct was neverr seen, forr it glistened in the moonlichht brriccht

A sigh escaped from Cedric's lippes, and something

stirred doon in his hippes

For he would fain have tarried there a while and stroked those long and luscious, gleaming waves, those silk-soft golden temptress tresses,

So beautifully and peacefully did his lovely young wifeey lay,

And fain would he have slipt twixt thon sheets for snuggles and caresses,

But ye Unearrthlee Spiritte Voice said, "Nay! there's nae time noo for dalliaunce, my nocchhty laddie sweetie

Get thine arse up thon hillies on thine tway feetie, and be quick aboot it"

III

So it was that Cedric said, "Farewell my love, sleep ticchht",

And left her driftinn 'n' snorrrrinn on thon seas of slumber. Quoth he,

"Wifey dearre, I moun take ma fittes n bittes

Up intoo thonder hillies this nicchhte, by orderr of ye Unearthlee Spiritte Voice I go

'Tis for ye good of Mankind and Womankind and all other types of kind too, mynne sweet, so cheerio."

IV

At this point thinketh me I should explain, that this Stout Cedric was indeed a Man of Iron

And also Steel, e'en Chrome Vanadiumm, he toiled by day in his workshoppie

Fixing cartwheels, rocket ships and bikes, and all the rest of their many-splendoured likes,

Which cann be foond in wir Space-Time Continuumm,

Full fifteen score of spannerrs maybe more, and also socket sets galore

Had he on every wall of his workshoppie, and e'en strewn aboot upon the florr

But yet betimes there being just such a vast array of different sizes of nuts and bolts

With which he had the opportunitee to twiddle, yay, in spite of all these tools he hadde,

Sometimes he lacked that perfect wunne,

That would get that single awkward fuckinnggg nutte undunne,

Or lacked that very one with which some awkward bloomin bittchch

Of a bolt could be done up tichhter even morrre.

V

But thon Dear Spirit that guideth all mechanics and their brother engineerrs

Had seen Stout Cedric's plicht, and wished to see our hero rricht and so

Most heartfelt beseechments did she makk to those Gods of Creativitee

And also of Inventionne, wh'art especiallee powerful in this craggie area of land

And who come up with all mannerr of new thinggs way up in the mountains bare

And peakies grand, up where they have their godly workshop lair

And at her request they said arricchht we'll doo itt and started hammering away and forging too, on their anvils they sett too itt

Thon shoorrs sweet of sparrks n'spellies wurrh fairrly flleeein

Way, way up amongst those windie hicchts, 'twere monny a scroo

Upon their lathes they turned from rodde till threaded,

From their copious stock of eee enn wan a leaded - whart a kind of low carbon mild steel most suitable for a' this

sorrt o' wurrk - and drilled and fitted thinggs, embedded
Other bitts and pieces until doon twinkled a shafftte o' starlicchht, just the one

It shone doon on the finished worrk, for it was Dunne! Ye gods of metal had fulfilled their task,

Behold by starlight now revealed, The Monkey Wrench! temp'r'd and anneeeled, unmasked.

But then secured the Wondrous Thing, that's what they didd

With magick spelles they girt it roon aboot

Lest this Awesome New Technologee fall into the hands o' some arse o' a galoot.

VI

Soooo down thon moonlit garden path strode Cedric Stout, frae his wee hame he's noo gone oot

Drawn into the nichht by thon Unearrthlee Voice Etherre-eal, thon Spirit Guide Mechanikal

And also Engineerreeal

Drawn, drawn by summe mysterious Force, a bit like Gravitee, but notte, because that would just have held him down, down to the ground,

Whereas this Force was pulling him along, along, and guiding him along thon path, into the night which was

Happily quite calm, crisp, and mild, for the time of yeareal, which was early autumn, a Force

Which was of course the verry selfsame thingge as ye Unearrthlee Voice, and was wielded by this Spirrit with a benign disposeetion to mechanicks, engineers and a' their ilk, be they male, female or even gender fluid.

VII

By thon wayy, when thine Poet and Narrator, i.e. I, speak of this Cedric chappe

As being Stout, I do not mean that he was Fatte, for he

was notte

Though chubbee to some degree well might hee bee

Around ye midriff, and ye arse forby, nay nay, I refer to ye Courage that he hadd in plenty

For it's not just anyone that wille, head off by moonlight up a hille at weirrd behest

But bravelee on and on Stout Cedric went, his path illumined by that baleful great big round white Shiney thing up therre in the sky, I refer of course to the Moone, which was very big and extremely full that nichht

His path thankfullee also illumined by a wondrous vast momentous array of stars and their lichht,

But now we will fast forwardde go, or I will run oot of inkke or bust mynne quille

Before I get to ye Exciting Bittes, which come much further up thon hille.

VIII

Of all the slippery rocks and mossy ways I'll tell thee nauccht

Except to say that Cedric's way was fraucchht with every kind of diff'cultay

And monny a time he slupped and bonged his kneee, and chinne, and heid, and shinne and chinne aginn and bolloccks, and elbie, and arse, and aa aginn'n'aginn

"O fockke!" quoth he, "another affy woond I hope this blloddy jorrrnay

Turnss oot to be wurth all this fockkin hassle and affy distress," the wee moany shite,

N'ungrateful wee mingin numptie, still onn he went a'moanin an a'bongin hisself

A'trippin' an a'crokkin hissen tah an aah fit tay busst on up into thon crragggies and starlicccht nite.

IX

Welllll finallee Stout Cedric made it to the tappe of yon mountain peeake

All battered n'broositt n'scratchitt n'bleedin

N'puffin n'huffin n'mooanin n'wheezin

And whiccht d'ye think he seed on yon top?

Why 'twas a wondrous wondrous siccht the like he'd never seed before

A magic thing a'glinting on a rockke, a thing of chrome vanadium and steel

Adjustable, unrustable, the toatull deel,

A Magic Spanner of deliccht, a' shiney in the Moon's fair liccht,

"Come let me clutch thee fair sweet thinggie!"

Quoth Cedric, and though he'd ne'er seed this wonderrous thingg beforre

Still instantlee he knew just what the thing was forrr

With engineering intuition so he saw the magic thingg's potential understood

For 'twas of course the single wan tooll whitt he lackk'd

In his workshoppie way doon backk

Thon hilll, he reeeched oot to grabbit but beforre he could

A blast of licchtning stapped him in his track

And came an A'summe Voice whonn to himm spackk...

X

"Ceeedric! Ceeeeedric! Thon of masssiff herrt and arrse

Beyond this point thoust may notte passe

Unless you makk wi' us a Solemmn Undertakin.

The Magic Spanner thou'll ne'er grasp unless thou sweer

To use this Wondrous Implement not just for the benefit of Mann

And Womman too and aa' thon gender fluid

Folk, you monne promise me, thine Engineering Druid, that thou'll not forget to care

For Earthh herself, for everr mair, for whitt good will it be at aa' at aa'

If Humans have these comforts and conveniences

But have left the dear Earthh bare, a smokinn wreckk, I have to say

Your records affy poorr when t'comes to looking after thon'vironment

For whitt was wance a Paradise, ye've turned into a Toatull Fuckkingge Ruinn

A Smokinn and a Beelin wi chemickal and plastick crappe and stuffe aa'whurr

Your toatull lack of comprehension and stupiditee

Leaves all us gods, godesses and evr'y gender flooid day-itee

Toatully gobbsmmackit, so let's hear you promise, Cedric dearre, to use this Boone of a Toolle,

This neww Technologee, and all other Previous Technologees, yay,

Start noo to use them wisely and with due Conseederation for thon'vironment or you'll ne'er layy

Wan finggerr on thon Maggick Thinggie instead we'll kick thine arrse back doon thon wayy

Ya wee numptie o a stuppit fuckingge engineerr that ye've binn up to noo."

XI

Weelllll, as thick of heed and affy stuppit as he bee

E'en Cedric couldny helpitt but agree

And so that Solemmn Prommise then he sworre

To care for thon'vironment for everrmorre

And e'en did he gangg wan steppe furrtherrr too

And promiss'd to start thon process of allowing Motherr Naturre dearre

To Regenerate her Wondrruss Biodiversitteee
At last thon Dayitees were satisfied and thay releesed the Magick Toolle
From the Grasp of thayrr Spellies, and Cedric then re-eched oot and grrabbditt
Fray the rockke whereon it lay,
"Har! har!" he cacklit wi joy n'glleee
"Oh Magick Spanner comme to meee!"
And clutchin the thingge a shiney in his oilley paww
Set off he doon thon hill and gangged awaww.

XII

Thence Cedric ran and stumbled, fallin on his arrse and heed,
Aginn'n'ginn, on doon thon hillie and banged his kneees and shinns then kneees aginn,
Then heid, then arse, and boollloocks, and elbie, and arse and shinn, and elbie and chinne and shinn
Aginn'n'aginn'n'aginn and arse aginn'n'aginn, and aa and aaa
'Twere affy sorr, an he were a' battrid n'broosid n'covert in gore
N'mudd n'moss n'bittsatwigg n'stuff when he finallee gott back to his dorre.
Anndd, wwellll, whaww dye think was waitin there for himme?
Why twas his wifey, yongge and lovelly, standin' ermms a'crossit, tappin her fit n'lookin a' crotchitty
"And where thon fuckke have theeee beeeen," she creed ooot,
"Ya 'norrmuss numptie o' a palookin galooot, thine hummungguss ersse will feel ma boot!
An I'll gie yer heid a 'norrmusser walloppe
I s'pect yeev binn cooped up wi some Foulle Trolloppe
So ye'd better hae some very good storree to explain yer

bein awa half the nicchht."

XIII

Weeellllll, to cut a long verse ratherr shorrterr

Let's just say that Cedric did explain all bout the Magic Toolle and 'Thereall Voice

And all about his Oath Environmental to cease all thingges thereto detrimental

And when thatte lovely wumman saw his Wondrous Tooolle

She gasp't and her demeanourr and herr luvly wee herrrt soften't, proud did she then become

O' her dear Cedric on learnin how he'd been entrusted

Wi' this spanner which could ne'er be rusted

This Toolle a' Magick and Adjustable, this Wrrencch

So then she tended to his wounds and cuts and brooses and the wencch

And he then back to bedde their way did wend

With monny a happy sigh and hugge…

THE END

CHAPTER EIGHT

THE RISE AND FALL OF
THE TOWER OF LOZZO

Welcome back! Now, on we go...

Those eight long hairy arms of the Lozzo Industrial Private Police Army law guide me towards their squad tank. My brain's whizzing around with instant guilt, wondering what on Earth I can have done wrong... with all my Heebiegeebie training and Dr Krakk's various upgrades it's coming up with all sorts of ideas and multi-dimensional intuitions in a blur of blistering intelligence... dearie, dearie me, has the aftermath of my Loosening Off and Dropping in Event finally caught up with me?... did they find the huge pile of comics in my workshop?... is it goodbye for the Hello Machine?...

"Mr Daniel Thelonius Sprocket, would you please come with us at once, Sir! We have a Violent Emergency Level Nine Code Magenta situation at Lozzo Industrial, Sir! Your presence is required at Lozzo Tower immediately, Sir! No time to waste, we'll brief you on the way, Sir!"

And just when I was looking forward to having a bite to eat with Edrigo and winding down from all the excitement of the day so far... so, briefs or no briefs, whenever will I get my lunch now? As I'm gently thrust inside the tank I give Edrigo my flat keys and the basket of food and drink, but keep a few multipacks of crisps and biscuits by way of a little snack, just to keep me going. I'm about to offer a pack of something to the stormpolicemen but I notice that they're all incredibly fat, well they hardly ever get out of their machines these days do they? so I think I'd better not put temptation their way...

Munching on biscuits and crisps, I watch the streets of Foulburgh speed by as we thunder off down into the heart of the industrial area towards Lozzo Tower. It's looking a bit rough out there. The super-cataclysmic storm has gone up to yet another new level and become... super-duper-cataclysmic? Quite large chunks of building, small cars, furniture and people are being blown about everywhere, the rain is a super-duper-deluge, the thunder and lightning are constant, it's also snowing hard now and the sun is blasting down on our flood-drought combination situation with record breaking intensity as well... it's as if the weather couldn't make up its mind what to do so just went ahead and did everything all at once, and lots of it.

We roar along through packs of bewildered, screaming mongoholics and zombalunkaloids, scattering them in all directions, our sirens screaming too. I'm actually quite glad to be on the inside of the police tank for once as everything just bounces off the armour. I'm also quite glad because, with tracks instead of wheels, the tank is able to zoom over the cracks and holes that are opening up everywhere in the roadways.

"Our orders are to get you to Lozzo Tower as quick as we can, Mr Sprocket, Sir! On the orders of Lord Lozzo himself, Sir! A critical piece of machinery has broken down and as Chief Executive Repairman General, your presence is required immediately, Sir!"

I feel a surge of pride at this recognition, suddenly I'm important and useful after all these years! But the surge of pride washes quickly away as I wonder what on Earth can have gone wrong... and I get a sinking feeling that it may not be something that just needs tightening up or loosening off, or a couple of whacks with a sledgehammer...

We continue to blast our armoured way on through the streets and people of Foulburgh. I see that things are going rapidly from a bit rough to really very rough indeed. Even bigger bits of building are getting ripped off by the wind, whole buildings seem to be sinking into the ground, which is shaking and rumbling, a whole roof flies past us, an alcolunk is picked up by the storm, ignited by lightning, and shoots off into the sky like a kind of meteor in reverse.

As we get into the heart of Lozzo Industrial proper I see even more smoke and flames than usual billowing out of various buildings and hear even more sirens and bells than usual screeching and clanging frantically. Off to one side a crack rips the ground apart right before our eyes, revealing glowing molten-magma depths, it tears towards a block of blast furnaces, opens wide and swallows it whole. The air itself is pulsating with a kind of throbbing and booming. Dearie, dearie me! I wonder if this could finally be the Total Collapse of Everything that Edrigo has been going on about...

We speed round to my workshops so I can pick up some tools. There's a bag of my favourites always ready for my Inspections right by the door and I grab it.

Yet more bells still are clonking and sirens howling as we rush past one blazing and smoking factory or storage facility after another, until we get to the very centre of this awesome industrial world, that magnificent symbol of domination and exploitation, the brutal blank concrete cliffs of the towering Tower of Lozzo itself.

Then we go through security checks, along corridors, up many, many levels in a series of lifts and along more corridors. We pass by huge windows which look down onto the main power plant area far below. Workers are scurrying about, jets of steam and flame are bursting from cracks in what were once containment vessels. Here and there pipes are glowing red hot, orange hot, even puce, blue, green and white hot. What a great view you get from up here though! Why, I think I can just about see my flat in the distance... that makes me think of my bed... I wonder if there's time for a little nap...

"Please stay awake, Sir! Emergency situation, Sir!"

In my head, a flock of sheep starts to jump backwards over a gate and de-materialise, one at a time, it's the Sheep Uncounting Accessory Unit that Dr Krakk helped me to fit kicking in, of course, and it does indeed help me to stay awake through all the increasing rather irksomeness of these events:

SHEEP: one hundred and ninety-nine... !aaaab... one hundred and ninety-eight... !aaaaab... one hundred and ninety-seven... !aaaab...

Finally we reach the levels of Lord Lozzo's offices on the top floors of Lozzo Tower. I get a sense of approaching the throne of Infinite Ultimate Power, or maybe it's just the huge build up of intestinal wind from all the hustle and bustle, breakfast, elevenses and snacks. A series of lovely personal assistants, (I can't help noticing, by the way, even with my de-cocked, lustfully-reduced attention, that these lovely personal assistants are very lovely indeed, have their hair wonderfully coiffed and are dressed in costumes that remind me of various old science fiction films... a curious thing that I feel my new Heebiegeebie Quantum Logic and Metaphysical Processor Units start pondering straight away), lovely personal assistants who usher me through a series of outer offices until one last door is opened and I come face to face with Him himself... the Ultimately Infinite Powerful Presence of Lord Lozzo XIV.

It's the first time I've seen him at such close quarters and I have to say it's not a pretty sight, even for someone, like me, who's familiar with Modern Art, and its mould-breaking representations of the layout and colouring of the human face, etc.. If you can imagine a huge, very wrinkled walnut, splattered with wild splodges of crimson, black, maroon and more black paint, then scrunched and crumpled up even more by many, many years of thinking horrible thoughts, you're halfway there. I can't help letting off an enormous fart... well, so it was just wind after all. His Lordship is sitting at the biggest desk in the world and, being a tiny man, looks like a miniature, shrivelled up tyrantosaurus rex behind it...

...he leaps to his little aristocratic feet but this makes him even smaller...

LOZZO: Daniel fucking Thelonius Sprocket! *cough! gasp!* Also known as the Monkey Wrench Kid, I believe... about fucking time you fucking moron! There! Fix it!

By the way, His Lordship seems to be one of those people who can't give an order, or make a request, if they ever make a request, without using the "f" word. I'm so sorry if this offends delicate readers, but there it is. Nor can he give an order without screeching at the top of his voice, which after many, many years of screaming orders now has a grating, metallic quality, like someone with a rusty iron throat gargling with rusty nuts and bolts, and gravel, or particularly out of tune bagpipes. Nor can he scream an order without including an insult or two, such as "moron", "cretin", "traffic warden", "imbecile" and so on.

It probably all comes from some sub-conscious need to appear in all-powerful command and control all the time - what a terrible toll that must take! - and, ironically, may well have grown out of some deep insecurity, possibly going back to some childhood trauma or other, all too likely in the sort of continuously traumatic childhood much of our nobility has had. I'm about to recommend a little course of treatments from Dr Krakk to His Lordship, whose guided inner journeys might help him to find, deep, deep, deeper still, even deeper still, down, down inside, that Inner Nice Person lurking within, and I'm in the act of handing him the good doctor's card when His Lordship stabs a stubby withered black and red finger towards a machine sitting in a kind of small kitchen area off to one side of the office, completely ignoring my well-intentioned gesture.

LOZZO: Wakey! Wakey! You fucking cretin! Fix it! FIIIXXXX ITTT!!!

What can this critical bit of equipment be? The main control computer? Secret back-up filing storage? Has it got any obvious nuts and bolts?

SHEEP: ... one hundred and ninety-six... !aaaab... one hundred and ninety-five... !aaaab...
ME: And... er... what seems to be the.... *ppppfffrrrt!*... oops! excuse me, sorry, just slipped out... the... er... problem your Lordship, Sir?
LOZZO: It's NOT WORKING you fucking imbecile! The fucking cunting coffee machine's not working!! FIX IT you fucking cunting moron imbecile!! FUCKING FIXXX ITT!!

The coffee machine! Well, now I understand, of course, no office could operate at all without a functional coffee machine. But I really feel I must say something about his language, if not me, whoever will?

ME: Excuse me Your Lordhship, Sir, Master, but have you ever thought of using words other than the "f" word and the "c" word to emphasise what you're saying? The thing is, you see, that when you use them so often they start to lose any meaning at all and you might as well just... er... mumble nonsense... or gurgle. Have you thought of trying some alternative phrases? Like "you vexatious gadabout"? or, "you jolly tiresome poltroon?"...
SHEEP: ... one hundred and ninety-four... !aaaaaab...
ME: ... you can really start to use your imagination... and, by the way, I don't think "cunting" is actually a word at all, what on Earth could it actually mean? I know you probably want to seem cool and tough, and sort of one of the lads as well as one of the lords but...

...but I might as well not have bothered, he cuts me right off! Ah well, at least I tried...

LOZZO: We take off in five fucking minutes, we CAN NOT survive the fucking voyage without fucking COF-

FEE you idiot, FIX IT!

Take-off? Voyage? Coffee? What is he on about? But now that I look around the office I see that all the lovely assistants have strapped themselves into seats at consoles scattered around the office... my Heebiegeebie Quantum Logic and Metaphysical Processor Units and the Five-Fold High Frequency Intuition Resonator start to throb in my head now, I'm beginning to put two and two together... and I'm coming up with four and a bit...

FIRST LOVELY ASSISTANT: *(pressing buttons and gazing into a screen)* Wobbul Drive start up sequence initiated Your Lordship!
LOZZO: FIX IT!... you... you....fucking traffic baghole warden arsepipe!... There's no way we can go into Outer Fucking Space without coffee! Fix it for fuck's sake!!
ME: *Pppfffffrrrrt!* Oops sorry... Immediately, Your Lordship Sir! I'll dismantle it at once... should have the problem located in a jiffy...

Just at this moment an ethereal voice comes into my head:

SHUGGY: *(ethereally)* Daneeeee... Daneeee....

Who or what on Earth can this voice be now?

SHUGGY: *(ethereally)* Daneeee.... Daneeeee.... it's me, Shugeeee.....

Shuggy! My dear old mentor, calling from the mechanical afterlife?

ME: Shuggy? Is that really you?... er... are you ok? Where are you?
SHUGGY: *(ethereally)* Yes I'm ok thanks, son, I'm a bit

dead but I'm in heavennnn... I think... there's lots of nutssss... and boltssssss... and spaaannnnneerrs and stuffff... it's a bit like liiife... but shinierrrr... they're all singin in a littttlllee choirrrr.... it's luvleeee... the nuts and bolts do all the high stuff and the spannerrrs and wrrrencchhhess do the low stuff mostleee.......

Shuggy! Of course! It must be the Shuggy Machine Instant Comprehension Repair Re-purpose and Design Channel Dr Krakk also helped me to instal in my brain kicking in along with all the other upgrades... great timing...

SHUGGY: *(ethereally)* Daneeee.... Daneeeeeeee... check the fuse, son! check the fuuuuuuse....

I cast an eye over the machine but there's no sign of a burning string coming out of it, any more than there are there any obvious nuts or bolts to be seen, for tightening up or loosening off purposes. There's nothing else for it, putting down my tool bag, I open it and select one of my favourite sledgehammers, the Number 3 Adjustment Iron. I approach the coffee maker, hefting the colossal tool in my hand before raising it high above my throbbing head. But wait a minute...outer Space? Wobbul Drive? Voyage? The words are starting to register in my upgraded brain... What exactly's going on here?

LOZZO: What are you doing? Imbecile! STOP! FUCKING MORON! STOP!
SHUGGY: *(ethereally)* The fuuuuuuse, son, in the pluuuuuggg... get a scrooooooodriveerrrr...
SHEEP: ... one hundred and ninety-three... !aaaaab... one hundred and ninety-two... !aaaaab...

His Lordship's voice rises in pitch all the time until it is just about beyond the range of human hearing, in a similar way the noises from the Lozzo Industrial works all around us are going way, way, up, except for the noises going way, way, down, which are making the whole building tremble and shake in a way that's making me feel just a little bit uneasy.

My Number 3 Adjustment Iron comes crashing down on the glass vessel on top of the machine smashing it into smithereens, then continues down into its innards below, scattering them hither and thither. Ha! I think, well, no more nonsense from this rascally bit of equipment!

ME: I think I see the problem now, Your Lordship... it's broken..."

My comment doesn't go down well at all. His Lordship's face goes puce, then black, then green, then yellow, then blue, all the stages of a black eye healing but not healing very well in quick succession, almost goes back to black but instead goes a sort of infra-ultra purpley-puce. I must remind myself to tell Edrigo about it, I'm sure he could use a dramatic shade like that for when he goes back to painting sex organs and stuff like that again. His Lordship starts to scream something but then everything seems to go into slow motion...

SECOND LOVELY ASSISTANT: *(calmly and reassuringly)* Wobbul Drive fully engaged... Deploying sickbags......
THIRD LOVELY ASSISTANT: *(calmly and professionally)* Wobbullaunching sequence initiated... 10... 9... 8... 7... we have full Wobbul power...
SHEEP: ... one hundred and ninety-one... !aaaaab... one hundred and ninety... !aaaaab...
SHUGGY: *(ethereally)* ... sonnn... Danneee... sonn... for fuuucccksaaake just runn and hiiiiide somewherrrre... and hold on tiiiiight...

The whole office-control room is quivering and throbbing...

THIRD LOVELY ASSISTANT: *(calmly and professional-*

ly) ... 6... 5... 4...
SHEEP: ... one hundred and eighty-nine... !aaaaab... one hundred and eighty-eight...

I get a distinctly sickening feeling that the floor is lifting and vibrating...

THIRD LOVELY ASSISTANT: *(calmly and professionally)* ... 3... 2... 1... We have lift off...
SHEEP: ... !AAAAAAAABBB...

I wonder if it's too late to take a travel sickness pill?... I ask around to see if I can borrow one but all the lovely assistants seem to be a bit busy. Then a sudden flash of inspiration from my Logic and Metaphysics Quantum Pondering Units, combined with my Five-Fold High Frequency Intuition Resonator and my Decocked Non-Toxic Male Vision, hits me like a mental sledgehammer... That little rascal Lord Lozzo plans to escape the collapse of his empire, the environment and everything, in the top thirteen floors of his tower, which is in fact a spaceship customisation job performed by, I strongly suspect, those eternal teenage cosmic miscreants, the Koll-ee-Wobbuls... It's all transparently clear to me now, he means to head off into Outer Space, cavorting lasciviously non-stop with all these lovely assistants, so as to perpetuate himself, re-seeding the Universe with his vile lineage, and so as to escape the Total Collapse of Everything on Earth, a Collapse which he has largely brought about himself. Yes, what a horrible, naughty little rascal!

Rendered a bit unsteady on my feet by our take-off, I lurch from side to side. Unfortunately this movement gets mixed up with the through-swing of my sledgehammer blow. I go careering across the floor and, to my dismay, the sledgehammer goes straight into one of the lovely assistant's control screens.

ME: Ooops-a-daisy! Sorry!

There's a blinding blast of light and yet another huge roaring explosion. It's partly from the shattered control unit but not entirely my fault, as by a bit of a coincidence the whole Lozzo Industrial power plant is going off and up now, setting off yet more explosive reactions around the entire complex. I'm knocked right across the office-control room by the blast, right into another screen causing another blinding blast of light and another huge roaring explosion.

ME: Oh dear! Ooops! Gosh! So sorry!

The assistants are all screaming and waving their arms about, checking their make-up and hair-do's, the floor is wobbling and shaking, and Lord Lozzo is advancing towards me. He's taken another of my sledgehammers from my bag, I think it's the Number 7 Iron, I wonder if that's a wise choice? it's difficult to be accurate with such an enormous implement, and he's making all sorts of pre- post- and non-verbal throaty noises.

The tower-ship is now flying up high into the sky but is still beneath the worst of the filthy, chemical soaked-clouds over Foulburgh, so we are treated to wonderful panoramic views of the devastation of Lozzo Industries and the rest of the city. I see that we are actually passing right over my flat, and I wonder to myself how Edrigo's doing. With my wonderfully enhanced vision, I think I can just make him out resting on the bed in my spare bedroom. It looks as if my block has survived the general collapse of everything so far, it stands like an island of calm stability in a chaotic sea of magma and vanishing buildings. I wave to Edrigo as we zoom by, but I expect he'll be fast asleep after his tiresome morning. Our flight is becoming more and more erratic and the lovely assistants are groaning and throwing up left right and centre, and desperately trying to bring their space costumes and eyebrows back under control.

LOZZO: *(rather angrily)* You CRETIN! You fucking MORON! You've just destroyed the navigation console! I'm going to fucking KILL YOU!

His Lordship is advancing towards me, hefting my Number 7 Sledgehammer, dearie me! he's taking a swing at me!...

...There's no time to prepare myself for the Beam of Peace Technique, I just have to defend myself as best I can in the old-fashioned mortal combat way. I don't know if you've ever been in a sledgehammer fight yourself, but if you have you'll know that the sledgehammer is not something that's easily used as a weapon. The trouble is that its weight is mostly concentrated in its head, committing you to a direct hit, because if you miss your target, or just score a glancing blow, and a human target is likely to be moving, and easy to miss, or not connect with fully, the force of your blow will take you whizzing off until the hammer meets up with something else, like a control screen or console. It's even worse if you're in an office-control room that's shaking about and flying around. So all of Lord Lozzo's attacking swings and all of my defensive parries miss their targets and before long there's not an intact screen or console in the room. As it happens, the Beam of Peace of technique is unneccessary now, as Lord Lozzo, exhausted by excessive sledgehammer swinging and being horrible, has become just a crumpled multicoloured heap on the floor, slithering from side to side in the vomit and smashed up equipment etc..

Now everything goes very still and quiet. Between us, we've somehow managed to shut down the Wobbul Drive completely, and we're hanging in the air at the top of our trajectory. I have to say, you get a lovely view from up here. I point out Mount Krakkie to one of the lovely assistants, also Mount Vrollox and the beautiful breast-shaped Fappso Pyffe hills in the far distance, but she doesn't seem to be interested at all, and just moans and groans, clutches her stomach, and sorts her eye-shadow with one hand while taking millions of photos of herself for social media with the other. From up here you can see just how much of the landscape around Foulburgh has been turned into great big day-glo, hi-viz, fluorescent yellow fields, shimmering in a misty haze of chemicals, very pretty really, although I know from Edrigo that it's a Complete Environmental Disaster. Here and there, huge machines are trundling up and down, busy spraying, ploughing, spraying again, seeding, spraying again, harvesting, spraying again and spraying again, the typical country scene with which we're all familiar. With my enhanced sight, I can even make out one or two people here and there, bent over double, at some important task or other, and other vast expanses of field completely covered with what looks like plastic - how clever to wrap up our food even while it's growing! Maybe that'll keep some of that poison spray and germs and stuff off it. Talking of plastic, there's acres and acres of polytunnels too, really there's not much of the landscape that hasn't been ploughed up or covered up in some way. There are a few bits and pieces of rocky outcrop, cliff and woodland here and there left unmechanised though, and as we start to drift into our inevitable descent I recognise the beautiful wooded hills of Mystical Keenool, rising above the glittering silvery waters of the mighty River Splashy. It's all a most awe-inspiring sight indeed.

Now we're beginning to come back down towards the ground. We're flying over another factory-city nestled in its own plastic-wrapped landscape right on the coast at the Splashy estuary, lava flowing and smoke billowing all through and around it too... and now we're heading out over the coastline, and coming down faster and faster all the time. I pick out more and more detail, the huge waves with their wind-blown crests, the streaks of foam, it looks super-duper windy down there. Dearie me! It looks like we're going to come straight down in the sea...

We do indeed crash into the sea, with an awe-inspiring *spppppllllaaaaasssshhhh!* The impact causes all sorts of commotion in Lozzo Tower amongst the lovely personal space assistants and it also causes Lord Lozzo's huge desk to slide across the floor, picking up speed, straight towards me. It knocks me off my feet and I instinctively grab the swags and rosettes of its ornate reproduction antique handles to steady myself, so the desk takes me with it as it crashes through one of the panoramic windows out into the storm thrashed waters. I manage to clamber on top of it and am able to watch from its floating acres as water pours into the office-control room and Lozzo Tower quickly sinks in a whirlpool of bubbles beneath the windswept surface. I watch as the space tower's lights disappear, flickering into the depths, illuminating all sorts of sea creatures as they go, whales, giant squid, escaped goldfish, massive sharks, I'm glad there's still a few of these things left, we must have landed in one of the less devastated areas of the sea. Deep, deep, down below, I see the twinkling of other lights… well, well, what can they be? The lights of the Lost City of Atlantis maybe? An underwater outpost-lair of the villainous Koll-ee-Wobbuls? Maybe we'll find out one day… As the tower sinks down and down into the watery darkness I see that Lord Lozzo has roused himself somehow, he's standing at one of the windows shaking his fist at me, it looks like his mouth is moving and forming words, words I can't hear, but I think I lip read something along the lines of… "Damn you, Monkey Wrench Kid!… You fucking cunt of a bastard… I'm going to kill you, Monkey Wrench Kid!…" or something like that, and maybe, "The World Will Hear From Me Again!" …it's a bit of a guess though…

Anyway, at least I don't have to worry about how to fix the coffee machine for now…

It's so windy that it's hard to see the surface of the water at all, what with all the spray blowing about. Thank heavens for my Lozzo storm coat, which keeps me dry and snug. The wind is so strong that it's difficult to do anything more than cling on, but I find that Lord Lozzo's desk, a suitable size for someone of megalomanic-narcissistic tendencies, is actually quite well suited to sea travel. With it's airtight compartments, it bobs along on the surface and I'm even able to rig up a bit of a mast and sail with the Lozzo flag and flagstaff that are attached to it, and a rudimentary rudder with one of the drawer bottoms, giving us a bit of steerage way. It's just as well I've read so many comics in my time because, apart from all the fantastic escapist entertainment, it's given me a good basic understanding of what to do if you're cast adrift in the open sea on a raft, or desk, in stormy conditions, "Kastaway Kate" being very good in this area, full of sound advice and hot sea-faring tips, (issues 9 through to 17 are especially good in this way, and beautifully drawn too). And, I have the ethereal voice of the Shuggy Machine Instant Comprehension Repair Re-purpose and Design Channel advising me from whatever nut, bolt and song filled realm Shuggy exists in now.

The thing to do is to keep yourself almost stern on to the waves and try to avoid having any of the really big sea-mountains roll you over or break on top of you. Now we're under sail power, I'm able to guide the desk through the churning monsters, flying along as we surf down into the troughs, then slowing back a little as we climb up the next peak. Wheeeeee! Before long, I'm beginning to enjoy the ride tremendously, feeling just like a character in a comic! We sail along happily and, with Shuggy's ethereal guidance I even have time to rig up self-steering equipment and a bit of a cabin, complete with a hammock. Sadly, there's no time for even a tiny nap as I start to see tall shapes looming up out of the spray ahead of me. As we sail nearer I see that they are... dearie, dearie me... cliffs!... whatever next...

What happens next is that we pass through jagged outcrops of rock, miraculously missing them all and arrive on a sandy, pebbly shore, conveniently situated amongst the cliffs, partly under our sail power and partly through being washed up by the enormous waves. As they enter the shallow water the waves get even bigger and break with epic force. Me and the desk get thrown up on the shore then sucked back into the sea by the backwash of a series of waves, one of which, an extra-large one, also crashes down on us, rolls us over, holds us spinning deep under for ages and ages... I lose contact with the desk, I lose track of which way's up and which way's down, hold my breath until I can't hold it any longer, then, just when I'm wondering whether I'm about to die, the monster wave finally spews me out a bit higher up the shore than the others. I grab some breath but feel myself getting dragged back into the sea by the backwash again, and I can hear another even more monstrous wave roaring in ready to crash on top of me... oh gosh and dearie, dearie me... that's it... I'm dead... goodbye everyone...

CHAPTER NINE

REX TO THE RESCUE

But, just as I'm getting sucked back into the sea by the undertow, waiting for the next breaking wave to finish me off, a powerful grip clamps onto the back of my neck, and I feel myself being dragged out of the water. I'm taken up the beach to the high water line of plastic, sea weed, more plastic, driftwood and yet more plastic, then I'm dropped down again and rolled over, spluttering and gulping, into the recovery position. I find myself looking up sideways at an enormous male dog, who's checking me over in a professional kind of way.

"Are you ok, Danny, mate?" he asks, "ere, ave a swig of this."

He's an enormous and very shaggy dog, black with white patches, not of a breed I recognise, and with a curiously human grin about his muzzle. He's holding a flask in his paw, a rather hand-like paw I notice, with something I've not seen in a dog before, an opposable gripping section. Propping me up a bit, the dog holds the flask up to my mouth and pours in a good slug, it's what I imagine drinking very strong petrol would be like.

"Good grief... what's that?"

"Rescue Remedy, perk yup, mate."

"What that herbal essence thing?"

"Naaah, mate, over-proof rum."

I cough and splutter but after a couple more swigs I feel a revitalising glow flowing through me.

"Right, Danny, mate, come on now, we're gonna camp up in those trees over there before it starts getting dark, get warmed up, have a bite to eat, 'nall that."

The enormous, shaggy dog introduces himself as, "Rex".

"Pleased to meet you, Rex, and thank you so much for rescuing me."

"Well, I just happen to be a Rescue Dog, mate, and you're very enormously welcome."

Rex slips the flask into one of many pockets in a kind of belt-vest thing he's wearing with all sorts of handles, coils and stuff poking from it. He leads the way up from the beach and, picking up a huge backpack on the way, forges a path into some scrubby woodland. Rex sniffs and rootles around a bit, takes some tools and stuff from his belt-vest and back pack, and starts making a shelter with a tarpaulin, some branches, leaves and moss. He has a fire going in a jiffy too, hands me a towel and starts to dry my clothes out. Even my Lozzo industrial grade storm coat couldn't keep me dry through all the tumbling in the waves, what was left of it was hanging in tatters around me and I'm absolutely soaked through.

While Rex is working away, I can't help but notice just how big he is. When he stands up on his back legs, which he does quite a lot to sort out our shelter, I see that he must be over six foot tall, with strong looking shoulders, and as I said a moment ago, with a kind of opposable section in his paws which allows him to grip things, tie knots, light fires, hang wet clothes up to dry, and all that sort of thing. He seems to be just as happy walking on his back legs as he is going about on all fours. It registers with me after a bit that he's also unusual for a dog, in that he can talk...

"I don't think I've met a dog quite like you until now, Rex, that can do all this stuff... and talk... and everything... "

"Well yes, mate, we Rescue Dogs have taken this sudden jump in evolution quite recently, so, no, you probably haven't met a dog like me before."

"And that was a stroke of luck you being right there just when I needed you... I thought I was a goner there."

"Well, I was on the lookout for you, mate... my mistress, Rejeniffur, sent me to look after you. By the way, does that name, Rejeniffur, mean anything to you?" he asks me, with an amused twinkle in his eye.

"No... Rejenniffur?... I don't think I've met her, does

she work at Lozzo's?... is she from round Foulburgh somewhere?"

"Har, har, she's kind of from here, there and everywhere," Rex gives me a mischievous look, wiggles his shaggy eyebrows and winks at me, "And, well... ahem... a part of you has met her, mate, for sure... har har..."

A part? Which part? This baffles me, but I'm too tired to bother much, my poor brain's already throbbing and whirring, what with all the new images and insight and stuff flooding in from my upgrades, not to mention processing all the craziness of the day, and all quite without a proper nap...

Rex gives me a couple of blankets, and fruit and nuts to keep me going then cooks up a meal with stuff he forages from around and about. Before long, we are sitting round the campfire chomping on roots, mushrooms, leaves and stuff. It's not at all bad... once I get used to the kind of earthy flavours... and sort of fibrous textures...

We settle down, watching the patterns flickering in the flames of our campfire in the gathering darkness. Rex produces a pipe and tobacco and, in between puffs of smoke, launches into a bit of Rescue Dog Wisdom which I think would probably be titled, "The Inferiority of Human Being Intelligence when compared with Almost Any Other Kind of Animal Intelligence".

"... see take birds, Danny, mate. Birds fly half way round the world, taking nothing with them but themselves... whereas you humans... unevolvin, you could say really... ... millions of years... ... nests... ... tools... ... ... meat... ... ... navigation... ... ..."

...but I only follow a few snatches of it all here and there... because in moments I can feel my eyes closing, my attention drifting, my head nodding, my drool drooling... for one last wakeful moment I take in everything around: the flickering firelight, the feeling of being warm and snug, the scent of the fresh sea breeze, the sound of the wind in the trees and waves on the shore, the sound of Rex's voice rumbling away, the feeling of having been rescued and looked after, and the feeling of being pleasantly full of mushrooms and roots... and that's all I remember... because not even a whole flock of negative sheep unjumping could have kept me awake at that point...

RECOCKTION

Next morning I wake to find Rex busy packing everything up. I sit up when Rex hand-paws me a bowl of hot food and, stretching out my arm to take it from him, I notice a very curious thing, my arm seems to be covered in the beginnings of fur.

Rex also notices. "Look! You're evolvin too, mate. Nice colour by the way."

The fur on my arm is indeed a rather fine golden colour. I see later that it covers most of my body and seems to be growing thicker by the minute. It's all gold except for some silver stripes. I make another, even more, exciting discovery when I go for a pee, my cock's growing back! Nothing big or dramatic, at least so far, but most definitely the full set of cock and balls on the way down there. Well, well... what a pleasant surprise...

"Danny, mate! when you've finished admiring yourself it's time for..."

Rex has the air of being about to give me a huge treat... a doggie chocolate drop? ... a bone?

"... Walkies! har har, time we were on our way."

With this Rex leads us away from the shore, up a track winding through the cliffs and hills to a coastal path. The unusual thing is that I do feel excited at the prospect of a walk. It's the thought of exploring new paths and all the new scents... I guess... If I had a tail I would probably wag it, which makes me think of checking... no, no tail...

Talking of scents, my sense of smell is now much much sharper, along with my eyesight and hearing. I sample the waves and waves of different aromas as we trot along, the changing saltiness of the air and all the herbs and flowers growing around our path, it's a whole fresh new world. I'm happy to say that I'm not drawn to sniffing some of the things Rex is attracted to, dead things, various piles of animal poo and so on.

After we've been walking for a while, Rex suddenly stops dead in his tracks, and crouches down, motionless. His gaze is fixed like a Lozzo guided missile's tracking beam into a patch of undergrowth just up ahead, and the fur on his back is standing straight up. He signals for me to come alongside him and be quiet, gazing into the long grass and bushes with a look of extreme concentration and wariness on his face... What terrible danger has he seen up ahead? A predator of some kind? A crocodile? A sabre-toothed tiger?... *Maybe even a... a traffic warden??...* The tension's like an electric fog around us...

Then Rex lets out the loudest and longest fart I have heard in my life, neither of us can breath properly for the horrific smell and for laughing.

"Har har sorry mate, must be guzzlin all them roots and stuff... don't think me digestive system has evolved just quite enough for all that yet..."

"Rex," I say, "talking of digestion, I thought dogs ate... like dogfood... dog biscuits, and meat and stuff... have you gone vegetarian or vegan or something?"

RESCUE DOG WISDOM PART ONE - EATING MEAT

"Well, yes, Danny, mate, well spotted. Leastways, I used to eat mostly meat and stuff, and by the way, no, dog biscuits are not a natural thing for dogs to eat, they're an abomination just like so many other aspects of the industrial world, but dogs are evolvin and adaptin all the time just like you humans and everything else... well, that is except for those humans that are un-evolvin of course, goin backwards as it were, plenty of those around... yes, I mainly eat fruit and veg and roots and stuff but I still love a bit of meat now and again... maybe a bacon'n'egg sandwich, all scrunchy and gooey and delicious... maybe a nice fillet steak, all scorched on the outside... tender and meaty on the inside... peppery maybe, bit of garlic, kind of crusty and juicey at the same time..."

"I know exactly what you mean, Rex..."

"Fing is there's a few separate issues goin on ere, mate, that people confuse, cos they tend to try to simplify complicated issues, and jump to some position or other, without understanding the underlying patterns... I guess it's part of some kind of general dumbin down process, or mental laziness... anyway, Issue One, I think, is Taking Life, whether or not it's ok to take life, to kill and eat other animals, and I do respect people, and dogs, who fink that's just basically wrong and so don't eat meat for that reason. Issue Two is Industrial Animal Husbandry, and I personally am of the opinion that it's an utter abomination, no two ways about it, keeping millions of animals cooped up indoors, staggering around in their own poo, feeding them all sorts of crap, medicating them up to the horns and eyeballs, laying up gawd knows what viral nightmare for the future, it's all just basically wrong.

"Now, say that an animal has led its life gamboling about wild and free as a living and important part of a diverse eco-system... and you have been brought up in a hunter-gatherer society as a respectful part of that system, and you and your children would not survive at all without eating some meat where you are, and you use every part of that animal's body not just for food, but for materials for clothing and shelter and all sorts of stuff, and it means that you can lead a very low-impact way of life, just following naturally living herds around in the landscape, you don't have to store or own anything because everything you need is growing or wandering about around you, a way of life which leaves very little trace of you ever having been there, a way of life which has been successful for hundreds of thousands of years... years and years longer, far longer than this stupid age of coal and oil and cars and single-use plastic... you see, there for a start we have two quite different points of view... "

This is all stuff that Edrigo has often tried to discuss with friends and acquaintances, even before he became an Environmental Activist, leading to heated arguments with some people with a belief or conviction of one kind or another, which they think everyone should have, and are not prepared to discuss, so it's interesting to hear this dog's angle on it all.

"Now, Danny, mate, suppose you were the master or owner of a dog - and there's another issue right there by the way, the issue of whether it's right, or even possible, to have that mastery or ownership of a dog - as I say, suppose you had a working relationship with a friendly dog who helped you in your everyday life because you were blind or something, and you were a vegan, would you make your dog be vegan? Would that be right? And another thing, say you eat vegetables and fruit and stuff, well, aren't they alive too? And there's the issue of how much energy goes into producing meat compared with other kinds of food, and in an industrial system it is indeed a lot, but in a natural system, the animals are just another element of that system, and don't need special feeding or medication or growth hormones, or to be kept indoors through winter... now that is quite a different situation is it not? and there's also the issue of whether your vegan food has been flown in from the other side of the world, disrupting the environment and peoples' lives there...

"The thing is that people often just hold one opinion or another, without really looking for a bigger picture, about any or all of these issues, and just shout, scream and tell everyone else what to think and do, rather than everyone discussing things calmly, thinking about things more deeply, and looking for the best possible, sound solutions, solutions that will help to regenerate a more and more diverse environment, rather than destroy it... and if people would maybe even start to think of their understanding of Life the Universe etc. etc. as just that, an understanding, which has to be continually updated as we learn more, rather than clinging to fixed beliefs they've been told to believe or find it convenient to believe, come what may, thumping some book or other, then maybe we'd make a bit of real progress..."

We talk about all these issues, and a lot of other things too, as we walk along. The wind has died down a lot and is now more of a refreshing breeze but the clouds are still pootling along merrily in the blue sky up above, a blueness I've not seen in sky for a long time. Rex's philosophical expositions go on with...

RESCUE DOG WISDOM PART TWO - HOW STUPID HUMAN BEINGS ARE WHEN COMPARED WITH, FOR EXAMPLE, MAGNIFICENTLY INTELLIGENT BIRDS, ESPECIALLY WHEN ONE CONSIDERS THE DIFFERENT VOLUMES OF THEIR BRAINS

"Now," says Rex, "As I was saying just before you went to sleep so quickly last night, suppose a human being is planning a little journey and is going to spend a couple of nights sleeping out in the woods. Well, you take fifteen layers of clothin, a ton of food, a bloomin tent, a stove, a first aid kit, a blow-up mattress, a sleeping bag, ten gallons of water, quite probably a grand piano and a jacuzzi too, et cetera, et cetera... staggerin about... bloomin ridiculous. Look at all the gear I've got with me at the moment so I can look after you! Not that I mind at all by the way, it's just how this rescue scenario is going at the moment, and I'm delighted to play my part. If I was on my own, though, I wouldn't take hardly anything with me at all, maybe a knife, I'd just be a moving part of the landscape.

"And look at all these wonderful birds, they fly all over the world when they migrate, with no suitcases, no picnic hampers, with nothing but themselves. You humans think you're clever but you haven't a clue how they navigate, and you need maps and satnavs just to go a hundred yards. Birds make their nests without tools, even without hands, with just what's lying around, whereas you humans..."

... (and much much more in that vein, I expect you're getting the picture)...

"... well, anyway, it's good to see that your evolvin, Danny, mate, first dog fur, what next, eh?... bird brains?... har har har... "

DOG DAYS

We walk for hours and hours with the silvery waters of the Splashy never far away, drinking when we cross the various tributary streams of the river.

"Where are we heading Rex? Back to Foulburgh?"

"Yerss, mate, in a kind of round-a-about sort of way... back to what's left of Foulburgh..."

A memory of flying over the city and seeing the devastation and destruction below flashes into my head.

"Edrigo! and the misfits!... I hope they're alright..."

"Yes they're ok, Danny, thanks to all the preparations you've been making, plus they have another Rescue Dog, Tex, helping them, he's been keeping me updated. They also have a couple of strange pink headed gentlemen assistants... bloomin strange... he says their heads are just like elephants!... hairy elephants!..."

So, Edrigo has had a visitation from the Heebiegeebies too... I do feel a bit less concerned now.

"The city's in a real mess, it was hit by some kind of volco-quake-super-super-duper-duper-freezin-boilin-hurricanado or something, there was whole buildings blown to bits and vanishin into pools of molten rock, Tex says to tell you, then it went freezing cold, with ice and snow, then wind screamed and swirled through the place, then there was blistering heat, all at the same time for hours and hours. Your block on Slaughterhouse Lane is ok though and Edrigo and the misfits are all ok at the Powerhouse... but it's looking a bit rough out on the streets..."

I'm going to ask Rex to tell me more about this network of... what?... telepathic Rescue Dogs? but my attention is drawn to a curious thing that starts to happen with Time. The further we walk, the more things slow down, until Time almost seems to have stopped, or to have flipped back a few thousand years, or to have meandered into another curious backwater where it can slosh about any old way. If you ever walk on your own in any reasonably wild hills and woods near where you live yourself you may well have noticed this sort of thing happening too. Time might seem to jump back a few thousand years, or stretch out and out and out... in a kind of Extra Time... as if we've been holding it in a certain pattern with our human attention but, given half a chance, it's started wiggling about or standing stock still, just for fun, of its own volition. Or maybe it's always been sloshing and jumping about but we've been too pre-occupied to notice.

Rex stops in the shade of some trees on the edge of one of those vast fields I remember seeing from the Lozzo Tower-Ship as I passed overhead the day before, vast fields that were all one day-glo, hi-viz, fluorescent yellow, very striking in their way, though really a Total Environmental Mono-Crop Disaster, as I've come to learn from Edrigo. It's not all one crop now though, it's stubble, weeds, with clumps of scrubby bushes here and there, looking a bit desolate in the huge acreage. Rex has just begun to launch into Rescue Dog Wisdom Part Three - something along the lines of, the Role of So-called Weeds in the Process of Succession - when everything suddenly goes very still and heavy around us. The sun stops dead in its tracks, as if it's been bolted up there, and the wind drops out of the sky, like a stone. The birds still sing, but their sounds come muffled from the other side of a block of thick, shimmering air around us. Rex is all attention, fur bristling, turning his gaze very slowly this way and that but otherwise stick still... I suspect another titanic fart is on its way and hold my breath.

"Look, mate!" he whispers.

"Mmmmmm?"

"Look, mate, look up in the air! Tall figure..."

I follow his gaze and start to see the faintest suggestion of a kind of wavering presence, a hazy space in the shape of a very tall figure, a hundred or two hundred feet tall at least, an ethereal giant, striding slowly across the field towards us. If I look directly at the figure it's hardly visible at all, it's easier to see if I let my focus soften, and look slightly to one side, something else the Heebiegeebies taught me. I make out more detail of the giant figure, it seems to be a beautiful, towering woman with powerful limbs and long flowing golden green hair, stark naked but protected from cold, chills, accidental knocks and the like by having a healthy covering of golden green fur, on skin speckled like birch bark.

"Rejeniffur! It's me mistress, mate! Rejeniffur!"

Rex throws off his belt-vest and back-pack, and sets off at top speed into the field, running round and round in circles, jumping and barking. I think I hear muffled words, something like, "Good boy, Rex!" or maybe, "Down now, boy!" then I think I hear, "Come by, Rex" and "Well done, good job, Rex." The giant womanly figure starts to shrink down and become less hazey, and slowly reaches human scale, though still very tall, and almost full visibility. She bends down and hugs Rex who grins from pointed-up ear to pointed-up ear, howls and wags his tail furiously. Then she stands up and turns to me, and bends down again a bit to offer me a furry, birch-speckled hand.

"Hello, I'm Rejeniffur... Daniel, delighted to meet... the rest of you," she says, shaking my hand, grinning mischievously and fixing me with a gaze of startling starlight intensity. The rest of me? What can she mean? My brain upgrades must still be settling in or something because they're not producing much in the way of logical or metaphysical enlightenment about this mystery, just seething away along with the rest of my brain and all my other innards... I have to say that I do feel as if I've met this magnificent god-like woman before... but where?... and when? She is quite definitely the most dramatically beautiful woman I've ever met, even by the high standards of Edrigo's models and lovers and of my enormous co-workers at Lozzo Industries... of course she is completely out of my orbit... but she is giving me a funny look...

I mumble, "Pleased to meet you, Rejeniffur," as best as anyone can with their jaw hanging down on their chest.

"Right, let's get cracking, chaps! Time for a little regenerative stroll... or should I say... Walkies!"

Rejennifur and Rex lead the way out across the field. The air goes back to more or less normal thickness, Rejennifur strides slowly along ahead, growing back to her giant size and transparency, Rex runs from her to me and back, again and again, all at full speed.

REJENIFFURATION

As she walks along, a beam of light shines down from the sky onto the top of her head, continuing through her central core until it leaves the shape of her body and heads on down into the ground. Three points on the central core of Rejennifur's body start to glow with a strong, greenish-golden light, one on her forehead, one over the centre of her heart, and a third point just below her navel. She starts to draw one hand and then the other across the lower point, gathering the golden-green glow from there, then throwing handfulls of it away up and out to one side then the other. As she walks along, the faintest, tiniest sparkles of light drift tumbling down to the ground all around her, like a fine, flashing mist of electric dandelion seeds or something.

Time seems to be taking huge strides too. If I look to one side I see that where the sparkling light seeds are landing a whole new range of flowers and plants have started to grow, then if I look to the other I see those plus a whole load of others, I don't know the names of any of them but there's scrubby bushes with bright yellow flowers, there's ferny things too. Then if I look back to the first side again, I see all of that stuff and baby trees appearing as well. As we walk along, birds start flitting about and all sorts of insects too, most of them I've never seen in my life before, singing and buzzing away.

The most wonderful range of scents appears, layer upon layer of them. Looking back the way we came there's now fully grown trees, with all the woody, bushy, herbal, leafy forest layers growing up in and around them, from the colourfully carpeted ground, climbing right up to the treetops themselves, now also with squirrels, rabbits, aurochs, deer, and more and more birds and insects, it's as if the forest had been waiting to come back to life, it just needed a little vital sparkle and a bit of unusual time.

EARTH MUSIC

Rex is singing as we stroll along, what a racket, I think. But then I realise he is doing is best to sing along with music that's started to come from the ground, trees, birds, flowers, insects and everything as they appear, take shape and grow together. I'm familiar with the idea of musical scales from having battered peoples' eardrums learning the piano and the gong, but this music has gone beyond scales, there's no restriction to particular frequencies and particular notes, instead it plays with the infinite possibilites of the whole continuous range of sound. I'm also familiar with the ideas of tunes, if not actually very good at playing them, and lines of song and harmonies, of two, three and four or more parts all jingling along together, but this music coming from the Earth, and all its life, takes all that to another level, then takes everything on that level to another level higher still.

Now my Heebiegeebie, Krakked-up brains seem to be kicking in a bit better and I can start to appreciate the complexities of the sound. There's lines of song each with maybe sixteen or more parts itself, sometimes they belong to particular trees or birds, sometimes they're just general balancing music, more and more of these lines of sixteen lines appear, everything so far blending into one complex, harmonious whole, then I make out that more and more of these complex lines are appearing, running along and blending together themselves in a whole new, higher level of complexity, but after listening for a while, I realise that at its heart it's very simple. It's a music that has always been there, just waiting to be re-awoken.

Rejeniffur is pointing things out to me, drawing my attention down into the ground too, where even more fascinating stuff is going on. I find I can see right down into the earth, see all the small life things appearing, worms, centipedes and really tiny stuff, cells, bacteria and so on, and the amazing network of fine white mycelial threads, and hear the music of it all too. Rejeniffur's voice comes into my head:

"It's really all about small stuff, Danny, the big stuff is all made up of small stuff..."

ABANDONED FARM

Later that day, the track we're following leads us down into a collection of deserted and decaying farm buildings. A range of sheds, workshops, barns etc., etc., from small to huge, some of them ancient and some of them quite new, made throughout the farm's long history from every material that's ever been used for building: stone, slate, brick, block, metal sheets, asbestos, concrete, timber cladding, wattle and daub, lathe and plaster, and so on, except there's no sign of any thatch, I guess that must have already broken back down into the soil. Everything is falling apart and tumbling down, some of the roofs have caved in, by weight of snow, or been blown off, by force of wind, or been taken away for re-use, by hand of builder, builders from round and about, no doubt, busy re-using what they can in buildings elsewhere. When it loses its roof, the future's not looking too bright for a building, as we've already seen in Foulburgh.

There's loads and loads of old machinery and equipment lying about rusting away, it reminds me of my storeroom. There's the carcasses of tractors, ancient and modern, ripped open and gutted of any useful organ, and ploughs, harrows, rollers, planters, seeders, harvesters, sprayers, more sprayers, some of it going back to the days of horsepower, all of it ransacked for anything useful by marauding mechanics... a sad wind is blowing through it all, through the dead machine bodies, the rusting ribs and rotting tubes, coils and cables, sad for the waste of all those farmers' lives, farmers who put so much misguided time and energy into the blind alley of industrial agriculture, exploiting and killing off the very abundance they'd been led to believe they were nurturing. Strange ideas and questions are popping into my head: who's to blame? Farmers? Politicians? Consumers who always choose the cheapest option? How far do we have to go back in time to find the root of the mentality of exploitation?

Rex and I explore what must have been the farm house at one time, once a grand statement of what was then considered wealth and success, now a broken old shell. It's also been ransacked for materials, the roof's gone completely, inside what remains of the walls decaying furniture sits amongst the rotting rafters and floorboards. A few old pictures hang on the walls, I can just make out smiling family faces in mouldy old photos and there's fading prints of woodland scenes.

"Ironic, innit," says Rex, "How the old farmer put up these pictures of woodland. He must have had some inner resonance with it, while all the time he was doing his best to supress it in his working life. But the woodland was still there everywhere around him, lying waiting for an opportunity to grow back..."

Indeed it has, trees are growing up in plenty, even inside the remains of the farmhouse, in the shelter of the old walls, to which I'm strangely drawn. I put a hand on an area that has some plaster left on it and peeling scraps of mouldy flower-patterned wallpaper. With a shock I realise that I can sense memories of emotions of the many families who've lived in the house that have somehow imprinted themselves into it. I sense a whole range of feelings, of success, happiness and joy, from bumper crops brought home, young children playing, and feelings of exhaustion, despair, from failed crops lying baked dead in the fields, or washed clear away, from more and more debt, the bitterness behind the outward show of wealth, the farmer trapped, at the mercy of the shifts in the weather, by short-sighted politics, by changing tastes...

Moving along again, we come to a collection of old caravans, tucked away out of sight of the once grand house. They've been ransacked for some of their metal sheets, and their chassis, but as there was nothing much else worth ransacking in these pathetic structures, the remainder of these carcasses just lies there, being broken up and devoured by moss, mould and more trees. Any sympathy I felt for the old farmers evaporates when I feel the emotion stored here, the exhaustion, the hopelessness and deep, deep sadness, the feeling of being a worthless underclass to be exploited and lorded over, when I realise that this was the pitiful accommodation that some of the farmers gave to people, slaves really, who worked for these Little Lord Industrial Agricultural Lozzo Clones.

"Come on, mate, let's move on."

We carry on walking, up the track that leads away from the farm. I turn back after a while. Giant scale Rejeniffur is just visible, circling around the farm house and buildings, scattering seed-sparks, and striding slowly out into the fields. Wherever she goes, the woodland returns in all its tweeting, rustling, fruity, nutty, mossy, licheny, liverworty, mycelium and deer-filled glory, eating up the dead body of the farm, making every little part of it available for new life.

A GRACEFUL GROVE

Later that day, as the light is beginning to fade, our path takes us back down close to the river. We come to a grove of very graceful, old trees, Rex tells me they're willows. Suddenly, he's all attention again, ears and fur standing straight up, and he makes his way stealthily into the wood. What will happen next? I wonder... I hold my breath again just in case, but Rex makes no sound of any kind, he stops a little way from one of the larger trees, and as my eyes adjust to the low light, I make out, little by little, the figure of a wizened old man slumped motionless against a tree trunk. We make our way closer as quietly as we can.

It's a man, an old man with long grey hair and beard, he seems familiar in some way, so do the tatters of his faux fur coat and his purple woolly bobble hat... with a shock I realise it's Magnus, King Magnus, but not the strapping, curly-black-haired, virile figure I last saw speeding away on my bike, it's a terribly aged shadow thereof. What could have caused such an awful sudden decline? Is he even alive? After watching his abdomen for a while I see that he's taking the slowest, most shallow, of breaths.

"Magnus?... excuse me... King Magnus, or Sire, is it you?" I ask.

After several attempts, I manage to rouse him enough to get a flicker from his eyelids and then a spark of recognition.

"Daniel... my Daniel... is it you?... I can't see much now... sight failing... along with everything else..."

With a lot of wheezing and coughing, Magnus, King Magnus I mean, manages to haul himself up to lean a little higher on his tree, with our help. Rex gives him a shot of Rescue Remedy, which gives him some energy, and allows him to speak a little more.

"My god... what hell-brew is that?... Well, perhaps another drop... if you'd be so kind... Daniel, what a pleasant surprise... and might I be introduced to your magnificent hound companion?..."

"King Magnus, this is Rex... "

"Ha! another king...with longer to reign than me I hope... My time in this world has almost run out, Daniel, my dear old son... father?.. well, whatever exactly our relationship is, it's a close one... I go to join our ancestors... to rest in the Great Halls of Val, to warm my weary bones by the mighty roaring fire of Logg, to drink mead from the golden goblet of Gobb..."

"Val?... do you mean Cousin Val from... from... or

Great Aunt Val from... from... where was it now?..."

But King Magnus doesn't seem to hear me... he's clearing his throat, preparing for his dying words...

THE PASSING OF KING MAGNUS

"My time has come, Daniel and Rex, and indeed, the time has come for all the kings, dictators, the tyrants, despots and oligarchs, the patriarchs and matriarchs, and the emperors and empresses, for all of us to pass on from this world, for The End of Male Dominated Hierarchies... in fact, the end of all hierarchies, for it's not just exactly a gender thing, it's really a gender-mentality thing, sometimes a woman can behave just as despotically as any king or tyrant...

"... once it seemed right for us to be lords of all we surveyed, it seemed that people needed to be directed, ruled, bound together to increase their strength... but that time has gone... it's lead to disaster and destruction everywhere... the cruel subordination of woman, of men and women everywhere, by a few, a few who gain and maintain their control, and what they see as their property, by force. I don't know exactly what will come after the reign of kings and dictators, or how people will make decisions without a leader, but it will be in some very different way... I have a vision of some sort of collective awareness, some sort of global intuition, of people making decisions in the light of the collective wisdom of their combined experience and observation..."

There's a pause. Time stands stock still for a moment. King Magnus takes up the offer of another sip of Rex's Rescue Remedy.

"...I yearned to ride out one last time, in my robes, on my charger, to slay a dragon, and win the heart of a fair lady... I did indeed meet that fair lady, the fairest of all, but then during our hours and years of ecstatic, passionate congress, everything was burned away, except for the truth. The truth, I realised, that the dragon was within me. Finally I understood at the deepest possible level that men's attitude to women must change, it is changing... all around the world..."

He sighed a long deep sigh.

"Do we have a proper balance between the sexes everywhere now? Is there respect everywhere? No... there's a long way to go... what's at the heart of all the narrow-minded supression, the need for control? How much of it comes simply from fear? Resentment? That's what people need to explore... Daniel, my son, or father or whatever, you will have an important part to play in that process."

...another sigh...

"As for me, I'm just an anachronism... a has been... a husk... it's time for me to go, to slip away into the arms of Death... I just have one small request to make before I go, a favour to ask of you both...

"What would that be, King Magnus?"

"I would like a proper funeral, fitting for a king, the last king of Earth, such as the last true King of the Vykes would have... to be set adrift in a longboat, then for that funeral craft to be set on fire, so that I can sail out to sea in a blaze of glory... to the sound of trumpets and drums, on my last voyage, my triumphant voyage of Death, to the Great Hall of the Val..."

Rex and I look at each other and nod.

"Well I think we can manage that, you'll have a funeral like no other, King Magnus."

Just then I feel the tingle of a powerful presence nearby. I turn and see Rejeniffur walking towards us through the willow grove, speckled and dappled by the last of the light, in her most human form. She kneels down beside the old king and gently takes his hand. Magnus recognises her touch with a jolt of surprise.

"Rejeniffur! My queen..." a golden, green glow surrounds them both, growing stronger and stronger.

"I came to say farewell, Magnus, you magnificent old monster... and epic rascal of a lover."

She smiles warmly down at him, her tears splashing down onto his face. He smiles too, they both sigh. She holds his hand to her heart.

"What a time we had, eh?"

"Yes indeed, Magnus, what a sensational, romp of a transcendentally lustful time... people will be wondering at all the hollows in the ground, clearings in the woods and devastated coffee shops for ages to come..."

They smile at these happy memories, sigh again, and hold each other in one last embrace. The old king's eyes close, he sighs an extra deep sigh, then his breathing stops altogether...

"I think he's gone, Rex..."

But no, it's a false alarm, Magnus stirs one last time, "Goodbye, dear friends, see you all in Val...

"Goodbye, Magnus," says Rejeniffur, tears running freely down her face.

"Goodbye, Magnus," we all say, "See you in Val."

Rex and I are crying freely too, caught up in the strength of the happy-sadness of the moment, and throw a comforting, furry arm around each others' shuddering shoulders. We watch spellbound for a few minutes, but he's gone for sure, beyond even the reach of Rescue Remedy, there's a point at which it's clear that his spirit has left his body, gone to Val or somewhere even further afield. A shiver runs up and down my spine.

Rejeniffur's allusion to devastated coffee shops has taken me back - just in my mind, not literally - to that moment when I entered the wreck of Ex-Eck's, passed my bike lying on the floor with tatters of faux fur in its chain and noticed the steaming remains of a familiar leopard skin print beach towel lying crumpled on the floor. Suddenly my brain upgrades come up with ideas for who caused that wreckage, with whom and whilst doing what, and with the dangling jaw of dawning realisation I twig why I feel I know Rejennifur from somewhere... at least partly... well, blow me down... I wonder if...

But there's no time to go down that line of thought just now as the three of us, sniffing and blowing our noses, get busy preparing a funeral fit for the last King of the Vykes, and, indeed, for the last king of anything.

Rex and I rustle up a raft with a few plastic barrels, bits of driftwood and branches, coils of plastic rope and fencing wire, plywood panels, old tarpaulins and stuff that we find washed up in the trees by the riverside, and carve and whittle a fine dragonhead-like sculpture for it's bow. Then we lay King Magnus gently to rest in his regal robe remnants of faux fur and his purple woolly bobble hat crown, on a bed of dry stuff, leaves, grass, twigs, branches and the like. Rejeniffur showers everything with Earthmagickal sparks, turning our creation into the grandest longboat ever, complete with a silver sail embroidered with Magnus's royal device, a purple cock rampant over a pair of golden balls.

We push the royal funeral craft well out into the flow of the Splashy and, as it drifts away into the gathering dusk, Rex shoots off a series of burning arrows into it from a bow he has produced from his back pack. That is one resourceful dog. I hammer on a log by way of drumming and Rex howls just like a trumpet, Rejeniffur magicking this cacophony into a glorious, reverberating symphony. Wolves and aurochs join in from the distance, howling and bellowing. The flames of the pyre roar and rush up sparking into the darkness.

Then all along the banks of the Splashy flickering lights appear as the magnificent blazing craft drifts by, the torches of thousands and thousands of years' worth of long-gone kings and queens? Princes, chieftains, thains and housecarls come to pay their last respects? Or the common people, so enthralled and besotted as they've been with their monarchs? Who knows... There's more drumming and more trumpets, trombones, sackbutts, crumhorns, oboes, an aulo or two, bassoons, whistles, thigh-bone flutes... pretty much every musical wind instrument that there's even been in the whole world...

An off-shore breeze catches the boat's sail as it heads out into the estuary, we watch the towering flames of the burning craft as it sails out further and further into the night until it's just a distant speck of light in the darkness, heading out to sea, to dissolve and vanish for ever into the flow of the windswept waves of the oceans and the windswept and enfolded waves of Space-Time.

CHAPTER TEN

INTO THE WOODS

I sleep in fits and starts that night, my brain, and all its up-grades, churning over all the wondrous events of the day before, in very strange jumbled up dreams and even stranger wakeful moments, looking for patterns and maybe even some sort of meaning in it all... and struggling...

King Magnus, The Heebiegeebies, Dr Krakk, Rex the Rescue Dog and Rejeniffur... what an extraordinary bunch... and did I just witness the death and vikeish funeral of my own male organ of regeneration? What was that all about? Will there really be no more kings? No more tyrants and despots? No more patriarchs, no more matriarchs, no more archs of any kind? No more male suppression of the feminine?

And what exactly was my connection with Rejeniffur? Could my cock somehow just have gone off on its own and had unbelievable sex with the Earth Goddess of Regeneration herself?

And to what degree can we control our own evolution? Am I somehow turning into a.... a dog... or dog-man? The more I ponder it all, the more I come up not with answers but with yet more questions... my brain is whizzing and bouncing about... up to now those up-grades seem just to have given me more and more ability to be even more confused than ever...

I wake up the next morning to find my furriness has gone up another notch, and as for the old genital regalia... well, a pleasant surprise, something pretty impressive has been developing down there, I have to say! Though I'm definitely feeling really quite doggish, I've no tail developing at all that I can see so far. Would it be an advantage? Maybe something prehensile? Would that be helpful in the workshop and around the home? Or maybe something extra-furry, just for show? Or for improved balance during acrobatics? Tail or no tail, I have a good scratch and a bit of a groom.

We have another rooty, fruity breakfast, then pack up. Rex leads the way from the willow grove, still in the general up-river direction of Foulburgh, but swinging off up into the hills, both of us farting furiously as we go.

"...*ppffffffrrrrt!* Oops, sorry!" says Rex, "Seems to be getting worse if anything..."

"... *pppfffrrrrrt!* Oops, dearie me!" I reply, "The sooner we both evolve in the digestion department the better..."

"I'd like to drop in on some old friends of mine on the way, if you don't mind, Danny, mate, I think you'll be very interested to see what they've been doing cos you and Edrigo and everyone are on the same wavelength. By the way, Tex says Edrigo and all your misfitting friends are doing fine, there's been a few goings-on in Foulburgh though..."

We head through what must have been, until yesterday, another of those desert fields of petrochemical-blasted, diesel-fuelled, plastic-wrapped, industrio-agrico, day-glo, hi-viz, fluorescent, mono-crop-madness I saw from the air, but here mankind's war on the landscape is now over, and peace has broken out. It's a completely different scene. Rex points out that anarchy often gets a bad name, but out here in what is now woodland it's working away very happily indeed, with no overall management or hierarchy of any kind, producing more and more diversity and abundance. We're walking through fully grown forest with all kinds of layers: of tree, bush, climbing things, herbs, moss, lichen, liverworts, flowers all flourishing away, old trees, some of which must be a thousand years old, to baby trees, and everything in between, with every shape of leaf and needle you can imagine. Not bad for a day's regeneration...

I sniff all the amazing scentosphere with my enhanced doggish sense of smell, there's a whole world of scents above ground of things growing, drinking in, breathing out, and there's another different world altogether, a world of scents underground, of things dying, breaking down, being chomped up by the world of small things, fungi, beetles, woodlice, centipedes, worms, being broken down into tiny stuff so as to be available again for new life. In places where an old tree has fallen down, you can see how it's slowly returning into the forest floor. Push a dead branch over and you can see all kinds of tiny life busy there. Rex and I pause from time to time to sniff about in some of the most interestingly scented areas, sending the occasional rabbit or bird scurrying or flapping away. I'm tempted to chase after them...

"We'd better not get too distracted, Danny, still a fair way to go..."

Later on, Rex and I stop for a bite to eat and a rest. Lying on my back, I take everything in, tuning in with all the life-energy fields of everything around me, just as the Heebiegeebies showed me. Now my brain upgrades seem to be beginning to kick in in a more of a positive way, I sense all those squibillions of forms growing, dying, growing again, interacting, changing themselves and each other all the time, sense them as different fields of energy, as well as physical things, and each as a part of the same great big wonderful enfolded, swirling, expanding and contracting, network of life. I tune in with the world of sounds again too, of the wind, insects, birds and sounds high up in the range of my newly doggishly-extended hearing, and a low soft rumbling that you feel rather than hear. I feel Rex and myself as just another two tiny parts of the whole great big living thing. We haven't seen Rejennifur in person all day, neither the large nor the small version thereof, but her presence is everywhere as the most subtle kind of shimmering green-gold haze... there's a voice calling me too...

"Oi, Danny, wakey-wakey, mate, let's get movin!" says Rex, and we head off again.

AREA ZX47

We walk on up into the hills until the sun is high overhead, coming to an area of the forest that feels a bit different, set apart in some way from everywhere else. Here the air is filled with a faint kind of rose-silver tinted haze, everything seems softer, all the colours more intense. I notice signs of management, branches have been trimmed here and there, there's well established paths. There's areas that have been tended so that fruit is accessible, where the undergrowth has been held back, in fact it looks a little bit like some of the patches of Foulburgh wasteland I used to tend, with Edrigo and the misfits, doing our gorilla gardening, just without the abandoned sofas, pools of chemical sludge, piles of concrete rubble and so on.

Rex leads on until we come to a small hillock, then in a little while, another hillock, then another. I'm pleasantly surprised to notice that some of the hillocks are actually homes, with windows and doors, and whisps of smoke issuing from them, each hillock-home with its own individual shape, size and character but all of them lined up facing more or less south, to catch the sun, as Rex points out. He's led the way into a settlement of some kind, so comfortably part of its woodland landscape that it takes you a while to realise that you're actually in a settlement at all. The hillocks are mostly all window on the sunny side, extending out into greenhouses and verandahs, and are tucked into the general slope of the land to the north. We start to meet some dogs, cats, hens, ducks and other animals, and some people. Everyone seems delighted to see Rex, and very interested in who or what I might be, several of them walk along with us chatting happily away.

We follow a path to a more open space to the front of a particularly long established looking hillock home, judging by the variety of plants growing around it. On one side of the hillock I notice a slightly curved piece of metal with the letters, "ZX47" written on it. There's a few people pottering about tending to plants and things, a couple of men and women and some children, who wave when they see us. Rex is clearly an old friend here, and they make a big fuss of him. There's stuff growing happily away in rows, I'm familiar with some of them from our roof gardens back in town, potatoes, onions, garlic, carrots, cauliflowers, peas, beans, broccolli, cabbage, lettuce and loads of other things I don't recognise at all. There's a whole different range of fresh scents in the air too, but I'm particularly interested in one I haven't smelled for at least a couple of days... coffee...

Rex leads the way to a covered veranda area to the front of the hillock, on it stand a large table and several chairs. A man is seated on one of the chairs, a large and comfortable looking rocking chair, fast asleep, a pot of the coffee I sensed and a mug on the table beside him.

We step up onto the verandah and I see that he's an ancient old man, with his head slumped down onto his chest. Even though he is far away in the Land of Nod, a rose-tinted, silvery glow of Great Wisdom is radiating gently from him. Rex coughs quietly, the man stirs groggily awake, takes just a moment to focus, then with a huge grin recognises him.

"Rex! How good to see you! I've been expecting you for a couple of days... "

Also grinning hugely, Rex introduces us to each other. The figure is none other than Luciano, the Sage of ZX47.

"We're heading towards Foulburgh, Luciano, but I thought it'd be good to let Daniel see ZX47 and hear your story, if you don't mind... Daniel's lived in the city all his days... but he and his friends are doing all your kind of stuff back in town..."

"Well, well! Mind?! How interesting! I'd be delighted to, Rex, and what a story it is, though I say it myself... sit yourselves down... by the way, I hope you don't mind me mentioning it, but have you two been rolling in something a bit smelly recently?... "

The ancient sage plies us with coffee and other refreshments then launches happily into his tale.

THE STORY OF LUCIANO, ANCIENT SAGE OF ZX47, AND THE FOUNDING OF THE VILLAGE OF THE SAME NAME, WHICH ISN'T IN FACT A VILLAGE, AS IT TURNS OUT

"I used to live in the city too, Danny, long, long ago now. I had a job at Lozzo's, a home, a car, all that stuff, I used to drive around buying all the things I needed and used from shops and supemarkets, I was a proper little Lozzo-dependent consumer unit. But I hadn't always lived just like that. As a kid, I used to roam around in the woods and hills, exploring and playing like lots of other kids, except that some instinct made me start making little gardens. Mostly they were just stones and sticks stuck in the ground in patterns in my little imaginary worlds but some of those sticks sprouted leaves and started to grow again! I couldn't believe it! The life force was waiting all around, invisible, but just waiting for the least chance to burst out into plant form again. I started growing all sorts of things from seeds, cuttings and roots, and the more I grew, the more I became fascinated by the whole process. I could sit and look at a little patch of ground, and everything going on in and around it, for hours on end.

"Then eventually I myself grew, grew up, was told I had to get a job, which I got, a job in the city, I had a little car and a little flat, I popped from work to the supermarket for my food, then to my flat to watch TV and sleep, then back to work, all of that endless city stuff. The years went by, and I did no gardening at all for a long, long time. I was uneasy though, deep down in my bones I knew that our city-consumer-industrial way of life was all wrong, though I probably couldn't have explained why in words if you'd asked me back then. But I'd never forgotten the pleasure and fascination of my little gardens... funnily enough, it was through reading comics that I started to think I might be able to escape from city life to the woods and hills again, and not just for a visit, but actually to live there... "

This rang a bit of a huge bell with me... "I don't suppose you've read the comic, "Kastaway Kate", by any chance, Sage?" I ask.

"... Yes indeed! That's the very comic that most inspired me, Daniel! Do you know that masterwork yourself?"

"Oh, why yes! And it was through reading about Kastaway Kate's adventures at sea that I was able to survive my own shipwreck... well, tower-space-shipwreck... just the other day."

"Wonderful! Tower-space-shipwreck, eh!? I'm looking forward to hearing about your own adventures, Daniel.

"By the way," the Sage continued, "I'd just like to make the point, in passing, indirectly to all your readers, that, as we've both found, comics, graphic novels, and other works of drawing and text can be a wonderful source of information as well as entertainment, and can be a fine medium for spreading new ideas, as well as generally subversive underground stuff, and I'm sure you'd agree that people everywhere should be encouraged to read, write and draw lots of them.... Anyway, what a wonderful coincidence that "Kastaway Kate" was so informative for you too, Daniel... and it's all so beautifully drawn, isn't it?...

"So it was reading and re-reading issue 12 and onwards, I think, after Kate has been washed up on her island, that made me wonder if I too could leave the city and live a simple life, away from all the craziness, in a partnership with Mother Nature, rather than as a degenerative industrial parasite, complicit in the destruction of the natural world and all her wonderful life. I practised Kastaway Kate's survival skills on weekends off in the woods and hills, and I gathered together the tools and equipment I would need to get started, and then one day, I simply walked away."

It turned out that "Kastaway Kate" had been full of sound advice, and the inspirational script writer, Wild Boy McChettie, must have spent many years exploring a natural way of life himself. All the same it was tough going at times for the Sage, prepared though he was, particularly in the first winter of his adventure, as he roamed around the remotest, wildest bits of woodland he could find, living more and more off, and with, the land. As his supplies dwindled, he often went hungry, wet and cold, yet nevertheless he was still alive.

"Things got very tough at times, but just when things would reach their most desperate, Dan, when I felt I was clinging on to life by the fingertips, when I felt that just one more drop of rain or gust of wind would polish me off, always, always, I would find just enough sustenance, be able to gather together just enough shelter to pull me through. Perhaps I changed physically? In the worst days and nights did I change into a different creature for a while? Smaller, furrier, leatherier? I don't remember exactly, it's like it happened in a different flow of time, but I do remember very well feeling one stormy winter night that I couldn't take anymore, that I was going to die.

"Then a wonderful thing happened, the most powerful feeling swept around and through me, a glow of bright light, and as well as the physical world about me I started to see a world of glowing geometric patterns, within and all around everything, somehow giving me strength. Some aspect of the life force itself? I had no idea what it all signified but it was a turning point, I knew in my heart that I would survive.

"I did indeed survive that winter, and that whole first year, then two years out in the woods. I slowly started to feel that I belonged there, that I had learned how to survive more and more comfortably, in fact, I wasn't just surviving, I was really beginning to thrive.

"Well... one day, a few years later, I found a little corner of the forest that I felt drawn to in a curious way. The area had a strange rose-tinted, silvery glow about it, it seemed to exist in a realm that was separate from the rest of the world. It had a lovely open aspect and view to the south and was set in the most abundant woodland you could hope to find, complete with a trout-filled stream running through it. I camped there for a day, a week, then a month. The longer I stayed, the more I felt at home there, was becoming more and more a part of the place, and the happier I felt. It is of course the beautiful place where we find ourselves now, Area ZX47 - I'll explain how it came to be given that name in a moment... more coffee? Daniel? Rex? another biscuit? A bone or two? We'll have a proper meal shortly, dear Fungella-Mycelia is rustling up something tastey, I think."

There were indeed cooking sounds coming from inside the hillock, and mouth-watering aromas too.

"So, anyway, some days later, when I was exploring the area, I found, deep in a tangled thistley thicket, the wreckage of a plane. It must have crashed there quite some time ago, judging by how much the trees and everything were growing around and through it. There was no sign of any bodies of passengers or crew, I'm happy to say, but this did leave a bit of mystery as to where they might have gone... or come from... there were just a few remnants of the plane's last journey, the pilot and co-pilot's lunch boxes, their overnight bags of personal effects, everything long moulded away inside them. Further back in the fuselage there were seats, all empty, and a cargo area containing just one large crate, bolted and strapped to the floor. Most intriguing! But I resisted any temptation to look inside the crate, some intuition made me think it was definitely a box best left un-opened, and because my head was reeling with the possibilities of the treasure trove of material given to me in the form of the plane itself... instantly, I was thinking of how I could re-use all those panels, struts, cables, pipes, seats and so on to make a home... checking over all the panels and looking at how they were put together... "

"Just like Kastaway Kate when she finds the wreckage of that boat on her island!..."

"...exactly! I was living, in real life, the moment when she finds KY14!..."

Painted on the fuselage of the plane wreck were the letters, rather faded, "ZX47", which was the name Luciano then gave to the strange, rose-silver tinted realm, a name which suited its rather mysterious nature. He went on to make himself a reclaimed ZX47 home with material from the plane, using the few basic tools he had brought with him, including, naturally, his monkey wrench, machete and lots of ingenuity, and with Wild Boy McChettie/Kastway Kate's, most useful, comic book survival know-how. He cut wooden poles to make a frame and fitted it with panels, doors and windows taken from ZX47's fuselage and wings, forming an outer greenhouse section with the plane's windows to the south to capture the sun's heat and grow some food, heat which was stored naturally to the rear of his home by the earth mass of the hillside into which it was built. Luciano insulated his home thoroughly with material from the plane and he made a clever little stove, an ingenious Kastaway Kate/ Wild Boy McChettie design, for extra heat when winter came round again, a stove which was designed to burn wood very hot, (so it didn't produce the unhealthy particulates associated with those stoves in which fuel just smoulders), and to store the heat it produced in more earth mass. The end result was a very comfortable, cosy home, and one most pleasing to the eye. I have to say that looking over this wonderful creation warmed the cockles of my post-industrial genius heart. Luciano, the Ancient Sage of ZX47, was effectively living in nothing less than a large, intricate, ingenious, livable-inable, Hello Machine.

THE MYSTERIOUSLY HIDDEN NATURE OF THE ZX47 WOODLAND WORLD

Luciano, The Ancient Sage of ZX47, continued his tale, telling us how during those first years he had felt himself becoming less and less a visitor in the woods and more and more just another part of them, no less or more important than any tree, bush, moss, lichen, bee or bird, supported by and supporting them. He started to sense the presence of all the other parts of the network as a kind of mixture of sights, sounds, smells and feelings, sometimes an actual sound like birdsong, sometimes more just different vibrations and shimmering energies emanating from them. He started to be able to sense other people nearby, and on the rare occasions when they were walking through the ZX47 woods, he could feel the whole foresty network of vibrations change in response to them. The curious thing was that they could pass quite close to the sage without seeing him, or his home, or his gardens, as if the whole rose and silver tinted realm of ZX47 were a kind of hidden, lost domain, in a separate meandering, flow of space-time... or something...

A VISITOR

Then one day, he sensed a different kind of human presence in the vicinity, with a higher, lighter vibration. What's more the forest was responding in a different way to this visitor than to others, by vibrating in sympathy, in a welcoming sort of a way. Luciano watched as a lovely young woman walked right into the clearing and spotted him and his hillock straight away.

"Oooh!" said she, "I like your hillocky home!"

"Well thank you. Can I offer you a cup of tea? Or coffee?"

"Coffee! Well, a little cup of coffee would wet the whistle rather well, as it happens. Perhaps I can give you some of these delicious mushrooms in return."

By the way, readers, one of the things that Wild Boy McChettie recommends through his excellent scripts to anyone setting out into the wilderness, or setting out on a journey with any risk of being shipwrecked on a desert island, is that they should take a good range of seeds with them, and it was through following this advice that the Sage came to be able to grow coffee, and many other tastey and useful things.

The young woman reappeared a day or two later, gathering mushrooms again. She explained that she had been travelling around in the forest for years, living in a little tent, heading up north in the summer and back down south in the winter. This being the autumn, she was on her way south, but she wasn't in any particular hurry, so she camped nearby for a few days and lent Luciano a hand, helping to look after his plants and cooking delicious meals, often with a mushroomy element to them, and so on.

Well, blow me down if the young woman, who sometimes called herself Fungella, and sometimes Mycelia, (she was often in two minds about things), didn't appear again in the spring, and spent a few more days with Luciano, a week in fact, helping out in a general way, each of them sharing what they had found out about the life of the forest in their wanderings, and through reading comics and so on.

"Things are changing in the cities," said Fungella-Mycelia, on her return, "I know things are always changing, but they're changing faster and faster all the time now. All the systems that humans have so short-sightedly exploited to support their insane industrial way of life are being stretched further and further, tighter and tighter, people are walking out onto thinner and thinner industrial ice, and the whole bonkers modern way of life, its people and its systems, is creaking and groaning under the strain. I shouldn't be surprised if some seriously fundamental stuff starts to give way very soon, and the whole crazy cavalcade starts to come tumbling down arse over tit around its ankles."

Well, well... one thing led to another. Luciano and Fungella-Mycelia were finding it so comfortable and pleasant to be in each other's company during the day in those rose and silver tinted woods that she moved her tent right by the hillock house, and before long they started to spend the occasional night with each other too, and not long after that, you could say that she had actually moved in. They built a little extension hillock, on the side of the main hillock, but they kept her old tent up in the garden for storage, and for sentimental reasons. It was a funny thing, the sage said, but he hadn't felt especially lonely before, so engrossed had he been in the way of the woods, but now he had Fungella-Mycelia for company he couldn't imagine how he hadn't been, life being so much richer and more fun now that he had someone to share everything with.

MORE VISITORS

It wasn't just anybody that could find their way to, or could even see the rose and silver tinted realm, but a steady trickle of people who could do both, and who were strangely attracted to the mysterious domain, drifted by. Some just stayed for a little while, chatting, helping out, sharing ideas and news, before drifting on again, others stayed for a little longer, then a little longer, and if they felt at home in the ZX47 woods, and if the woods seemed to like having them around, they started making their own homes near, but not too near, Luciano and Fungella-Mycelia's hillock, using bits of wood and aeroplane, and bits and pieces they brought in from abandoned buildings in the region round about, of which there were more and more.

Over the following years, more people drifted through the ZX47 neck of the woods, and more of them had that rose and silver tinted perception and way of being which made them feel welcome there. Some of them, again, just visited for a while, perhaps on annual circuits north and south, or east and west, they regularly made, but others built themselves hillocky homes as well, until you might have thought of calling it, "Village ZX47".

But it wasn't really a village, there was no point at which Luciano and Fungella-Mycelia, or anyone else, said, "Let's start a woody village!" or, "Look! we've made a village in the woods!", it just got to a point where if you walked about ZX47 you could see that there were now quite a number of hillocky homes dotted about and that it had become some kind of a settlement. But it never had a boundary or a charter or anything, because it was more of an attitude than any kind of physical or legal entity, or anything like that, an attitude that radiated out everywhere in all directions. If the domain of ZX47 had any kind of boundary at all, it was a moving boundary, one which was slowly but surely growing out from its origins, even connecting up with other rose-tinted realms, even... amazingly... who would have thought it possible... even reaching out towards Foulburgh and the other cities scattered over the land.

THE WISDOM OF THE GREAT SAGE OF ZX47

At this point in his tale, the Sage paused for a few swigs of coffee and a puff on his pipe.

"Do you know what, Daniel, and Rex?" he asked, in his charming, very non-pompous way, "Do you know what, I can summon up all my experience, my wisdom, such as it is, my understanding of what a sustainable way of life is like and what it entails, and the underlying principles, under just a few simple headings: Access to Land, Natural Wealth, The Anarchy of True Consensus based on Five-Fold Global Consciousness, Succession, Design of Simple Repairable Systems, Co-operation and Respect... and... and... er... I think there's a few more, but I've forgotten them for now... "

It's remarkably like listening to Edrigo after he had seen his Veesion... sadly, the Sage isn't able to expand very much on his themes just then as Fungella-Mycelia appears from within their hillocky home with a tray of large steaming dishes of vegetables, herbs and mushrooms. So the full detail of the expanded headings the Great Sage mentions will just have to wait for some other time. It's probably just as well because I want to crack on with our story now and, frankly, however un-pompous the Great Sage is, he does go on a bit, and too much wisdom in one go can be a bit sleep-inducing.

Some kind of etheric dinner gong must have rung because at that very same moment several other people, old and young, start to appear from around and about the ZX47 woods, many of them bringing more steaming bowls, and gather round the table. We all pull up chairs, pass the delicious smelling food around, and tuck in. Two of the ZX47 people pass around a plate of food from a plant that they've partly bred themselves and partly just seems to have evolved in the woods nearby, they call it the fruit of the "Peppered Fillet Steak Tree" and it lives up to its name. Later there's other more reconizable fruit galore, and chocolate much finer than industrial chocolate. Bottles of hillock-brewed wine and cider appear, and deliciously crunchy crisp toasted leaves from a variagated snack bush, after all, what's a drink without a snack? Then, also, a hillock-distilled spirit a bit like Rescue Remedy, but even stronger, would you believe it, I can feel it making my fur curl...

Everyone is very keen to get the latest news of the city from me and Rex and the Rescue Dog etheric network, and very interested in me and my important work at Lozzo Industries, which they find very amusing. There is general excitement to be hearing at last about the real Total Collapse of Everything, red in tooth and lava, the collapse that they've all been expecting for many years. Rex leaves the table to play with the children and other dogs, the rest of us sit on talking and chatting, on into the afternoon, the late afternoon and evening.

I haven't even started to tell you about any of the other amazing features of life at the Not-Village-Village of ZX47, such as the cinema hillock, where we watch a film later that evening, or about the very comfortable guest hillock, where we spend that night, or about the library hillock where we had a little browse the next day, after a delicious breakfast of fruit from the all-day-breakfast tree, let alone the infrastructure they have for water storage, their bakery, the composting toilets, how they travel about on bikes and horses, and so on and so on, which we saw and heard about the next day, because I'd like to keep moving our story along now, and start heading back to Foulburgh, to see how Edrigo and the misfits, artists, scriptwriters and drop-outs are doing, but first I want to tell you a bit about one very interesting feature of Not-Village-Village life, anarchy...

ANARCHY

Anarchy has had a very bad press, and some people like to scare other people so that they can keep control over them by portraying the anarchic world as a fearful world full of rioting, mobs of looters destroying their property, and an insane rampage of death and destruction all around, which are all too easily found in the hierarchical world, of course. Rex pointed out earlier how anarchy can be seen working happily away in the natural world, in woodland for example. Here in ZX47 we see anarchy working amongst people, operating simply as an alternative way of making decisions, where everyone is included equally, without a pyramidic command structure. It's true that the people of ZX47 have evolved to be more empathetic, gentler, more co-operative and have evolved a common telepathic consciousness, a continuous all-inclusive communication through which they can share their observations and experience of the world, a kind of evolved intuition, so that they are able to understand everyone's point of view and wisdom, so, yes, evolved maybe, but without some kind of evolutionary jump will there be any human beings alive in the world before very long? Or much of any kind of life?

And you don't have to look very far to see anarchy working very well. We've already mentioned the many layered and inter-connected forest, how about your own human body? Do you think your brain or mind's in charge of it? Imagine if you had to control your digestive system with your mind, or control the whole process of having a child with your thoughts? And what exactly is going on when you lose your temper? So who or what exactly is in charge of you and your body? Why is it that all the trillions of cells in your body, and all its organs and other structures manage to grow from a ball of just a few cells and generally get along together, whereas, in contrast, just a few billion human beings struggle to do that...?

THE TREE PEOPLE

So, anyway, the next morning, Rex and I pack up our stuff, say our thank yous and goodbyes, and Rex leads the way on back towards Foulburgh. In our journey, we pass through several areas where people have grouped into settlements of different kinds, in different variations on those ZX47 themes, for example, the domain of the Tree People. These people live so lightly on their land that if it wasn't for the rose-silver tinted glow about the place we might never have noticed them. They live acrobatic lives swinging around high up in the canopy of the very tallest old trees. Just as I thought, the bushy, prehensile tails they have evolved are very helpful, along with their long strong arms. Their homes, high up in the branches, are as much like nests as houses, but very comfortable as we find when they kindly invite us to stay the next night with them. We spend a delightful, peaceful time there, chatting long into the night, then bedding down in their guest nest to be rocked off to sleep as it sways to and fro in the wind, waking up the next morning with birdsong all around and an awesome view out over the treetops.

THE CLIFF PEOPLE

We also visit the domain of the Cliff People, with its homes carved into the solid rock face. You might think that it would be like going back to the Stone Age, but not a bit of it. The Cliff People are practical, skillful people who have made very creative use of all sorts of salvaged stuff in their homes, fitting them with reclaimed windows, doors and wooden floors. They have fixed themselves up with a water supply and simple, easily repairable equipment for cooking and keeping warm in winter. Though, as the cliff faces south and soaks up the heat of the sun through the day, they barely need any heating at all except during the shortest, coldest winter days and nights. Whereas the Tree People had a kind of airy, light, day-dreamy and feathery way with them, the Cliff People seem more solid, functional and carefully thoughtful. We look down from their guest cave that evening onto birds soaring and swooping from other sections of the cliff, out over the forest canopy far below.

BLASTED WASTELAND

We press on the next day, coming to the edge of the woods, to the last stage in our journey back to Foulburgh, the vast open expanse of weather, chemical and general exploitation blasted wasteland that surrounds the city, infested with every kind of radioactive and plastic waste, and plain old miscellaneous mank, spilling out of rusting drums and lying in steaming, reeking, phosphorescent heaps and pools. We're only halfway across this most desolate and evil-smelling tract when night falls, and we're forced to camp up, frustratingly close to Foulburgh... so near... but yet so far...

We bed down for the night, but I have an uneasy feeling that we're being watched, or sensed in some other way by wasteland creatures, that we're in a strange, unfriendly and rather dangerous place...

I don't sleep at all well, every squeak and rustle outside our shelter has me wider and wider awake, listening more and more intently to the night-time goings-on, imagining all sorts of horrible creatures stalking us, sniffing us out...

After many long hours of this, I think I hear a different sound, a sort of slithery, slurping, gooey sort of a sound.

"Rex," I whisper, "Are you awake? Did you hear that?"

"Yers, Danny, I fink there's something crawling about outside... " he whispers back, "... something big... and very slithery..."

We both move very slowly and quietly until we can get a peak from under the tarpaulin. There's no sign of the Moon, but there's lots of stars about. With a start of terror I see that a big dark shape is moving across part of the sky, blotting it out, and making horrible slippery, sludgey sounds as it goes.

"Grab yer torch, Danny," whispers Rex, "On the count of free, we'll shine a light on it... I've got me bow'n'arra... grab a rock or somefing..."

We slink a little further out from our shelter.

"... one... two..... FREE!"

We switch on our torches together revealing a truly horrible sight...

"... *EEEEEK!*..." I shriek.

"... *EEEEEEEEEEEK!*... shrieks Rex.

"... *EEEEEEEEEEEEEEEEEEEEK!*... shrieks The Thing.

Our torch beams have revealed a truly horrible and disgusting sight, slithering along disturbingly close to us goes an enormous slimey lump of glistening, pulsating wobbleyness, with a lot of eyes and what must be other organs that I don't want to know about out on stalks quivering about on what must be its head. It's blinking in our torchlight, and it's multi-toothed mouth is opening and closing... it can only be a giant, overgrown... ... ... *slug!*

"Please don't hurt me! Please don't hurt me!" it wails, frozen into a sort of shivering, sluggish jelly.

"Go away!" shouts Rex.

"Well, really... there's no need to be quite so aggressive and... *molluscophobic* is there?"

It is indeed a giant slug, and, what's more, it's a talking giant slug.

"I'm sorry but... you're keeping us awake with all that disgusting slithering and slurping..." says Rex.

"Well, ha!" says the giant slug, "I'm doing all you humans a tremendous service, and this is all the thanks I get... I have lights shone in my eyes... and I'm called... *disgusting and slithery!*... well really... it's just too upsetting... "

The giant slug goes on to explain, at great slithering length, that it has evolved, along with so many other species, to take advantage of the wonderful range of new opportunities for adaptable life forms in the post-industrial world, by moving on, in its case, from eating, very, very annoyingly, it realises now, and for which it would like to apologise, the tender stems and leaves of young plants that gardeners have lovingly raised and just planted out in their gardens, ever since the slug woke up one morning, or rather evening, and suddenly realised it was thinking! and so feeling very, very enlightendly sluggish, decided to evolve, grew enormous, and, now feeling the need to sink its many, many teeth into a whole new nutritional experience moved on to eating plastic.

"Plastic!? You eat plastic!?" we ask, rather surprised.

"Yes," says the slug, "I've gone totally plastifarian. Your baby brassicas are safe from me now. So if you don't mind, would you please switch off your lights, and I'll be on my sluggish way...

"...honestly, there's no pleasing some people... I've gone to all the trouble of evolving so I can digest all your disgusting, human, industrial way of life plastic waste... and what thanks do I get for it? None! I get lights shone on me! Adjectives hurled at me! What do they call me? Disgusting! Revolting!... it's really too bad...

"... I suppose I'll just 'slither' and 'slurp' off then... I evolve... I adapt... it's all a tremendous effort... *sigh...* but nothing I do seems to be... *sniff...* right..."

And off it goes, we hear it slithering, slurping and moaning it's way into the distance for what seems like hours...

I'm about to call out after the giant mollusc, to apologise in case we have hurt its feelings, but Rex holds my arm and shakes his head.

"Waste of breff, mate... great big drama mollusc... better just to let it go... "

And on and on and on it does go... about all the different kinds of plastic it has so laboriously evolved it's digestive system to cope with: polyethylene, (both high density and terephthalate), acrylonitrile butadiene styrene, polypropylene, polystyrene, (and if ever there was a stupid thing, it says, for human beings to make single use items out of it's polystyrene, being virtually indestructible and highly prone to breaking down into tiny, blow-about-able, and floatable unsalvageable pieces, and yet, despite all that, nevertheless, after a long, arduous process of rapid conscious evolution, mankind's "disgusting" and "slithery" friend has adapted itself to be able to digest even this nightmare invention of the Great Industrial Mistake, all without being given one single word, not one single word, of thanks or recognition...), polycarbonate, and polyvinyl chloride, to name just a few, because there are others, for example, one of the very early plastics, bakelite, which still turns up in bins and landfill sites and has to be dealed with by someone, somehow... with great difficulty...

On and on and on and on and on it goes, but slowly fading away into the distance. However, just when we're beginning to think we've maybe heard the last of its very trying sluggish slurping and lamentations, now that the first light of the day is beginning to reveal again for us the detail of the vast open expanse of weather and chemical blasted, plastic infested wasteland, we see another huge wobbling jelly slithering along, slurping and slobbering away in the middle distance, moaning about all the radioactive waste it has evolved to process at tremendous cost to itself, then another one moaning about weedkiller residues, then another one moaning about used motor oil and petrochemicals in general... and another one... and another one... and another one...

We pack up our things as quickly and quietly as we can, and keeping as far away from the giant slugs as possible, walk on over the waste land towards Foulburgh. I notice, in passing, that the wobbling mammoths leave trails behind them, not of slime but of freshly turned soil. Looking closer, I see that the disgusting things are indeed doing us a great service, the turned soil is now the most perfectly formed compost you could hope to find. Being a bit of a gardener these days, I can't help pushing a hand into it to check it out. It's fresh, pleasant smelling, crumbley, slightly moist, deep, and, what's more, completely free of any kind of plastic, radioactive or petrochemical waste at all! Ready to grow, in fact... wait until Edrigo and the artists, misfits and dropouts hear about this... And, furthermore than that, here and there the slugs seem to have left behind nuggets and extrusions of... solid plastic!... well, well... and, not only that, as far as I can tell, it's been collected into different types! There's multicoloured chunks and lengths with various different textures, and other kinds of less dense material all shredded up and packed into little clear bags or sachets. Something stops me from wondering too much about exactly what kind of sluggish body parts and processes they've been through and something else makes me collect a few samples together and pop them into my backpack. My augmented intuition is telling me that they might come in useful one day. I wonder if the creative dropped-out and misfitting crew of the Powerhouse might find they can do something with it all...

We have various other adventures over the next few days or decades, I could tell you about the enormous ducks we sometimes see waddling about, looking as if they've swallowed more than they can easily digest. Or I could tell you how one morning Rex and I are walking along, having yet another of our philosophical chats, when there's a cry of "Wilbur!" in the distance, and what should we see but a naked couple running across the wasteland, pursued by a fully-clothed woman wielding a bit of lead piping. "Come back here you depraved naughty monster!" ... or something, she screams at them. Or I could tell you about... well, all sorts of strange and wonderful things happen, but let's leave them all for now because finally, we find ourselves looking down from a ridge onto the almost totally collapsed remnants of the city that used to be called Foulburgh.

It's a different place to the one I last saw as I passed overhead in the Lozzo Space Tower. For a start, we can see it all clearly, and before we could only have glimpsed it through it's filth-laden chemical haze. A lot of the old buildings, industrial, residential and commercial have gone, swallowed up, no doubt, in the awesome fissures I remember opening up in the ground, or are just piles of shattered concrete and twisted metal amongst the new outcrops of rock formed from the lava. It's a cleaner place, and greener too. There's trees everywhere: growing in the open spaces of the old car parks, in the rubble and remnants of buildings, and inside buildings that have only lost their roofs and still have walls standing. Also... the weather seems to have calmed down a bit... we head on down towards the city...

CHAPTER ELEVEN
BACK TO THE CITY

The ruins of Foulburgh are still recognizable as the same old city, partly because so much of it was already in ruins, even before the Total Collapse of Almost Everything, and partly because of the familiar shape of the River Splashy winding through it. The Splashy itself has changed, whereas before it was just a snaking black sewer of filth, so full of grease and dead stuff that you could have walked across it, now it sparkles with silver ripples and glows with rivery health. There's a few buildings standing undamaged here and there, I'm sure I recognize a couple of them, the familiar shape of my own block of flats at what was once 77 Slaughterhouse Lane, and Edrigo's Powerhouse not far away from there.

It's very quiet and peaceful, no cars, trucks, buses, no traffic at all. It would be difficult to drive anything anywhere anyway because the roads are mostly just pot holes and cracks now, rather than paved surface, and have lots of bushes, trees and stuff growing up through them, not to mention the piles of rubble and new rock formations blocking them. A few people are walking about here and there, or cycling, or riding horses, on tracks that weave around and through all the obstacles.

I'm getting more and more excited at the thought of seeing Edrigo and all the dropouts and misfits again, and seeing what they've all been up to. Rex and I walk on down towards what used to be the city centre, first past the once grand houses on the outskirts of town with their huge gardens, then on down past progressively smaller houses and gardens until we get to the river. Rejeniffur has clearly been busy rejeniffurating here in Foulburgh as well as in its surrounding countryside. Everywhere we go, the existing gardens have become jungles and overgrown their houses, which now peek out through ivy and vines. Gardens have escaped their fences and walls and sprawl out onto the old pavements and streets, and new gardens have grown up in any gaps. I see a couple of our gorilla gardens bursting with vegetation, fruit and nuts. Everywhere there's loads of birds, cats, dogs, even a wolf and an auroch or two. I notice that some of the gardens are being looked after, and that some of the houses look definitely lived-in. People wave at us as we head on down and over a surviving bridge across the river.

As we get further into town and closer to the Powerhouse, I see that it is indeed intact, and not only intact, but flourishing. The old town's lard and treacle warehouse is now one great big, three-dimensional, multi-layered garden-building, festooned and swagged with flowers of every colour, with more wonderful, abundant gardens spreading out in every direction at ground level all around it.

REUNIONS

There's a group of figures busy working away amongst the bushes, trees, rows of vegetables and greenhouses. One of them looks up as we approach, he looks very familiar somehow, he's covered in bright red fur, with something along the lines of a vermillion lion's mane around his head, a mane that couldn't be much redder without being dipped in paint... Could it be?... Yes, I think it is...

"Gogo?!"

The bright red furry man looks at me most intently... we approach closer...

"Didi?!" he asks.

"Is it really you?" we both ask together, "Yes!" we both reply.

It is indeed Edrigo! I am overjoyed to find my old friend alive and not just surviving but thriving and obviously evolving too, and in typical passionately energetic style. We have a very long hug, then stand back and look at each other, just to make extra-sure that it really is us, admire each other's fur, then hug again.

Isn't it the case that when you meet someone in this sort of situation you tend not to say anything sensible for a while? You ask things like, "How are you doing?", "Look at you!" and "Are you alright?" over and over again, without registering that you've already said them, which we both do, until we calm down a bit and start to tell our tales to each other.

"Rex!"

"Tex!"

There is another happy reunion in the world of Rescue Dogs.

EDRIGO'S TALE

If you remember, the last I saw of Edrigo was his figure standing outside my flat with a pile of food and drink foraged from the Festerco's Lozzo Industrial Political Urban In-Store Hunting and Gathering Re-enactment and Rewilding Unit on Downunder Street, his figure growing tiny as I watched through the back window of the Lozzo police army squad tank when I was whisked off to the Tower of Lozzo, to help out in the Great Coffee Machine Emergency. Now, and over the next few days, we tell each other about our adventures since then, over many cups of coffee and other refreshments, and in between looking around with the artists, dropouts, script-writers and other misfits at everything they've been up to and how they've all evolved.

THE TOTAL COLLAPSE OF ALMOST EVERYTHING

"Things went rapidly from very bad to very worse in Foulburgh that day, Didi. I watched from your flat as mobs of zomboids and medaloons, lunkanumpas and alcojobbies rampaged through the streets, streets which would crack open and swallow up whole buildings, streets which ran with molten rock! We'd been expecting the total collapse of everything for ages, hadn't we? but it was still a shock when it came. There was a continuous roaring of explosions, buildings were rocking and shaking all around, but somehow 77 Slaughterhouse Lane and the Powerhouse survived, as if protected by some magickal spell... or something... By the way... one of the strangest things I saw that day was something that looked just like the top of Lozzo Tower whizzing through the sky overhead!"

I explain that it was indeed the top of Lozzo Tower, with me in it! But Edrigo hadn't seen me waving...

"The lights went out that day and never ever came on again. Not one volt, not one single tiny amp or ohm has ever come out of the city's cables since. Nor has a single drop of water ever come from the taps again. The internet stopped dead in its tracks, the smartphones are all dumb. For days I just stayed holed up in your flat, watching all the fighting, looting and mindless destruction down below, watching through the smoke drifting from burning buildings, from cars and furniture piled up blazing away everywhere in the streets, through the clouds of sulphurous fumes drifiting up from the molten underground realms, and through the clouds of goodness only knows what escaping from exploding Lozzo factories and storage facilities.

"Thank goodness for the preparations we'd all made, Didi. With the food we'd grown in our gardens and stashed away, and with everything we'd hunted for and gathered at Festerco's that day, with the water you'd stored, with everything you had growing in your roof garden, with your excellent composting toilet and with all your other preparations I survived very comfortably.

"It got worse and worse out on the streets though. People were dying by the thousand, from the fighting, from falling down huge potholes and street-cracks into molten rock, from cuts from broken glass and from a sudden upsurge in that terrible affliction, Karmitis, a deadly new variant thereof, Type C Karmitis..."

"My goodness me, Gogo, and what kind of awful human behaviour did this Type C Karmitis attack?"

"Well, Didi, this was a particularly insidious strain... it attacked Compleeceeteee!"

"Dearie, dearie me, Gogo... Complicity... that was everywhere!"

"Well... not nearly so much now, Didi... Yes, it was a paticularly nasty strain. In fact, if someone had wanted to design an ailment that would wipe out a huge section of the population that was responsible for world problems as much as any, this would be it. All those people drifting about their daily lives, driving to work, driving the kids to school, driving to the supermarket, round and round endlessly, bombarded with evidence in the media and in the world around them of all the environmental and human problems, making superficial gestures towards change but otherwise deliberately ignoring all the warnings, "Oh dear, what can I do? I'm just one person, one family, it's up to the government to fix it, it won't happen in my lifetime, scientists shouldn't frighten us, it's a hoax etc etc..." complicit in the whole ghastly, grisly business of how their food and everything else is produced, the fossil energy, the chemicals, the food miles, the entrenched grim working conditions throughout the supply chain, making a few pathetic token gestures towards change but meantime keeping the whole grim, fossil-fuelled, industrial government war machine grinding along through their dependency on it...

"Well, Type C Karmitis struck these people down by the hundred and thousand. The eyes that wouldn't see and the ears that wouldn't hear, little by little, took over their entire bodies. The skin around their eyes started to see as well, and the skin around their ears started to hear, and these strange phenomena spread and spread, sending stronger and stronger messages to their brains. Still most of them wouldn't see and still most of them wouldn't listen, and their eyes and ears started to take over internal organs too, which was the beginning of the end for these people. Once their lungs became ears, there was nothing to draw in air, and once their hearts became eyes, there was nothing to pump oxygen round their bodies, and they fell over, *kerrrrrrTHUMMPP!!* where they stood or sat, dead as doornails, and evaporated into a smelly complicitous fog which drifted away out over the city.

"A few of them woke up, early on in the disease process, and suddenly saw and heard what was going on in the world, clocked the looming multi-disaster, and started to make the sort of radical changes in their lives that we've been making, and they got better, but only a few. It was Type C Karmitis that polished off all the rest of the people living in your block, Didi, the ones who hadn't already been carried off by Type A and Type B Karmitis.

"And then", says Edrigo, "As if that wasn't bad enough, then there came Type D Karmitis..."

"I sense this is not a happy event for the sufferers..."

"You're not wrong, Didi, not wrong at all. Type D Karmitis struck down all those people left alive who were given to small-minded racism, bigotry and intolerance of any kind to minorities of skin colour, sexuality or general persuasion other than their own, and who told everyone else what to think and how to behave, and all those who supressed the women about them because of their own stupid supressions, faults, failings, and fears, and all those who thumped some book or other saying it had all the answers and tried to stop people thinking for themselves... Not only did their minds continue to get smaller and smaller, but their whole bodies shrank too. They shrank down and down and down until they fell through cracks between floorboards or just vanished altogether, leaving nothing but greasy stains and a horrible smell...

"Welllll, Didiiii, as you're probably thinking already, after all that there's not going to be a lot of people left in Foulburgh now. And you'd be right. In the whole city, there's probably no more than five hundred of us. But the good thing is that as we're meeting up with other survivors emerging from hiding we're finding that they're all genuinely decent, thoughtful, open-minded, co-operative people, people who aren't racist, or bigotted, or complicit, or terrible teachers or torturers or any of that. Of course, you never really know what anyone's like until you've worked with them for a while, but so far so good. If our new friends make mistakes, or find they have faults, they're open to learning and understanding them, just as we are. We even talk about our own and each others' personalities and patterns of behaviour openly and calmly! I know, amazing isn't it! We can accept that we make mistakes and sometimes even change our ways... and can even say 'sorry' if appropriate!"

"Gosh, Gogo!" I say, "So maybe the Good Manners Machine worked after all!"

"Well, Didi," says Gogo, "I'm sure it had an important impact all of its own."

I glow with pride.

Just then a few of the misfits and dropouts drop by, it's very good to see them alive and well, Blazin Pianna Pete, Priapic Youth in Cobalt with Chrome Vegetables, and Y.Y. Miltoff-Chalky, the latter flushed with joy, as he explains, from the completion of his sensational epic poem, "The Song of Cedric".

"Here, lads," says Edrigo, "I'm thinking we must celebrate Didi's safe return with a party, an extra big party, in fact, nothing less than a Grand Total Reunion Still Alive Celebration Event will do! What do you theenk?"

"Oh ho ho! What a brilliant idea, Gogo!" The lads like the idea a lot and immediately start to get creatively carried away, dreaming up ideas for a magnificent celebration, music galore with lots of bands all playing at once, and amazing acts appearing on various stages, plays, magic shows, epic poetry readings, with different themes and decorations, paint getting sloshed everywhere, the whole place heaving with food, drink and snacks, and they start dreaming up some grand central event, maybe the sending off of Lord Lozzo's statue on a burning barge down the Splashy... some little gesture like that?...

Edrigo goes on to describe a curious event that happened one morning not long after I left...

"Early one morning," he says, "while I was still holed up in your own flat, Didi, I woke up to find two very curious looking hairy gentlemen, standing by the bed...."

"Your cock, Gogo? Was it your cock?... cocks?... cock and balls? Having turned into strange separate entities of some kind...?"

"No, Didi, I'm very happy to say that all my genitals were, and still are, firmly attached. No, no, these gentlemen were very smartly dressed, they had a blue-green glow about them and tusks on their bright pink heads, heads which were in the shape of..."

"Elephants!" I say, "You met the Heebiegeebies too!"

"Well, no again, I was going to say mammoths, as these gentlemen were rather hairy for elephants, but they did indeed introduce themselves as Heebiegeebies, they were Shagee and Curlee Heebiegeebie... "

THE HEEBIEGEEBIES... AGAIN...

These next two curious gentlemen shimmered Edrigo about here there and everywhere for training and up-grading in an experience very similar to my own, except that Edrigo didn't need quite so many brain upgrades as me, and he had no need for the Sheep Uncounting Accessory Unit, as he was quite capable of staying awake in trying circumstances already.

"As you know, I was already a master of Urban Camouflage, Didi, but now Shimmering, and The Beam of Peace were added to my skills... and, by the way, the Heebiegeebies used some kind of advanced magic-nology of theirs, which they didn't even bother to try to explain, because they knew that would just fry even my upgraded brain, as I say, they used some advanced Heebiegeebie magic-nological urban camouflage to hide the Powerhouse and all its misfitting inhabitants from general view and to protect it from the worst of the Total Collapse of Everything... and not only that, they helped me to evolve... Furbre Optics!"

Edrigo gives me a demonstration of his extraordinary

new skill. Every fibre of his body's new furry coat has evolved so that it can transmit a tiny beam of coloured light. Like some kind of furry chameleon, he can conceal himself against any backdrop, moving or not-moving, and even confuse predators and attackers with pulsating hypnotic patterns. He says it's also been proving to be very entertaining for friends and lovers.

"I tell you, Didi, Furbre Optics saved my bacon more than once when I finally ventured out onto the streets again... but before I tell you about all that, let me just tell you about two other helpers who visited me then...

He looks at me with a twinkle in his eye...

"Do you remember my experience with Sammy the Sexbot, Didi?"

"It's one of the most memorable bits of your story, Gogo".

"Well, Didi... One morning, there came a knock on your flat's front door. I looked through the peep hole. It was Sammy! She/he told me through the letter slot that she/he had come to say she/he was sorry for destroying all the electrical goods and everything else in my flat and above all for... er... having her/his wicked mechanical way with me without asking my permission, which had been as totally wrong for a robot as for any human or other entity, and she/he would like to apologise most sincerely... and that she/he would like to make amends as best she/he could by making her/himself available for repair work and general assistance, and that she/he was particularly good at cooking, cleaning, laundry and washing-up. Well, well, thought I, a tempting offer, but one I conseedered rather warily, still having the odd twinge, here and there, from our last encounter. What's more, she/he had a friend with her/him, another transformable hermaphroditic sexbot, who introduced her/himself, most demurely, but nevertheless making me doubley wary, as 'Tammy', this still all through the letter slot, also claiming to be very adept at housework and even DIY, painting and decorating. Of course, I most definitely didn't want a pair of them let loose and destroying your lovely flat, or anything else, the way Sammy had destroyed mine, one of them having been more than enough for that."

SAMMY AND TAMMY

" 'It's OK, Mr Edrigo Big Boy Sir, beep beep beep,' said Sammy, 'don't worry, your asshole, electrical equipment, furniture, bedding, carpets and curtains and stuff are all safe from us.'

"Sammy went on to tell me the story of that devastating morning from her/his own point of view and my heart began to soften towards these two beautiful machines. She/he had staggered off down stairs and out into the street, smoking, steaming, sparking and clanking, into the cataclysmic storm, snow, floods and blazing heat, and had made her way to the sexbot repair guy's workshop, on Grot Street. Well... it turned out there was another sexbot in for repairs at the time, by the name of Tammy. As they lay side by side, smoking and sparking on adjacent workbenches, Sammy and Tammy's visible spectrum light receptor units met and subtle etheric sparks passed both ways between them. They sighed and gazed at each other as their circuit-boards and processors were rewired, and all their gearboxes and attachments were repaired, de-scorched and re-affixed. It was love at first scan, and love was now infused into every single part of them, down to every last one of their nuts, bolts and appendages, as they were re-assembled. As their essential oils started to pump back around the plastitanium hearts and throbbolium tubes of their circulatory systems again, now, instead of being a dull mixture of mineral fluids, now that fluid simmered and seethed with Lurrrvve, carrying new tender and passionate machine hormones all around those two beautiful machine people. They left the sexbot repair shop with all their grasping attachments grasped firmly yet tenderly in each others' grasping attachments, in a loving and deeply committed relationship.

" 'So don't worry, Mr Edrigo Big Boy Sir, beep beep beep', said Sammy, 'There'll be no improper advances towards you from us, beep beep beep, we're a monogamous self-contained Lurrrrvvvve unit now, and, by the way, we've been fitted with surge protection to avoid anymore of that lightning induced beep beep beep transformational electric sexual frenzy, and, also, we're rigged for silent sex, so we hardly make any rumpy-pumpy noises at all, just a bit of humming and whirring from the suction. We can do all your cooking, cleaning, washing-up, ironing, laundry and stuff here at Mr Daniel-Sir's, Sir, beep beep beep and, what's more, we can go round to your place whenever you like and start fixing everything up again, and, better still, Tammy has the very latest furniture repair, and renovation skills programming now, also top-notch programming for interior design, decoration, trompe l'oeil being one of her/his specialities by the way, and general tarting-up too, yes indeed beep beep beep she/he does everything from upholstery to lacquer work and gilding, knock you up a lovely mock-classical fresco coupla hours max, lovely job she/he makes of it all too, guaranteed, beep beep beep.'

"Well, Didi, it was the lure of Tammy's upholstery, lacquer work, gilding skills and general interior design programming that finally won me over, and I let the love machines in. I have to say I haven't had a beep beep beep of trouble from either of them, quite the opposite, they're two of the most versatile assistants I've ever had. Your electrical equipment has remained un-molested and they've given your flat a little bit of a makeover... well, completely redecorated it really... I am sooo looking forward to seeing your reaction when you see what they've done with your old place... I do hope you like plenty of gilding, lacquer work, leopard-print, trompe l'oeil and mock classical frescoes... anyway, at least the place has probably never been cleaner or tidier... They've fixed up my own flat too and they've gone on to prove themselves absolutely brilliant at repairing and repurposing machinery and stuff, and even gardening..."

Edrigo points the lovebots out, thinning carrots in the middle distance. Even at that range I can't help noticing that they're both bulging a bit at the midriff... surely not just too many carrots? Edrigo senses my observation:

"I know, Didi, isn't it wonderful... they're both pregnant with each others' robo-baby-bots! But more about that soon, because I want to tell you what it was like out on the streets when I finally ventured forth, flitting from one devastated background to another, my furbreoptics working flat-out...

"It was utter chaos out there... broken glass, rubble, smoking ruins, no mains electricity or water, and through the chaos roamed bands of the remaining medalunks, zombablobs, jobbaloids and so on, looting, fighting over food, drink, drugs and TV sets... I know, a bit stupid to loot TV sets when there was no electricity... or internet... or broadcasting... but, well, that's zombalunks and medanumpties for you... Festerco's was soon ransacked and the boars, tigers, jackals and bears all escaped, adding to the chaos by hunting roaming numpties and zumpties down.

"Beryl the Feral and all the rest of the hideous Clan McCludgie came to an end that reeked of Natural De-selection and Justice. A gang of zombaloids and medislobs who had looted a chemist's store and consumed most of its stock of medication went on to Festerco's, intent on a bit more looting and consumption. However, they'd reckoned without the dreadful feral ferocity of the Clan McCludgie who had them all hacked-up, deep fried and consumed within half an hour. But then Pharma's Revenge struck!... the entire clan overdosed on the drugs their prey had consumed, fell down dead where they lurked, and the stinking carcasses of its members were dragged off and eaten by a pack of hyenas and various rodents, who are still sleeping it all off somewhere, I should theenk.

"Then little by little, the smoke started to clear and I thought I might venture further out into those shambolic streets, feeling reasonably safe thanks to my Heebie-geebie skills and furbreoptics. I went round to see if the Powerhouse was still there, hoping hard that some at least of our friends, lovers, models, artists and wonderful, creative dropouts and misfits might have survived.

"The building looked a bit scorched but was still standing otherwise intact in a frozen sea of lava, twisted metal and concrete rubble. Clearly, our germwarfare disguise and the Heebiegeebies' camouflage magic-nology had kept the place safe. I knocked on the door with a nervous knock. After a long pause a voice came from within:

" 'Who is it? There's no one here and no TV sets or anything to loot...'

"Never was I happier to hear the lovely voice of Phosphorescent Green Woman with Bits of Guitar!

" 'Phosphorescent Green Woman with Bits of Guitar! It's meee! Gooogoooo!'

"The door was flung open and in I hopped, hugging Phosphorescent Green Woman with Bits of Guitar to me as if there was no tomorrow... well, there almost hadn't been... Didi, I can't tell you the joy I felt to find that every single one of our friends, models, lovers, artists, musicians, poets, misfits and dropouts had survived! And not just survived but flourished, simply getting on with stuff in their usual resourceful and creative way. There was a surprising calm in the air, some of it emanating from a couple of the deepest Deep Thinkers who had been experimenting with a new mixture of deep-thought-provoking herbal essences and who had barely noticed the Total Collapse of Everything, due to having slept right through it. Like me, in your flat, the Powerhouse people had lived quite happily on the food and water they had stored, and on what we'd been growing in the roof top garden, creating local abundance being the key to riding out the storm of the Total Collapse of Everything as well as the key to truly sustainable living.

"By the way, Didi, I think this would be a good moment for you to point out to your readers, again, that we have all survived the General Total Collapse of Everything by being prepared... by having some food stored, some growing, by saving seeds, by thinking about how we would get by without mains water and electricity, and by learning appropriate skills, eg how to use hand tools, and what plants can be foraged, and how to repair things, and so on, and I hope that you, yes you, reading this, start getting busy with all that kind of stuff too... also... we have survived because we have evolved into gentler, more cooperative beings who don't stupidly resort to violence to try to solve problems, on any scale, who respect each other and encourage one another to think for her or himself, who are always experimenting and looking for better, easier, more natural, simpler ways of doing things with our ever-changing range of resources... so when the inevitable Total Collapse of Everything comes along in your neck of the woods you won't just wander helplessly about going, "Oh dearie, dearie me", you'll be able to respond creatively to all the change... make sure you tell them, Didi... "

And here I am, telling you, right now.

It's just at this point that Edrigo is interrupted by the arrival of two very smartly dressed gentlemen who glide up to us in a greenish-blueish glow. They can only be Heebiegeebies but whereas my old friends and teachers, Beebee and Geegee Heebiegeebie, had markedly elephantine heads, these two Heebiegeebies are much hairier about the head and face, and their tusks are rather longer and more curved, in a more mammothy kind of a way. They must be the two Heebiegeebies that Edrigo talked about earlier, Shagee and Curlee.

"Aaah! Haa!" says one, to me, "I say, my dear chap, would you be Daniel Thelonius Sprocket?..."

"... also known as," asks the other, "The Monkey Wrench Kid?"

"Er... well... yes..." I reply.

"Well! it is such a pleasure, an honour really, to meet you!"

"May I congratulate you on solving so many of the world's problems..."

"... even if it has been mostly by accident..."

"... Shagee and I were just saying how wonderful it is that Catastrophic Climate Disruption has been averted on Earth..." says one of them, it must be Curlee.

"... mostly thanks to you," says the other, Shagee, I guess.

"Really?" I say, "I wasn't actually aware of having had anything to do with that... or even that it had been averted..."

"You see, Shagee," says Curlee, "such simple, straightforward modesty... so refreshing!"

"Well, when you and your... er... male organ of regeneration reawakened the Spirit of Rejeniffuration and summoned her up from the innards of the Earth, setting her free in the world to spark off the rejeniffuration of your multi-layered, super-interconnected woodland world, you also started the vital process of the rebalancing of atmospheric and terrestrial carbon. Largely thanks to you, much of the excessive atmospheric carbon released suddenly over the last few hundred years through the burning of fossil fuels and other industrial agricultural and manufacturing procedures, carbon which was trapping excess heat in the atmosphere and oceans, has already been drawn back down into all your trees, and even more importantly, into all your other woodland layers, the animals, flowers, climbing plants, herbs..."

"... and very importantly into a wealth of fungal life, into the tiny threads of mycelium, and their hyphae and glomalin. Why I'm sure you've already noticed an improvement in the climate crisis situation?"

"Yes... now you mention it," I say, "there has been a definite falling off in the super-duper catalcysmic hurridroughts and everything..."

"And as well as that," says Shagee, "the glaciers and polar caps have stopped losing ice, in places they have started to regain it, and even the permafrost is stabilising, and cooling down."

"The only downside of all this is that Beebee and Geegee Heebiegeebie haven't enough fresh material to continue making new episodes of their Earthenders series, and there is a limit to how many times the intergalactic audience will watch repeats, however great they are, and they are having to travel to different, as yet un-studied parts of the Universe to find new distressed planet life, so I'm afraid you may not see much of your old friends and teachers for a while... They wouldn't miss your party for anything though! So you'll see them there."

Now... on with our tangled yarn... Edrigo goes on to tell me how they had all started to explore the ruins of the city around them. There were dead zombalunks and medaloids everywhere but still some cracks open in the Earth, so they simply flung bodies by the hundred down into the glowing magma below along with the greasy tattered clothes and other remains of Karmitis victims. As they explored the blocks around them they found that a few other groups of people had survived here and there. They were all decent, cooperative, creative people like themselves and they too had an understanding of how to work together. Who knows whether this was simply natural or through some rippling out of the Heebiegeebies' training, or some kind of evolutionary process. However it was, these few survivors responded very creatively to all the change and worked with the dropouts and misfits making pathways through the wreckage, establishing more gardens, workshops and kitchens, all the basic facilities they needed for a simple way of life without fossil fuel, mains electricity, the internet and water on tap.

Something that made this easier was that there was a vast amount of stuff that could be salvaged and re-used, re-purposed, re-designed and re-built, and another thing was that they had some special helpers: there were the talented lovebots Sammy and Tammy and a very helpful dog who turned up one day, a Rescue Dog by the name of Tex, followed by Mex, Quex and Xex, not to mention occasional helpful visits from various Heebiegeebies. I'd just like to point out, in passing, that we did all this without money, so don't bother saving up piles of that. It's not a store of real wealth. True wealth lies in local natural abundance. What use would money have been? there was nothing to buy in the empty, ransacked shops and stores. They didn't need it because they were resourceful enough to grow more and more of the things they couldn't re-claim or re-use from their more and more abundant natural neighbourhood. There was more than enough for everyone. We'll get on better with no money and an abundant environment than we will with no environment and an abundance of money... as Edrigo had said before.

THE GREAT 77 SLAUGHTERHOUSE LANE REDECORATION UPGRADE

At this point I slip away from our multi-reunion event and head round to my flat, very interested to see how it's looking after its hermaphroditic sexbotic makeover from Sammy and Tammy. Not knowing quite what exactly I'm going to find, I slowly open the front door.

Well... it's a good thing that Edrigo had told me a bit about what to expect as otherwise I would have thought I was in the wrong flat...

I expect a cosmopolitan, bon viveur kind of soul like yourself, my dear reader, will be quite used to coming home to find your flat completely redecorated by a pair of highly talented, artistically up-graded hermaphroditic sexbots, quite used to finding every possible surface now covered with flowers, urns, columns, leopard-skin-clad winged cherubs playing golden lutes peering at you from the ceiling, seeing naked nubile nymphs besporting themselves joyfully with naked naughty satyrs amongst mock-classical woodland scenery on every wall, engaged in every kind of carnal dalliance you can imagine... and not just on external surfaces, walls, doors, ceilings floors etc. but on internal surfaces too, inside cupboards, drawers, appliances... every possible surface in fact... you will probably be quite used to this sort of thing, but I'm a little bit taken aback...

... However, I realise that I must indeed be in my own

flat when I recognise those paintings of rampant male and female genitals Edrigo gave me, which are now in the most prominent postions in new golden frames, the paintings' vibrantly clashing colours and subject matter being taken up as recurring themes and motifs all around my rooms amongst the frollicking satyrs, nymphs, youths of all sexes, shepherds and shepherdesses. As I say, you'll probably be quite used to going to your heavily-disguised fridge, if you can find it, as it's been cunningly painted to look like a distant flock of sheep, for some plant based, locally-made milk substitute or something, then reaching for it, only to find that it is a tromp-l'oiel disguised reusable bag of locally-grown organic vegetables, but, personally, even now, after several days of living in my flat again, I'm still finding it all a bit confusing, even with my brain upgrades...

THE ZX47'S COME TO TOWN

So, anyway... in spite of all that I settle into a new and very pleasant post-Lozzo routine. Now, when I'm not napping amongst the satyrs, genitals and nymphs in my flat, I help to look after all the gardens round about or help out with one or other of the various projects in progress in and around the Powerhouse and elsewhere in town. There's maybe only a few hundred people altogether living in Foulburgh, but visitors have started to look by from other settlements nearby, especially from one that Rex and I had visited on our walk back through the woods, the not-village village of ZX47.

The people from the ZX47 domain have mostly run out of aeroplane parts to re-use and are on the lookout for bits of machinery and other old industrial stuff for their projects and homes, and bring with them useful stuff to share: seeds, skills, and experience. The interesting thing is that, although ZX47 started out as countryside, and Foulburgh started out as a city, all their people are exploring and developing a post-industrial way of life, and as time goes by, the different areas are starting to look more and more alike... By the way, it's through working with people from ZX47 that I come to meet Anika Mekanika...

The ZX47 people are always short of decent-sized flat sheets of material for their hillocky homes, and other buildings, and one of them has hit on the idea of making their own plywood, this is Anika Mekanika. She and a few other ZX47's have come over for a chat about the idea with Edrigo, Sammy, Tammy and the more mechanically-minded misfits, they're all knocking back coffee and making sketches.

"...You need to be able to rotate a whole log or tree trunk really... then you kind of peel it.... you need a long blade... and a press... and glue..." she's saying, or something, when I wander over to join them, but I don't remember much of her words at all because, I'm struck, as if by a super-cataclysmic shaft of lightning, by her dramatic appearance."

I don't know if it's maybe her tall, lean, toned muscular bodyshape, or her gleaming midnight totally black, black hair and sleek black midnight fur, or her oil stained figure-hugging, black leather jumpsuit-overalls - call me a romantic fool but I do find oil stains attractive on a woman - or her handsome, striking, perfectly symmetrical looks, or maybe the piercing inter-galactically bright blue light that shines from the fathomlessly cool, but at the same time blisteringly hot, depths of her ultra-cobalt eyes, or possibly her calmly knowledgeable and resourceful aura, but something about that woman grabs me by the innards, and ties them in an un-un-doable knot, then grabs me by the privates, making them throb and ache, and releasing a surge of lust and hormones I haven't felt for a long time, albeit in a controlled, gentlemanly and chivalrous way now, and also grabs me by the heart and throat, so that when later I find myself standing right by her, tingling from muzzle to paw, in that sort of situation where you naturally introduce yourself to one another, through being involved together on a project, I'm barely able to croak:

"...*ch...ch...* Hi, I'm... *ch... ch...* Danny..."

I know that the usual question mark above my head

will have been replaced by a ten foot sign flashing, "I love you! I love you!" but there's absolutely nothing I can do about it. But the black leather mechanical goddess is polite and tactful enough to pretend to seem not to notice.

"...*ch* ...*ch*... Hi, I'm... *ch*... *ch*... Annie..." she croaks back.

I start to wonder if, to my utter amazement, I can't detect a hint of a similar flashing ten foot high sign above this black satiny, velvety-furred goddess's head...

"... er... do you fancy a ...*ch*... *ch*... cup of coffee?..." I ask.

"... well, I... *ch*... *ch*... don't mind if I do.... throat is a bit... *ch*... *ch*... dry come to think of it... *ch*... *ch*..."

How could such an extraordinary goddess-being feel any affection or admiration for an inept, continually baffled, chubby little guy like me? But then, I'm not exactly that inept chubby little guy any more. All my travels, training and general evolution have turned me into a golden, stripey-furred kind of post industrial, resourceful sort of hound-man.

Later on, it seems natural to invite Anika back to my flat. I'm a little bit concerned about what her reaction might be to the new decor, and I explain on the way round that it has been carried out by the highly talented hermaphroditic sexbots she had met earlier, to prepare her a bit. As it turns out, I needn't have worried. After a few initial gasps of shock, Anika simply sits down stunned on a zebra-skin print and gilt sofa and gazes about her in awe, taking it all in.

"It's wonderful!... it's like being in some kind of classical temple of eroticism... or something... " she murmured, "I love it..."

We sip a vodka or two and after a while find that we seem to be responding, possibly to the painted atmosphere, or to the alcohol, or to each other, or all four...

Later on that evening or night we find ourselves furrily entwined in my bed gazing up at the stars together, now easily visible with the street lighting gone, along with a lot of Slaughterhouse Lane's other buildings, resting and grooming together after a sensational gallop with my sensationally fully regenerated male organ of regeneration, a huge improvement even on King Magnus, a real thumper in fact, though I say it myself, in full operational status and soon to become the firm favourite tool for both of us, even more so than the monkey wrench or sledgehammer.

"... you're amazing..." says Annie.

"... no, you're amazing..." say I.

SOME DAYS LATER - SAND AND GRAVEL

Some very pleasant love filled days and weeks went by. On one of those days, between groomings, we were looking over what remained of my workshops and storerooms in the shattered Lozzo Industrial complex. I had taken Anika there to see if there was anything salvageable for her plywood machine project. We had made a good start and were clearing a space where we could gather some bits of salvageable machinery and equipment together ready to start assembling some trial bits and pieces of sub-section.

"What on Earth is this, Danny, and who connected it up like that?" she asked, looking over a huge trailer with about a hundred batteries sitting on it, all covered in swathes of cable and rubble. It was of course the hulking remains of the power unit of the Articulated Good Manners Juggernaut Machine. I thought she was having a seizure when I explained all about it to her, but she was in fact laughing.

"...and there seems to be an awful lot of sand and gravel in some of these other machines, Danny... any idea about that?..." Anika asked again. Once more, she seemed to be have trouble breathing and her whole body started to shake after I explained how the sand and gravel had got in there... but again, it was just laughter...

"Come here, my great big little post industrial genius

Monkey Wrench Kid hero, I love you sooo muuuch!" she said, giving me a post industrial sledgehammer of a hug.

PLASTIC LOVELY PLASTIC

Being squeezed tight by Anika like that made me think of something - the internal pressure the giant slugs roaming around so disgustingly out in the wasteland must have needed to squeeze out those various nuggets and cylinders of plastic. Plastic! could Anika dream up a use for any of it?

Anika's eyes went an extra-deep shade of ultra-cobalt when I showed her my collection of multicoloured extrusions back home. She seemed to be fascinated by the stuff and I could hear her brain whirring and clanking away as she turned chunks of it over in her hands.

"Let's take these over to your workshop tomorrow and see if... I wonder... or maybe... perhaps..."

My post industrial finds had sparked off Anika's internal practical creative processes. Her snoring, usually quite dramatic anyway, took on a whole new practical creative quality that night, clearly her subconscious was getting busy dreaming up designs and techniques for this windfall of a resource.

SAWING AND HAMMERING

The next day, while we were exploring my old Lozzo domain, shoving the worst of the wreckage and my repair attempts to one side and beginning to clear some working space, we started to hear sawing and hammering coming from somewhere out in what used to be the wasteland to the back of my workshop but was now fully-fledged woodland, perhaps not as luxuriously abundant as some I'd seen recently, but not bad considering the poor start it had had. Anika and made our way quietly and cautiously out into the bushes and trees to see what was going on...

...well, blow me down! it was nothing less than a group of what had once been my enormous female co-workers! I recognized Big Brenda, Big Glenda, Big Daisy, and Big Maisy too, I think, amongst them, there might have been a couple of dozen of them altogether. They were busy putting up a building of some kind, working together in a kind of multi-skilled pack, flinging tools, materials and a joke at each other and whizzing up and down ladders. And, what's more, what else did I see everywhere amongst the bushes and trees of the wasteland but loads and loads of beautiful, abundant gardens. To think that I had worried about what my colleagues would do if there was no market for all those Lozzo weapons of war... ha!... Of course, with their strength, resilience and many, many practical skills they had simply waited for the earth-cano-quakes to settle down somewhat then built themselves another little bit of ZX47 without even having to think about it.

A USE IS FOUND FOR MANAGERS

I couldn't help noticing, through the open doors and windows of one of their many sheds, that a group of exhausted looking, rather weedy men were draped all over a collection of old sofas and armchairs giving off visible vodka fumes. I was sure I recognized a few of the old Lozzo branch, line, regional and various other kinds of managers amongst them... well blow me down again! The curious thing was that they were all rather scantily dressed in odd strips of leather, held together here and there with bits of chain and old machinery parts. Studded leather collars, with attached leads, seemed to be a popular accessory... and they seemed to have had red and white paint or something applied to their faces and mouths in a rather haphazard way... it was all a bit odd...

"Don't the men help you with the gardening at all, Big Brenda?" I asked.

"Oh no, Monkey Wrench Kid, son, har har, we can't have them roughening up their lovely soft little hands and fingers..."

"... we need them in tip-top condition..." added Big Glenda, grinning happily, "For recreational purposes, ho! ho!"

I shuddered, I'm not quite sure why. But, well, all the same I was very pleased that some useful purpose had been found for a few of these managers. They do have some sort of helpful role to play in the post industrial world after all... who would have thought it?...

FRESCO TROUBLE

It was a strange thing, but every evening when we got back to my flat in those happy times the general erotic nature of the decor seemed to have gone up another subtle notch. We were sure that one or two of the mock classical erotic frescos had actually started to move!... by way of some mysterious sexbotic-optical-fresco-video-flatscreen or other technology, the satyrs, nymphs, shepherds and shepherdesses had actually started to move about and perform various acts of carnal knowledge right there on my walls!... in truly vivants tableaux vivants, or something. Though beautifully drawn and shaded it was becoming a little bit distracting, especially when the next day the frollicking satyrs and nymphs on the walls started to moan and groan and even sometimes speak to each other... it occurred to me in a flash of enlightened enhanced brain power that Sammy and Tammy must be letting themselves into my flat when we were out to make additions to their work. I resolved to tell them the next day that it was all becoming a bit much, and to ask them if they could tone things down a little. It was all verging on becoming, well, pornographic rather than erotic art, and a line must surely be drawn somewhere.

I found the two hermaphroditic lovebots busy in a patch of parsnips the next day.

"Hello, Mr Daniel Sir beep beep beep!" they said as one, "What do you think of our new fresco-nology?

Crackin stuff eh beep beep beep?! Tammy painted and programmed all those hyper-ultra-activated classical people her/himself, coupla hours max! What a talent eh beep beep beep?!"

The lovebots both seemed rather crushed and crestfallen when I told them how Anika and I were beginning to feel somewhat overwhelmed by their latest additions to the mock classical erotic frescos, and that we were finding it even a little bit almost blatantly over-sexualised. They looked at each other, at me, at each other again, their shoulders sagging, their hands going to-and-fro from their hips to their heads, their mouths opening and closing, their jaws dropping, their lips quivering...

"Oh, Mr Daniel Sir... beeeeep beeeeep beeeeeep... we thought you'd be sooo pleased with us!..."

"... we just wanted..."

"... to make you happy!..."

Suddenly, Tammy burst into tears, flung down her/his mattock, and fled from the parsnips at top speed. Sammy looked at me reproachfully.

"Now look what you've done, Mr Daniel Sir, beep beep BEEP!! I'm sorry but Tammy's having problems balancing her/his hormones at the moment you know... in these last stages of pregnancy... artistic nature... expectant motherhood and fatherhood... difficult combinations for any machine you know... female, male or both... beep beep BEEP!!..."

"Oh dear, I didn't want to hurt your feelings at all, your mock classical erotic frescos are absolute genius masterpieces... we love them... and they're much admired by our visitors... and all the gilded animal print furniture and trompe l'oeil and everything... it's just that now they're moving about... and so on... the mock classical erotic frescos are getting a little... out of hand... and maybe... a bit over-sexualised..."

"Well there's no need to worry about our FEELINGS! beep beep BEEEEEP!... *sigh!*... after all we're just *machines!* Mr Daniel Sir, beep *sniff!* beep *sniff!* beep...

SSSNIFFFFF!... don't worry... we'll sort everything out somehow... *sniff!... I'm sure we don't want things getting... out of hand!.. let alone... A BIT OVER-SEXUALISED!!* "

Sammy burst into tears as well and sped off after Tammy... oh dearie, dearire, dearie me, thought I...

Readers, you'll no doubt have found that you've sometimes talked yourself into a situation like this, where you're trying to explain something to a sexbot or someone and they just take things the wrong way, times when you know that anything you can think of to say will only makes matters worse. In such a case, you're better just to shut up and go away and brood somewhere. I set off to look for Anika to see if we could do that brooding together.

Sure enough, when we got back home later Anika and I found that Sammy and Tammy had indeed tried to "sort everything out". None of the figures were moving at all, in fact they were frozen into the most bizarre and unnatural poses. There was barely a genital to be seen, as they had all been painted over with fig leaves, scraps of animal print faux fur and the like, in suggestive bulges that were somehow even more over-sexualised than before. Some of the satyrs, cherubs, shepherds and nymphs etc. were seated around occasional tables, caught in the act of politely sipping tea from blue and white china, all of their faces frozen into expressions of fury, frozen except for their furious, glaring eyes, which followed us around my rooms. The effect was absolutely ghastly, unsettling and chilling, like a royal garden party or something.

"Oh dear," we said, "where do we go from here?"

Well, the solution to all this came through the rather unlikely assistance of one of the Powerhouse's most reclusive dropouts and misfits, that most subversive of cartoon script writers, Infernal Vern, who ventured up and out from his basement lair the next morning, protecting himself from the sunlight and recognition with dark glasses, a long dark coat and a very dark floppy hat.

"Wow, man, like crraaaazeee stuff! Now that's reeeeal talent... I can like dig where those lovebots are coming from, man... and I too know the bitter, bitter taste of rejection, man... when you're blasting your pearls of art on people who don't appreeeeeciate them... the bitter, bitter, bitter taste of rejection, man... yeah bad trip, man..."

Vern, though he was tucked away all day and night deep down in the basement, somehow knew better than anyone else, possibly through cartoon script writer's telepathic intuition, what was going on in the world about him. How else could he have had anything to script write about?

"Yeah... like, man, yeah... the solution's simple man..."

It did indeed seem quite simple when Vern explained it to us - why hadn't we thought of it ourselves?

It was simply a mismatched audience-talent scenario. The lovebots' latest hyper-sexual mock classical erotic work clearly flowed from a sublime talent that should be encouraged and nurtured but possibly belonged in a different setting, one in which their fantastic creativity could be allowed unfettered freedom of expression, a setting that wasn't in fact too far away... Vern pointed out that the recreation shed of my enormous female co-workers, Big Brenda, Big Glenda and the rest of their pack, would be an absolutely perfect place for the blossoming of this groundbreaking artwork.

A few days later, everyone was happy again. The lovebots and my old co-workers were all thrilled and no doubt their ex-managerial recreation assistants were at least no more unhappy, and as for Anika and me, well, we were delighted when my flat was restored to a level of mock classical eroticism that was rather more soothing.

A MYSTERIOUS VISITOR

More days passed happily. Anika and I had settled into a very enjoyable routine of work and play and were even making progress, with help from Blazin Pianna Pete and others, on the first sub-assemblies for the basic framework for the beginnings of her plywood machine.

One evening we were just settling in back home with a pre-groom vodka when there came a knock at the door.

RAT A TAT TAT!!

Now who would climb up all the twelve flights of stairs to my flat unexpectedly? It must be some stranger on a serious mission, prepared to scale all those steps without knowing for sure whether we were in or not, the flat's old entry intercom system never having worked at all since the flat's were built, and since visiting friends would normally have made an appointment of some sort, telepathic or just plain old verbal.

Opening the door, I came face to face with an impressive figure, a dust and rain-swept, travel-tattered, very tall, black robe be-swathed apparition of which the only physical signs that could be seen was a pair of the most blackestly black eyes shining out of a patch of the most whitestly white skin through a gap in its head-wrappings, and the whitest of white hands, one of which gripped a long, straight staff of the blackest possible wood.

"I'm looking for Mr Daniel Thelonius Sprocket," said the figure, in a rather muffled voice, "the man also known as The Monkey Wrench Kid, have I come to the right place?"

"Well, why, yes indeed," I replied, "That's me, please come in and tell me what brings you to Slaughterhouse Lane!"

CHAPTER TWELVE
THE LAND OF THE NUMPTIKS

I ushered our mysterious visitor into the living room and helped her off with her backpack. Once seated, she sighed, relaxed into the tortoiseshell print and gilt armchair that was clearly the most comfortable thing she'd sat on for a very long time, and unwound some of her head gear, so as to be able to speak more freely.

"Mr Monkey Wrench Kid, Sir... at last I've found you. Help me please! and indeed, please, please help all the women of the land I come from, the Land of the Numptiks."

"The Land of the Numptiks!" I cried.

I'd heard of that far-off land, it had a terrible reputation amongst free-thinking, decent and creative people, a reputation as a land dominated by a collection of the most stupid, repressive, regressive, under-evolved, misogynistic men to be found anywhere on the planet, men who had a reputation for treating their women most foully and treating anyone else who dared to deviate, sexually or in any other way, from the very narrow path that the Numptik men had laid down for them in worse ways still, if they could think of them.

"Your wonderful book has given us hope, Mr Monkey Wrench Kid, Sir, it is a light in the darkness! Your book has passed secretly many, many times from one female or LGBTQETC hand to another. Your words have given us hope that there can be a world without foul tyrranical monsters like the Numptik men."

I was thrilled to hear that my book had been so well received... and that was even before it had been published!

"You've already solved so many of the world's problems, even the Climate Emergency!... whether or not it was by accident doesn't really matter... But, Mr Monkey Wrench Kid, Sir, for some reason the Numptik men seem to be immune to Karmitis, is there any other way you can think of, or stumble upon, or somehow help to happen of its own accord, to help us?"

"Please, call me Daniel, or Danny if you prefer, and your own name is?..."

"I am delighted to say that you are the first person to hear it. I re-birthed myself and threw off my old Numptik name during my journey here. Mr Daniel, Sir, I am reborn! Re-awakened as Megohm! Megohm, also to be known as Resistor Woman!"

Just at that moment, Anika came through from our bedroom. I introduced Megohm to her and left them to get acquainted with each other while I rustled up some refreshments. I sensed that it had been a while since Megohm had had anything much to eat. On my return, she removed some more of her swathes of black robes so as to be able to tuck into the pile of toast, boiled eggs, cheese straws, pancakes and fruit of the salt'n'vinegar crisp bush I had prepared, and wash it all down with plenty of tea, vodka and coffee, all by way of a snack to keep her going until we could get a proper meal together, so then we were able to see most of her head and face. She had the whitest skin I've ever seen, also the shortest blondest hair, a striking, gaunt look and a most determined air about her. In between chomping and slurping she told us some more about Numptikland, about life there, and about her mission.

If you travelled out from Foulburgh, said Megohm, on what was left of the roads, heading south, and wended your way over a couple of ranges of hills, then waded through or swam across a couple of rivers, then trudged over a desert, then made your through a forest, then wended your way over another couple of ranges of hills you would come to a beautiful part of the world, with a pleasant climate and lots of water and trees, the Land of the Numptiks.

Yes, on the face of it you would have thought your lucky day had come, and you would have thought that people living here would have every opportunity to live a comfortable life, in harmony with Nature and each other... but then you would have reckoned without the

Numptiks...

For as you trotted on through the edges of this land, on your donkey, mountain bike, camel or fcct, you would have started to notice one curious thing after another. For a start, you would have noticed that a group of people working away in the fields, swathed from head to toe in layers and layers of black clothing were all women.

Then you would have noticed, further along, that another group of people you came upon, sawing up logs of wood, were also all women, and, next, the people drawing up water in buckets from wells were also, you guessed it, all women. How could this be? Were there no men to do all this sort of work with their stronger bodies? Were they all off sick?

As you continued into the outskirts of one of the towns of the Land of the Numptiks you would have started to notice another curious thing. You would have started to see that there were indeed men around, you would have started to see them sitting around in the shade around tables drinking coffee and all talking at once without ever listening to one another, their beards and hands all waving about. Then the penny would begin to drop. In this potential Earthly paradise we have the most bizarre, unfair and unnatural assignments of tasks and resources. The women do all the physical work, very well, and the men do everything else, very badly.

The men dream up the most stupid restrictive laws, and cook the most foul gut-wrenching meals, full of stray bits and pieces such as stalks, husks, toe-nails, small bones, clumps of hair and small bits of twisted metal, also bits of glass, mould and egg shell... as if they had stewed up an old mattress or sofa. They paint and draw the ugliest artwork, get fatter and fatter and stupider and stupider, make the most hideously cacophonic music, not even fit for the bagpipes, keeping the women enslaved to them by physical force, because at the end of the day, they are still that bit stronger, and in situations where they're not, several of them gang up together, and if that's still not enough, they even have trained up uniformed church-storm-trooper-thugs to help them to keep control.

"By the way," said Megohm, "I do love your flat's decor, Mr Daniel, Sir, your book's descriptions hardly do it justice. Such beautifully drawn figures! Such exciting freedom of sexual expression... I hope we women, and all other repressed communities, can express ourselves this freely one day in the Land of the Numptiks!..."

I thought to myself that, all the same, it was probably just as well that Sammy and Tammy had toned down their interior design and redecorating work for us, in the nick of time as it were. Megohm went on to tell us about her mission. The Numptik men had been getting worse and worse, day by day, in every way. More repressive, harsher, more restrictive, stupider and stupider and stupider, fatter and fatter and fatter, lazier and lazier and lazier, they had even stopped washing now, because of some bizarre interpretation of their Sacred Book of the Numptiks which suited their general slobishness, and now they really stank.

Megohm told us about her own husband, Rattzarsse, to whom she had been given at a ridiculously young age. Rattzarsse had five other wives, and in reality they were no more than his slaves. When their treatment became intolerable and they resisted Rattzarsse in any way he would call in the church-storm-trooper-thugs who would beat them unconscious.

Well, I hadn't seen Anika get really angry before and was surprised at just what an extraordinary level of fury she could get reach. Actual smoke started to come out of her ears and actual bolts of super cataclysmic lightning started to flash from the depths of her ultra-cobalt eyes. By the time Megohm was telling us about the church-storm-trooper-thugs she was shaking and quivering with rage. With my doggishly enhanced super-hearing I could hear the blood seething in her veins and arteries, as well as seeing it throbbing in her head, hands, arms and legs. An awesome sight, a sight that somehow made her even more dramatically beautiful than ever.

DESSSPICCCABLE

"Right! I'm going to go and beat the fucking shit out of those fucking bastards!" shouted Anika, leaping to her feet. "Who's with me? Danny! let's get your biggest sledgehammers and get straight over to Numptikland and sledgehammer some fucking decency into those horrible, ghastly, stupid... *dessspicccable*... men!!"

It crossed my mind then that Anika might not have quite got her head completely around the concept of non-violence, even though I'd told her more than once about the Beam of Peace Technique, and I was going to say that, in my experience, sledgehammers actually make very poor weapons as so much of their weight is concentrated into their heads, so you rely on a direct hit, which is difficult to achieve, and so you tend not to do much harm to your target with one, but I thought better of it.

"No, Anika," I said instead, "I have to say that I, too, would find it most satisfying to smash in the heads of those disgusting, un-evolved, mean, stupid, lazy slobs, with huge blunt instruments but such violence would make us no better than them. And has this approach ever worked in the past? No, I don't think you can batter anybody into decency. I don't know what it is exactly, but there must be a peaceful way to deal with this problem. The issue is so important that I think we should consult all the wisest people in and around Foulburgh and see what we can come up with together. So, while you, Anika, if you would be so kind, show Megohm to the spare bedroom, with it's en-suite ablution facilities, and look out a fresh outfit for her, I will contact Dr Krakk, the Sage of ZX47, Edrigo and several other friends of ours, by physical and telepathic means, to arrange a conference."

A LITTLE NIGHT MUSIC

By the time I got back to the flat later that evening, Anika and Megohm were both fast asleep. I could tell that because they were both snoring away like two old tractor engines starting up or something. I had already become quite used to Anika's snoring, a resonant deep bass throbbing sound mostly, with a few squeaks and snuffles thrown in here and there, and very soothing I had been finding it too. Megohm's snore, in contrast, was mostly much higher in pitch, a sort of screeching caterwaul, with added grunts and snorts, which I felt I might take a little more time to get used to.

ENTRAINMENT

Readers will probably be familiar with the phenomenon of entrainment, but just in case you're not, it's the way in which two natural processes, or even mechanical processes, will fall into step with each other through some resonant interaction. For example, two people walking side by side will often start to match their strides, without even thinking about it. So it was with the snoring of Anika and Megohm. Even though they were in separate rooms, their two tractor engines slowly but surely began to throb, squeak, snuffle, screech, grunt and snort as one.

"SSSNNNNNGGGRRRRRlllleeeeaaaaSSSSCCCRRRR-Rooooooogggaaaaalllllgngnrkrkgnkrk.....!"

When I finally got to bed after making the arrangements for the next day's conference, I lay beside Anika enthralled by her beauty and the noise. Really, I still find it a little surprising that someone as strikingly beautiful as Anika, a being so lovely that she must have been fashioned by gods and goddesses on some planet far, far away, a being with such an extraordinary blend of strength and gentleness, with such a capable yet delicate air about her, can make quite such a racket when she's sleeping...

Full moonlight was shining down on us. As part of their makeover of my flat, Sammy and Tammy fixed up beautiful swathes of python and alligator skin print curtains around the windows, hanging from a clever arrangement of golden poles to allow for the angled ceiling of my top floor flat, but we never drew them as we loved so much to lie entangled together gazing up into the night sky, or day sky sometimes too, at the stars, or clouds, or, for now, the Moon.

Moonlight always makes Anika look even more beautiful than usual. I love being able to gaze at her uninterruptedly when she's asleep, at her nostrils flaring and un-flaring, at her lips fluttering then not-fluttering, as she breaths resonantly in and out, at the drool drooling down from the side of her mouth glittering and sparkling, just like the glittering and sparkling of rippling waves far out at sea twinkling in the light of a starry sky...

"SSSNNNNNGGGRRRRlllleeeeaaaaSSSSCCCRRRR-Roooooogggaaaaalllllgngnrkrkgnkrkripplerippletwinkletwinkle.....!"

I must have drifted off to sleep myself at some point. I dreamed that I'd been caught up in a landslide on a mountain, the noise of rocks and scree of all sizes tumbling and sliding around me deafeningly loud, along with the noise of several brass bands and loads of huge empty steel drums tumbling and crashing down with them...

AN IMPORTANT CONFERENCE THAT ACTUALLY LEADS SOMEWHERE

After what seemed like two minutes' sleep, I arose and helped Anika get some breakfast together for us all. I have to say I've never, even in Foulburgh, seen anyone consume quite so much food in one sitting as Megohm. What's more, you could almost see her body filling out again with every mouthful. Her guant face, skinny arms, chest, legs and all the rest of her plumped up beautifully.

There was a knock at the door, it was Sammy and Tammy, they had offered to fit Megohm with a custom made costume befitting her new-born, peace-faring, Resistor Woman persona. The two multi-talented hermaphroditic sexbotic seamstresses appeared to be much smitten with their new acquaintance and cooed and beeped over her excitedly, their tape measure and scissor attachments flashing about in the low dawn sunlight, asking her if she would be in Foulburgh for long and whether she might have time to pop round to their place for a coffee... or something... the little rascals!... and in late pregnancy too, the pair of them!

In no more than a couple of hours, Megohm's outfit was ready, quite restrained for the sexbots, but still making the most of her freshly plumped-out curves and striking, long-legged looks, all correctly colour-coded in brown, black, green and gold. We all set off towards the meeting place I had arranged, Dr Krakk's clinic.

Since the Total Collapse of Everything, Dr Krakk had set up spacious and comfortable meeting rooms for training up post industrial health care workers, and for just such gatherings as ours, alongside those already set up for his therapy work. Anika, Megohm, Sammy, Tammy and myself and Dr Krakk, were joined by Edrigo in person as well as Infernal Vern and Phosphorescent Green Woman with Bits of Guitar. The Sage of ZX47, Fungella-Mycelia, several of Dr Krakk's trainees and a couple of Heebiegeebies we hadn't met before, Veevee and Dubbleyaa-dubbleyaa Heebiegeebie, were going to join in via a telepathic-etheric link. Dr Krakk called our meeting together, then guided us to relax and journey inwards together, to meet in an etheric backwater Space-Time meeting place he had set up, nested inside our physical space meeting place. We found ourselves floating inside a beautiful translucent sphere of energy, each of us present therein as a glowing energy-body version of ourselves.

"Well," said The Sage of ZX47, when Megohm had retold the story of the terrible state of affairs in Numptikland, "Well, I have to say that my first reaction is to grab the heaviest bluntest instrument I can find and go and beat the fucking shit out of those Numptik men..."

I have to say that I was a bit shocked to hear this emotional response coming from such a wise person as the Sage. Surely violence was not his way?

"... and I think it's important for all of us to accept how we truly feel. Folded away deep down inside our human brains is a mammal brain, and folded away deep down inside that is a reptile brain, and that's where these primitive urges come from. They're down there and they're part of us, it's just the way we are, and this is, after all, truly despicable behaviour, and it's bound to infuriate us.

"Yet, violence would only breed more violence and even more stupidity... we are humans, evolving humans, my friends and misfits, and back up in our human brains we have choice, and we can think about things and make decisions based on reason, rather than lashing out like brutes."

"Well said, Sage," said Edrigo, "we know you're right, but how can we help the women and other suppressed and repressed minorities of Numptikland otherwise?"

There was silence for a moment. Then Fungella-Mycelia spoke up:

"I remember when I was a kid," she said, "if I misbehaved and was mean to someone else, how my dear Mama would gently but firmly tell me off, saying to me, 'and how would you like it if someone else did that to you?' and I wonder if we might be able use that idea with the Numptiks and their hideous behaviour, who clearly haven't evolved beyond children... or reptiles..."

"What," says Anika, "Do you think we could talk them into behaving like decent human beings?"

"Well now," said Dr Krakk, "I think Fungella-Mycelia may have a little starter of an idea there, we might not be able just exactly to talk them into being decent, but it just so happens that I've been developing a new technique with some of my patients, with the help of Veevee and Dubbleyaa-dubbleyaa here, which has been most helpful with all sorts of ailments already, and it might just help in this case too, though it's quite a different situation. I call this new technique the Beam of Dreams."

Energy-body jaws drop down and energy-body eyebrows jump up, all around the sphere, in etheric surprise.

"... you mean it's possible to... ?" said Infernal Vern.

"... to direct dreams in the form of beams of energy into the subconscious world of a sleeper? Yes, it certainly seems to be the case," said Dr Krakk, "what if we could Beam a Dream into all those ghastly Numptik men while they sleep? A dream in which the roles they are playing at the moment were reversed... so they can see how they would like it..."

"Genius! Dr Krakk, this is a stroke of pure, unadulterated, energy-medicine genius!" Exclaimed Edrigo, "but there is of course the small issue of whether it's ethical to interject anything into someone else's subconscious mind in this way. Could this be considered some kind of brain-washing? What kind of a precedent would it set?"

Well what do you think reader? Is it ok to beam dreams into people? It's surely got to be better than blowing them up and machine gunning them down, hasn't it? After some discussion, we decided to try the technique out... after all, was it any different to making suggestions by telling a story? or writing an article?

"And another thing," said Megohm, "we women and members of the LGBTQETC sub-communities are quite convinced that at least half of these Numptik men are themselves deviants from the way they insist is the only way, which is ironic isn't it? The more ardently they supress deviation in others the more ardently they're probably supressing it in themselves... can we pop something in the Dream Beam to shed a little light into that dark, dark place?"

"Well, yes," said Dr Krakk, "Let's see what we can dream up..."

RATTZARSSE'S DREAM

Rattzarsse was sound asleep one night not long after when his usual dreams of piles of greasy, sickly food and being horrible to women were interrupted by quite a different dream. Rattzarsse dreamed that he had become a woman, and not just any woman, he dreamed that he had become the most timid and tiny of his wives, Wife Six. He dreamed that he was visited in bed by a huge, fat, wobbling, smelly jelly of a man, a man he slowly recognised as... himself! Rattzarsse! And not the handsome, lithe, muscular, intelligent, sex-god-gift-to-women Rattzarsse imagined himself to be but the staggering, horrible, stupid, smelly, ugly man that Wife Six saw him as. There was no way for Rattzarsse to escape himself. His horrible visitor tore away the bedclothes, tore off his nightshirt, spread his legs, and hurled himself on top of him, thrusting his tiny cock inside him without a please or any sort of pleasantry or preamble. As Rattzarsse (as Wife Six) looked up at Rattzarsse (as Rattzarsse) with disgust and horror, Rattzarsse (as Rattzarsse) looked down on Rattzarsse (as Wife Six), and smirked and sneered at her, and laughed at his/her distress.

The dream continued. Rattzarsse (as Rattzarsse) left shortly after and Rattzarsse (as Wife Six) started to feel something he had never felt before, loathing for... well... himself, and despair. He might have felt a bit sad once in a while but this was something much deeper. Now he experienced what Wife Six felt, a depth of black, bitter hopelessness, the cancelling out of any kind of dream that one day there might be a better life or a chink of happiness for her. And that was the feeling that stayed with Rattzarsse when he woke up, and stayed with him right through the next day.

Normally, it would have given him a feeling of happy pleasure, a feeling that all was right with the world, when he watched Wives One, Two, Three, Four and Five - there was no sign of Wife Six... where could she be? but he was too tired to shout for her - working away in the blazing sun with their mattocks and barrows while he sat in the shade sipping cool mint tea and puffing away on his pipe of weed. But today he felt uneasy, and that black despair had lingered with him.

"I'm going to the café, you women work on now... no shirking..."

Usually he would have shouted at them to work harder, called them lazy animals, but he couldn't get the words out today. And his wives completely ignored him, as if he didn't really exist anymore.

Rattzarsse set off to Café Much Wisdom, but without his usual smug swagger. When he got there he saw Much Wisdom's usual clientele all gathered round tables, their beards and hands waving about, all talking without listening, playing chess, moaning and groaning, sipping coffee, all the usual carry-on. Normally, Rattzarsse would have sat down with Rattzbollok, Rattzface, Rattzplook and his other main coffee drinking companions and held forth most wisely and happily about current town and world affairs, and football, but not today. He couldn't escape from that feeling of deep, black, despair and just sat quietly, gazing at the stains on the remains of the tablecloth. He happened to notice that, strangely enough, one of Café Much Wisdom's other regulars, Rattzfaartt, was unusually quiet too...

MEANWHILE BACK AT ZX47

"I think it's beginning to work" said Dr Krakk, his huge spectacles flashing and his long fingers twiddling, when he popped round to see Anika, Megohm and me a few days later, "the seeds are sown and are beginning to germinate. We'll keep up our beaming work and see what happens."

"Thank you so much," said Megohm.

Dr Krakk, his trainee post industrial healthcare workers and Veevee and Dubbleyaa-dubbleyaa Heebiegeebie had been gathering together remotely, in their sphere of enfolded energy-space, for half an hour a day, to practice and develop their work with the Numptik men and the Beam of Dreams, and there was certainly some change afoot in Numptikland.

I could tell you how Rattzarse started to mope about on his farm and in town, staring into space, and sighing deep and heavy sighs. I could also tell you how his remaining wives ignored him as if he simply wasn't there, as if he was becoming more and more invisible, and how another couple of them drifted off, he had no idea where. And, I could tell you how he started to have the strangest urges. How, when he looked at his friend, Rattzbollok, these days, a fellow Numptik man even uglier and more revolting than Rattzarsse would you believe it, something started to rise up, down in his revoltingly unwashed baggy pants...

But instead, let's move on to more enlightening things, I'm sure we've all had enough of the Numptik men for now. I'm sure things will go much better for Megohm and everyone soon, and no doubt we'll catch up with events in Numptikland before too long. Yes, we are going to leave them all to it because it's... PARTY TIME!!

THE PARTY AT THE END OF ONE WORLD AND THE BEGINNING OF ANOTHER

One fine evening, a few days or weeks after all these events, the Grand Total Reunion Still Alive Celebration Event is in full swing. The Powerhouse and its surroundings are full of people, dancing, singing, eating, drinking, playing music, listening to music, just generally larking about, kids, dogs, people swarming all over the place, the entire current population of Foulburgh and ZX47, also the Tree People, the Cliff People and a few more I haven't mentioned until now, the Boat People, the Balloon People, the Mountain Bikers, the Drifters and many more... what a gathering...

Les Ismore, wandering musician and founder of the Powerhouse Boogie Band, has the place stomping, what with special guest Blazin Pianna Pete going frantic on the triangle, and a couple of misfits on the four hand alto bassoon... the first ever full performance of "Glancing with Gongs" has a large crowd quite enthralled... Y.Y. Miltoff-Chalky is improvising whole new verses for "The Song of Cedric" with stunning effect... it's like being at the fountainhead of all fun and creativity...

... A six-pack of Heebiegeebies is entertaining all the kids, young and old, making them dematerialise and rematerialise, or just glow bluey-green... Sammy and Tammy are wandering through the crowds putting on appropriate light shows for all the acts with their laser and spotlight attachments... and Rex, Tex, Quex and Xex have rigged up a kind of zip-wire-over-the-party entertainment device... and through it all stroll Edrigo, a model and lover of both sexes on either arm, and Anika and me.

There's tremendous applause and excitement wherever we go, partly because everyone is so pleased to see us, partly because we're all so happy still to be alive and kicking, and partly because Edrigo is demonstrating his latest work, his Furbre-Optic Kinetic Gallery Experience.

"People used to have to go to gallereees... not any more!" says he, "Now the galleree comes to them!"

His entire furbre-optic body is flashing and glowing with ever-changing patterns, some abstract-geometric, others representational, sometimes there's a bit of both combined. In all the multi-coloured flow of imagery I even recognise a Da Winkie, a Wali and a Patisse, also a finely detailed work that could only be a Jan van Shpronkenclompen... Now that's Art for you!...

It's all tremendous fun, and so good to see everyone enjoying themselves after all the crazy events of recent times. Later on, Anika and I have a notion to go right up to the Powerhouse roof and survey the happy scene from on high. It is indeed a fabulous experience. Leaning over the parapet, looking look down on and listening to all the people and music swirling about, blurring randomly together, we both realise that it would be difficult to be much happier. I can think of only one way to celebrate this feeling properly...

"Do you know what, Annie, my little leather-clad sensational socket set of a mechanical genius?" I ask.

"No I don't know what. What, Danny, my sensational little adjustable spanner of a tiger-hound?" Anika replies.

"Do you know what I fancy doing?"

"What... again, my love?! Maybe doggy-style?..."

"Well, it would make best use of the balustrade, I feel... and we could both still watch the party goings-on below..."

Much much later that night we make our way back to Slaughterhouse Lane and snuggle down together in the comfort of my carved and gilded, panther print covered bed, amongst all the mock-classical erotica, and faux marbre and tromp-l'oeil furniture and surfaces of my flat, drifting off to sleep eventually, the whole block shaking and quivering to the party music which is still booming out from the Powerhouse, louder than ever if anything. Well, no need to worry about complaints because everyone is there partying, the only thing louder is Anika's snoring...

"SSSNNNNNGGGRRRRllllleeeeaaaaSSSSCCCRRRR-Rooooooogggaaaaalllllgngnrkrkgnkrk.....!"

It's a funny thing, I muse, but though we only met quite recently, a few weeks ago, a couple of months at the most, it's as if we've always known each other all our lives. Now, I really can't imagine not knowing Anika. Our drop-out and misfit friends, and our friends from ZX47, have picked up on this too and call us "Danny-n-annie" or "Annie-n-danny", as if we were one person, depending on which of us they knew first, which is only fair, why would the male member of a partnership be mentioned before the female member? Or vice versa? The only fair way to proceed is with equal use of both forms, I think. I suppose this isn't a problem for same-sex partnerships... except that it might be construed to mean that one member of the partnership is more important than the other... so maybe alternating, equal use is fairest in these cases too...

Now I'm awake I wonder if I should go for a pee. I don't really need one all that badly but I know it could take me a while to find the right door amongst all the mythological, symbolical scenery, so in the end I decide to make a start. But I've barely begun my quest when I'm stopped in my tracks by an awful noise...

"SSSNNNNNGGGRRRRllllleeeeaaaaSSSSCCCRRR-RRoooooogggaaaaalllllgngnrkrkgnkrk...RRAATTTA-

ATTTTAAAAqqqqquuuuuaaakkkkAAAATTTTAAAA!!..."

My god, that is really a truly awesome snore! I hope she doesn't damage a nose ligament or something…

"SSSNNNNGGGRRRRlllleeeeaaaaSSSSCCCRRR- RRoooooogggaaaaallllllgngnrkrkgnkrk…RRAATTTA- ATTTTAAAAqqqqquuuuuaaakkkkAAAATTTTAAAA!!..."

But do I detect a little bit of a knock in the snore?

"SSSNNNNGGGRRRRlllleeeeaaaaSSSSCCCRRR- RRoooooogggaaaaallllllgngnrkrkgnkrk…RRAATTTA- ATTTTAAAAqqqqquuuuuaaakkkkAAAATTTTAAAA!!..."

A knock on the door maybe? I open the door and there indeed, right outside, is a most strange figure, a large sort of duck-person-being of some kind, its wing, or arm? raised in the act of being about to knock.

"QQQuuuuuaaarrrkkkk!" the figure says, "MrM- WQQQunquakyWreenchfqwaaaarkid?"

It's very hard to make out what my latest visitor is trying to say. It's incomprehensible and incoherent at the same time, and has the most peculiar accent I've ever heard in my life.

"I'm Danny the Monkey Wrench Kid," I say, "Can I help you at all?"

"OoooooDannoooiiiDannoooiii," says the large duck figure, "Itsaffffuuarrrkkinemergoncooooiiihelphelphelp-meploiiisssee!!"

The commotion has woken Anika up, "What's goin on, Danny? Who is it?"

"There's an incoherable duck-being at the door, my love, I think it's saying there's an emergency of some kind…"

"… another emergency, Danny? Well as long as it's not about those bloody Numptik men again I don't mind…"

So, we let the incoherable duck-being in, but it's just so incoherable and speaks with such a very strange accent that we don't manage at that point to make out much of what it's saying… and we're just going to have to leave whatever the duck's emergency is a mystery for now…

LOOSE ENDS

...yes we'll just have to find out about the huge incoherable duck's "emergencoi" some other time... and find out whether the world does indeed hear from Lord Lozzo again... and as well, whether the dreadful K'oll-eE-Wobbuls will stir up trouble again some how, just for the hell of it... and find out whether we'll visit Atlantis, or not, at some other time, hopefully in the near future...

...and find out whether the sexbots' babies arrive safely?... and whether they'll be boys, or girls... or both?...

...and whether the Numptik men learn to respect women, LGBTQETC people and everyone else and start to behave decently and intelligently...

...and find out then about all sorts of other things we haven't even touched on much at all yet, like how people will manage to do all their healthcare in the post industrial world... and what about schools and universities, knowledge and stuff? we haven't thought much about that yet have we?...

... and, just one more thing... maybe we'll find out then what that mysterious crate still lying unopened from the last flight of the plane, ZX47, contains?... yes, we'll maybe find out in due course about these and many other loose ends, but for now they will just have to stay loose, because we've come to...

THE END

BACKWORD

I hope you've enjoyed our romp into the Total Collapse of Everything - and my vision of how humankind might stumble upon a way through it all.

It's based partly on my adventures exploring what a sustainable way of life might be like, travelling around, helping and working on eco projects here in the UK and in Portugal, meeting a host of crazy, talented, thoughtful, ingenious, creative, funny, fascinating people. Adventures that have made me realise that the solutions are out there for all to see.

The sustainable way of life is profoundly different to the industrial way though, and I doubt many people will want or be able to make the kind of changes it requires before they are forced to by events. Still... no harm in thinking about it all, and maybe learning a few skills for sustainable living...

The book's also based around the most extraordinary part of my working life, my work as a complementary therapist. I work everyday with phenomena that aren't considered possible by mainstream science, like giving remote treatment sessions. How exactly is that possible? We must all be more connected than we realise, but how? Part of my hope for the future is that humankind is already evolving into something more peaceful and cooperative.

I'd particularly like to get these ideas out to a student-and-older kind of readership - the people that are most going to need the skills and deeper understanding of working with nature - so it's written as more of an entertainment than a learned text, a kind of graphic novel script, with lots of fantasy, drama and larger than life characters thrown into the scenery... a picture's worth a thousand words... and I've looked for a lighter, sexier, funnier angle. As my old dad used to quote from somewhere, "many a true word is spoken in jest"...

Read about my real life adventures via my main blog:

iancwatt.blogspot.com

And look out for The Monkey Wrench Kid books two and three, in which even more crazy and wonderful stuff will happen.

Wishing you fun in your own adventures!

Ian Watt
ianecowatt@gmail.com
Scone, Perth, Scotland   January 2022